EXPECTING THE RANCHER'S HEIR

BY
KATHIE DeNOSKY

AND

TAMING HER BILLIONAIRE BOSS

BY
MAXINE SULLIVAN

He traced her perfect coral lips with his tongue, then coaxed her to open for him.

When he stroked her tongue with his, he could tell from her soft moan that she was as turned on as he was.

Unfortunately, sitting on a bale of straw in a stable had to be one of the least sensual places on earth. Cursing himself as nine kinds of a fool for starting something he couldn't finish, he groaned and reluctantly broke the kiss.

"I think it's about time we took that hot shower," he said, setting her on her feet.

"We?" she asked as he rose to take her hand in his and hurry her toward the stable doors.

He didn't even try to stop his wicked grin. "I've decided it's about time for the ranch to 'go green.' We'll save water by showering together."

Dear Reader,

When I was offered the opportunity to participate in the DYNASTY: THE JARRODS series, I was not only honored to be asked to write *Expecting the Rancher's Heir*, I was intrigued by the idea of a no-strings affair suddenly becoming a very serious dilemma. Then, when I discovered it was set in the beautiful Rocky Mountains, my imagination took off.

Shortly after returning to Aspen for the reading of her father's will, Melissa Jarrod entered into a no-strings affair with local rancher Shane McDermott, one of the investors in Jarrod Ridge Resort. They've managed to keep it from her family and the other investors, but when their liaison takes an unexpected turn, it's just a matter of time before their secret comes to light.

I hope you enjoy reading *Expecting the Rancher's Heir* as much as I enjoyed writing it. I love hearing from my readers. Please feel free to e-mail me at Kathie@ kathiedenosky.com or send snail mail to PO Box 2064, Herrin, IL 62948, USA. And don't forget to stop by my website, www.kathiedenosky.com.

All the best,

Kathie

EXPECTING THE RANCHER'S HEIR

BY
KATHIE DeNOSKY

Published in Great Britain 2011
by Mills & Boon, an imprint of Harlequin (UK) Limited,
Eton House, 18-24 Paradise Road, Richmond, Surrey TW9 1SR

© Harlequin Books S.A. 2010

Special thanks and acknowledgement to Kathie DeNosky for her contribution to the Dynasties: The Jarrods series.

ISBN: 978 0 263 88320 6

51-1011

Harlequin (UK) policy is to use papers that are natural, renewable and recyclable products and made from wood grown in sustainable forests. The logging and manufacturing processes conform to the legal environmental regulations of the country of origin.

Printed and bound in Spain
by Blackprint CPI, Barcelona

Kathie DeNosky lives in her native southern Illinois with her big, lovable Bernese mountain dog, Nemo. Writing highly sensual stories with a generous amount of humor, Kathie's books have appeared on the Waldenbooks bestseller list and received the Write Touch Readers Award and the National Readers' Choice Award. Kathie enjoys going to rodeos, traveling to research settings for her books and listening to country music. Readers may contact Kathie at PO Box 2064, Herrin, Illinois 62948-5264, USA or e-mail her at kathie@kathiedenosky.com. They can also visit her website at www.kathiedenosky. com.

This book is dedicated to the wonderful authors
I worked with on this series, Maureen Child, Maxine
Sullivan, Tessa Radley, Emilie Rose and Heidi Betts.
It was a pleasure working with all of you.

And a special thank you to Charles Griemsman
and Krista Stroever for asking me to be included
in such a great project.

From the Last Will and Testament of Don Jarrod

…And to my daughter, Melissa, I bequeath the third portion of my estate. In particular, I entrust you with executive oversight of the Jarrod Ridge spa complex. Though you may think I didn't notice, the success you've had with your fitness concern in Malibu truly impressed me. Ever since you were a little girl, I've been so proud of you, even though our family business kept me away from home, and from showing how much I truly loved you. I only ask that you make your younger half-sister, Erica, feel as loved and welcome in her new family. You always held your own among your headstrong brothers; now show her the way.

One

"**D**on't say pregnant. Please don't say pregnant," Melissa Jarrod whispered, afraid to open her tightly closed eyes. Maybe if she repeated it enough times she could will the white stick in her trembling hand to give her the results she wanted.

When she finally worked up the courage to take a peek at the pregnancy test she held, her eyes widened and it felt as if her stomach dropped all the way to her feet. The word *pregnant* in the little results window couldn't have been clearer.

"I can't be pregnant," she said disbelievingly as she glanced at herself in the bathroom mirror. "We've been careful."

But as her gaze dropped to her flat stomach, she

realized that the way her luck had been running lately, it was not only possible, it was highly probable. She and Shane McDermott had been in a physical relationship practically from the moment she returned to Aspen two months ago. She sighed heavily. Although they'd taken the proper precautions, there had been that one night only a few days after they'd started seeing each other when they'd gotten carried away and passion had overtaken them.

Hoping the results of the test might be wrong, she quickly picked up the box to check the directions. No, she had done everything correctly. She turned the box to the side to see if there was a disclaimer or some reassurance that the test could have given a false-positive reading. Her spirits sank further when she found what she was looking for. The percentage of error was so low, it was almost impossible that she wasn't pregnant.

Wandering into the bedroom, she sank onto the side of the bed. What was she going to do and how on earth was she going to tell Shane?

He had made it perfectly clear from the beginning that he wasn't interested in a serious relationship, and that had been just fine with her. When she'd first come back to Aspen for the reading of her father's will, she hadn't been certain just how long she would be staying. But she, her brothers and her newfound half sister had learned they were required to take over the running of the Jarrod Ridge Resort for at least one year or forfeit their inheritance of the thriving enterprise. Even so, it would have been utter foolishness to engage in anything long-term, knowing that she would eventually return to California at some point in the future.

But with the positive results of the pregnancy test, their casual affair had just taken a very serious turn and become a lifelong commitment. At least for her. But how would Shane react when he learned that in a little more than seven months he was going to be a father?

Lost in a tangle of disturbing thoughts and fighting a wave of sheer panic, Melissa jumped when her cell phone rang. Reaching to pick it up from the night-stand, she noticed the number for the Tranquility Spa on the caller ID.

"What's wrong this time, Rita?" she asked, taking a deep steadying breath.

Whether real or imagined, the assistant manager of Jarrod Ridge's elite spa had reported a crisis nearly every day since Melissa had stepped in to temporarily take over the manager's position. But for the first time in two months, she welcomed the insecure woman's concerns. Anything was a welcome distraction from her own current dilemma.

"I'm sorry to bother you, Ms. Jarrod, but the yoga instructor called in sick this morning and I haven't been able to reach our backup. We have a room full of guests and no one to lead the yoga class. What should I do?" Rita whined, her voice clearly filled with indecision, as well as a good amount of panic.

"First of all, breathe, Rita," Melissa said, rising from the bed to pull a leotard from her dresser drawer. "I want you to calm down, then escort the guests over to the juice bar for a complimentary drink."

"Then what?" the woman asked, sounding a little more in control of herself.

How on earth the woman had managed to land the assistant-manager position, Melissa would never know. Although Rita was very nice, she couldn't make a decision on her own if her life depended on it.

Melissa checked her watch. "I'll be there in ten minutes to teach the class."

The last thing she wanted to do was lead a yoga session this morning. She needed to figure out when and how she was going to tell Shane, as well as her family, about the pregnancy. But the choice had been taken out of her hands. The Tranquility Spa had a stellar reputation for giving Jarrod Ridge guests five-star treatment and she wasn't about to let that status slip on her watch.

Putting her long blond hair into a ponytail, she stuffed her things into her gym bag, then grabbed her car keys from the kitchen counter as she started out the door of the lodge. Since her return to Aspen, she had been staying in Willow Lodge, one of the exclusive log cabins owned by Jarrod Ridge Resort.

She could have stayed in her suite at the family estate, but that had never been an option for her. Jarrod Manor might have been where she grew up, but she had always thought of it as more of a prison than she had a home. She hadn't been back but a handful of times since moving out to go to college eight years ago and she didn't particularly care to go back now.

As she steered her SUV under the canopy of the resort's main entrance, she relegated thoughts of her dismal, lonely childhood to the back of her mind. Even though Willow Lodge was the cabin farthest away from the manor, she could have walked the short distance. But as soon as the yoga class was over, she fully intended to make the drive over to the next valley where Shane's ranch was located and tell him there had been an unexpected complication in their no-strings relationship. That is if she could find the place.

She had only been to Rainbow Bend Ranch once and that had been years ago. If she remembered correctly it was in a remote valley that was several miles off the main road.

When she parked the Mountaineer, her heart raced at the sight of the man standing beside the truck just in front of hers. Shane McDermott was handing his keys to one of the valets and she didn't think she had ever seen him look so darned sexy.

Tall and devilishly handsome, he was a cowboy from the top of his wide-brimmed black Resistol to the soles of his big-booted feet. Shane was the type of man she had always fantasized about, and if the expressions on the faces of the female guests standing by the resort's main entrance were any indication, he was the type of man they dreamed about, too.

No wonder he had a reputation for being a ladies' man. They were drawn to him like bees to pollen.

Her heart came to a complete halt when he walked over to open the driver's door of her SUV.

"Good morning, Ms. Jarrod," he said, removing his hat as any self-respecting cowboy would do when greeting a lady.

A slight breeze ruffled his thick black hair and it reminded her of how it had looked the other night after she had run her fingers through it when they'd made love. She did her best to ignore the tingle that coursed through her at the thought of what they had shared.

"Good morning, Mr. McDermott," she answered, getting out of the car to hand her keys to one of the uniformed valets.

"I thought Friday was your day off," he said, smiling congenially.

"It usually is." She breezed past him and hurried toward the resort doors. "One of the spa's yoga instructors called in sick this morning and I'm going to have to teach her class."

He fell into step beside her. "After you finish twisting the resort's guests into pretzels do you have the rest of the day off?"

"Yes."

She couldn't help but wonder where Shane was going with his line of questioning. In order to avoid gossip among the Jarrod Ridge employees and the disapproval of some of the older, less progressive-minded investors, they'd been extremely careful to conceal their affair. Not even her family knew about them, and they had managed to maintain the appearance of being nothing more than acquaintances by limiting being seen together. They hadn't even spent an entire night together for fear of someone seeing him leave her place. Thus far, they'd been successful by not being seen together at all.

But if Shane continued questioning her as they walked toward the spa, there was a very real possibility that someone would take notice, and by the end of the day, the rumors about them would be spread all over the resort, if not the entire town of Aspen. Or even worse, her nerves could very well get the better of her and she would blurt out in the middle of the crowded lobby that she going to have his baby.

Neither scenario was appealing. She knew for certain that she couldn't cope with the fallout that was sure to follow on top of everything else she had to deal with.

"I'll come by Willow Lodge later," he said, smiling. His icy blue eyes danced with mischief. "I have something I want to talk to you about, Lissa."

"Would you keep your voice down?" she hissed.

She quickly looked around to see if anyone overheard him. He was the only person who had ever called her Lissa and it never failed to send an exciting little thrill coursing through her.

"I have something I need to discuss with you, too, Shane. But I'd rather not go into it…" Her voice trailed off when a bellman seemed to take more than a passing interest in seeing them together. When the man moved on, she turned back to Shane. "I thought you were supposed to have a luncheon meeting today with some of the other Jarrod Ridge investors, Mr. McDermott."

"I do." He looked as if he didn't have a care in the world, and she couldn't help but wonder how quickly that would change when she shared her news.

"Then what are you doing here now?"

Melissa hadn't meant to sound so blunt, but if she didn't get to the yoga class pretty soon, poor Rita was sure to suffer a nervous breakdown and guests would start complaining. Besides, she needed to put some space between herself and Shane. The scent of leather and woodsy aftershave were playing havoc with her equilibrium and it was all she could do to keep from swaying toward him.

"I came early to see that the new herd of trail horses I sold the resort is living up to expectation." He arched one dark eyebrow. "Do you have a problem with that?"

Sighing, Melissa shook her head. "I'm sorry, I didn't mean to be so short with you. The yoga class was supposed to start fifteen minutes ago and I really do need to get to the spa."

"Then I won't keep you, Ms. Jarrod." His voice grew a bit louder as they reached the entrance to Tranquility Spa and she knew it was for the benefit of anyone who might be eavesdropping. He gave her a conspiratorial wink as he dipped his head ever so slightly and touched the wide brim of his cowboy hat. "It was nice running into you again. I hope you have a nice Labor Day weekend."

As she watched Shane turn and stroll down the hall toward the meeting rooms, Melissa sighed. The man looked almost as good from the back as he did from the front. His Western-cut, dark brown suit jacket emphasized the width of his strong shoulders and his blue jeans fit his long, muscular legs to perfection.

His well-toned physique rivaled that of a Greek god and she had intimate knowledge of the power and strength of each and every muscle when he had held her, kissed her, made love to her.

A tiny shiver streaked straight up her spine. She forced herself to ignore the sudden warmth that followed as it spread throughout her body. Opening the door to the spa, she took a deep breath and prepared to teach the yoga class.

Lusting after Shane McDermott was what had landed her in her current predicament. It would definitely be in her best interests to remember that.

"Melissa, did you hear me?" Avery Lancaster asked. Engaged to Melissa's brother Guy, the petite blonde had become a very close friend in the month since they met.

"Um, sorry," Melissa murmured as she took a sip of her water. With her mind still reeling from the results of the pregnancy test, she found it hard to concentrate on the conversation.

"I asked if you've tried the cucumber sandwiches Guy added?" her friend asked patiently as she pointed to the leather-bound folder Melissa held.

Perusing the new healthy-choices section her brother had added to the Sky Lounge lunch menu since taking over managing the resort's restaurants, Melissa shook her head. "No, I hadn't even noticed the new dishes."

Avery frowned. "Is something wrong?"

"Oh, just the usual stuff that goes along with managing a spa," Melissa lied, closing the menu and setting it on the table. She hated not being truthful with her friend, but she needed to talk to Shane about the pregnancy before anyone else.

"Still having problems with your assistant manager, little sister?" Guy asked, walking over to join them. He leaned down to kiss Avery, then seated himself beside her.

"Actually, Rita is doing a little better than she was," Melissa said, thankful to have something to focus on besides her own dilemma. "She did have a moment this morning when I thought her nerves were going to send her into a panic attack, but we got it straightened out."

"In other words, you took care of it," Guy said, knowingly.

"Well, yes," Melissa admitted. "But in all fairness to Rita, there wasn't anyone else to teach the yoga class this morning."

"Are you still taking the weekend off like you planned?" Avery asked.

"Blake thinks I should," Melissa said, shrugging. Guy's fraternal twin and the new CEO of Jarrod Ridge Resort, her oldest brother had pointed out at the last managers' meeting that she needed to back off to see if Rita could handle the assistant manager's position or if she needed to be replaced. "I'll only be a phone call away, so I don't suppose it would hurt to be off for a few days."

"You haven't taken any time for yourself since you started managing the spa," Guy pointed out. "We both know if Rita knows you're available, she'll call."

Melissa rubbed at the tension building at her temples. "I can't just leave her on her own. What if something happens like this morning?"

Guy looked thoughtful for a moment. "If Rita runs into something she can't handle, she can get hold of me or Blake. I'll be around most of the weekend, and you know that Blake will be, too."

"You and Blake both intimidate Rita." Melissa couldn't help but laugh. "Besides, what do you know about running a spa or teaching yoga?"

"Me? Intimidate someone?" Guy grinned. "Just

because I demand the best from my kitchen staff, it doesn't mean that I'm a tyrant." Reaching out, he patted her shoulder. "Don't worry. I'll take care of whatever comes up at the spa. You just relax and enjoy a little down time."

Never having been encouraged by their father to develop close family ties while they were growing up, Melissa and her four brothers had become a lot closer as adults. She couldn't help but wonder what it would have been like if they'd had a strong bond when they were children. Maybe growing up in Jarrod Manor wouldn't have been as lonely for her.

"Thanks, Guy," Melissa said, smiling. "If you need me…"

Her brother shook his head. "I won't." Checking his watch, he rose. "Break's over. Time to go back to the kitchen and see how things are going." He kissed Avery's cheek. "I'll see you this evening."

Watching Guy make his way across the crowded restaurant, Avery sighed happily. "Isn't he just the best-looking man ever?"

"You're in love," Melissa said, unable to keep from feeling a bit envious.

Although they'd had a rocky start, Avery and Guy had the kind of loving relationship she had always envisioned for herself. Unfortunately, what she and Shane had together would never go any further than what it was now—a strong physical attraction that would most likely cool considerably once he learned of her pregnancy.

As she and Avery finished lunch, they chatted about the upcoming dinner honoring the Food and Wine Gala investors. By the time they parted in the lobby an hour later, Melissa was more than ready to get back to Willow Lodge. Shane would be coming over soon, and although she had no idea how he would take the news about the baby, they needed to get used to the idea that in about seven months they were going to be parents.

Shane walked out of the meeting room toward the Jarrod Ridge lobby with a single-minded purpose— find Lissa and convince her to spend the three-day weekend with him at his ranch. The resort's annual Food and Wine Gala had been in full swing for the past couple of weeks, and everything had been extremely busy. The time they'd been able to spend together had been limited, and, now that the event was over, he fully intended to remedy that as soon as possible. He certainly wasn't looking for anything long-term to develop out of their affair, but he wasn't yet ready to give up on whatever they had going on between them, either. He had enjoyed spending time with her the past couple of months and looked forward to at least a couple more before they went their separate ways.

"Shane, my boy, it's good to see you again," a deep, booming voice said from somewhere behind him.

Stopping, Shane turned to smile at one of his

late father's oldest friends. "It's good to see you, too, Senator Kurk. How have you been?" he asked, shaking the man's hand.

"Can't complain," the senator said, smiling. Tall and commanding, the white-haired man had been a member of congress for as long as Shane could remember. "It's always good to get out of Washington for a few days and come back home to spend a little down time with my friends and family."

"I'm sure it is," Shane agreed. "I've heard they're keeping you busy these days with several important national issues."

Senator Kurk chuckled. "And if that isn't enough to keep me awake at night, I've been named the head of a new investigative committee." He looked thoughtful. "Aren't you an architect?"

Shane nodded. "I specialize in stables."

"Interesting," the man said. "I suppose your studies included other areas of architecture, as well?"

"Of course." When the man remained silent, Shane started inching away. "I'm sure you'll get to the bottom of whatever it is your committee is looking into, Senator," he said, hoping the man wasn't at liberty to share what the committee was investigating.

As much as he liked Patrick Kurk, the good senator could be as long-winded and boring as any other politician, and Shane had plans that didn't include listening to him drone on about what ailed the nation. The sooner he got over to the lodge, the sooner he would start what he was certain would be a very enjoyable weekend with one of the most exciting women he had ever had the pleasure of knowing.

"Excuse me, Senator," one of the man's aides said, hurrying up to join them. "The Rotary Club meeting is about to begin and your speech is first on the agenda, right after the opening remarks."

Relieved that his trip over to Willow Lodge wouldn't be delayed any further, Shane smiled. "I won't keep you, Senator. Maybe we can get together for some trout fishing on the Rainbow River the next time you're in town."

"I'll take you up on that the first chance I get," Senator Kurk said, turning to go. "It was good seeing you again, Shane."

Walking out of the resort, Shane forgot all about politicians and senatorial committees as he started out. He was on a mission to get Lissa to join him for the three-day weekend and he wasn't going to give up until he got what he wanted.

Given her concerns about feeding the gossip mongers at the resort, he was pretty sure it wouldn't be all that easy to talk her into staying with him at Rainbow Bend. But there wasn't a doubt in his mind that what they shared would be worth whatever he had to do to convince her.

Shane shook his head as he looked around to see if anyone was watching, then took the hidden shortcut back toward the luxury lodges. He had been jumping through hoops for the past couple of months just to please her, and it was beginning to get old.

Instead of going directly to the lodge where she was staying, it had become a ritual for him to head toward the stables, then cut back through a small patch of woods. She had insisted that no one would think anything of him going to check on the herd of horses he had sold the resort, and he supposed she was right. But he couldn't control other people's opinions of him and didn't give a damn what they thought anyway. Lissa, on the other hand, was a very private person and he respected her need for discretion even if he didn't completely understand it.

Slipping through the stand of pine trees behind Willow Lodge, he took the porch steps two at a time. Just as he raised his hand to knock, Lissa opened the door.

"What took you so long?" she asked, taking him by the hand to pull him inside.

As soon as they cleared the doorway, he took her into his arms and used his boot to shove the door shut behind them. "I don't know a man alive who doesn't want to hear a woman ask that question, angel."

She looked as if she had something more on her mind, but it would just have to wait. It had been almost three days since he had held her, kissed her, and he had every intention of immediately remedying that particular problem.

His mouth came down on hers, and she let out a

startled little squeak, but to his satisfaction, she didn't protest or try to push him away. Instead, she wrapped her arms around his waist and pressed herself against him.

Her response to him never failed to send a flash fire rushing from the top of his head straight to the region south of his belt buckle. Today was no different. In the blink of an eye, he was hotter than a two-dollar pistol on a Saturday night.

Shifting to pull her more fully into him, Shane deepened the kiss. As he stroked and teased, her sweet taste, the floral scent of her silky blond hair and the feel of her soft body pressed to his much harder one had him feeling as if his jeans had shrunk at least two sizes in the stride. He quickly decided that he would do well to end the kiss or there was a good chance he'd end up emasculating himself.

"I've been wanting to do that ever since I saw you at the resort this morning," he said, leaning back to smile down at her.

The dazed look in her vibrant blue eyes and the heat of passion coloring her creamy cheeks was one of the most beautiful sights he had ever been privileged to see. Soft and feminine, Lissa looked the way a woman was meant to look when a man kissed her.

She shook her head as if to clear it. "Shane, before this goes any further. We need to talk."

"Yes, we do," he agreed.

"There's something I need to tell you."

"Me first," he insisted.

He took her by the hand and led her into the great room. Settling himself into one of the oversize leather chairs in front of the stone fireplace, he pulled her down to sit on his lap.

"This is really important, Shane. There's been an unexpected development that—"

He placed his index finger to her soft lips. "It'll have to wait."

"This is something that can't wait."

He gave her a quick kiss to divert her. "I have something I want you to do with me this weekend."

The kiss distracted her just as he had intended. "W-what?"

"I want you to spend the next few days at my ranch with me." When it looked as if she was about to protest, he shook his head. "Hear me out, angel. Most of my ranch hands are off for the holiday weekend and the ones who aren't couldn't care less who I have staying with me. Cactus, my housekeeper, has already left to visit his sister in Denver for the next few days, and we'll have the entire house to ourselves. Unless you tell them, no one who cares will ever be the wiser that you stayed with me."

She looked thoughtful for several long moments before she finally nodded. "We need to discuss something at length and I think it would be a very good idea to have the privacy of your ranch to do it."

Surprised and more than a little pleased by how easily she had agreed, he hugged her close. "Talking wasn't what I had in mind when I asked you to go with me. But I guess we can hash over whatever you think is so important while we rest up from more pleasurable pursuits."

She gave him a warning look. "Will you be serious?"

"Angel, I thought you'd have figured out by now that when it comes to making love, I'm always serious," he murmured as he kissed the side of her slender neck. "But if you think it's necessary, I'll be more than happy to take a few minutes to refresh your memory."

"After I tell you what I discovered this morning, I think you'll agree that there should be less emphasis on teasing and making love this weekend and more concentration on making some very serious decisions about what we're going to do," she said, pulling from his arms to stand up. He watched her shoulders rise and fall as she took several deep breaths. "Shane, there's no easy way to put this and I doubt you'll be happy to hear about it."

His smile slowly faded. Her body language and the seriousness of her tone warned him that whatever was on her mind was most likely something unpleasant. But he had never been one to avoid an obvious problem. He preferred to hit the difficulty head-on, deal with it and move forward.

"Why don't you just tell me outright and get it over with, Lissa?"

"A-all right."

The slight tremor in her voice and the lone tear slowly slipping down her cheek when she turned to face him caused his heart to stutter and had him moving to get to his feet in the blink of an eye. But her next words stopped him stone cold.

"Shane, I'm...pregnant."

Two

Feeling as if he had taken a sucker punch to the gut, Shane stared at her as he sank back down into the plush chair. Rarely at a loss for words, he suddenly couldn't have strung two words together if his life depended on it.

Pregnant. Lissa was pregnant. That meant he was going to be a…he swallowed hard against the knot forming in his stomach…a daddy.

Un-freaking-believable.

He shook his head in an effort to make some sense of his tangled thoughts. He wasn't sure what he had expected her to tell him, but the fact that she was having a baby—his baby—certainly hadn't been it.

Hell, he had never expected any woman to announce that he had made her pregnant.

"The baby belongs to you," Lissa said, sounding a little defensive.

He shook his head. "There wasn't a doubt in my mind about that, angel. When did you see the doctor?"

"I haven't." She bit her lower lip to keep it from trembling and he knew she was thoroughly stressed. "I just took the home test this morning."

"Maybe it was wrong."

"I don't think so. I've missed one period and getting close to missing the second." Her shoulders slumped. "Besides, the test boasts the highest accuracy rate of all the in-home brands."

Suddenly needing a good dose of fresh air and a little time to come to grips with her news, Shane rose to his feet. Walking over to her, he used the pad of his thumb to wipe the tear from her cheek.

"Why don't you pack a bag for the weekend while I go get my truck?"

"But what if someone sees us leaving town together?" she asked, looking uncertain.

"We've got bigger things to worry about than what some busybody with nothing better to do than spread gossip is going to say about seeing the two of us together," he interrupted, anticipating her argument. Taking her into his arms, he pressed a quick kiss to her forehead. "Once we get to Rainbow Bend, we can discuss things, sort it all out and decide what we're going to do. For now, get your things together and be ready to go when I get back." Without waiting for her to change her mind or find an excuse to stay at the resort, he quickly released her and walked outside.

Pulling the door closed behind him, Shane stood on the deck for several mind-numbing moments and gazed at the panoramic view of the Rocky Mountains against the bright blue September sky. Splashes of gold from the aspen trees making their annual autumn transformation painted the slopes and quavered delicately in the slight breeze. He saw none of it.

He was too focused on the fact that he had done the one thing he had sworn he would never do. Hell, he had never even considered fathering a child as part of his life plan.

But he had just learned that particular horse had left the barn and there was no sense in closing the gate now. As he saw it, all there was left to do was man up, accept his responsibilities and do the right thing. It was what his morals demanded and his father would have expected of him.

Filling his lungs with the crisp mountain air, Shane straightened his shoulders and descended the steps. Walking toward the main part of the resort, he knew exactly what he had to do.

He had made Melissa Jarrod pregnant. Now, it was time for him to make her his wife.

The drive to Shane's ranch was mostly spent in quiet reflection as they both contemplated the ramifications of the unexpected turn in their no-strings affair. By the time they reached Rainbow Valley, Melissa felt as if her nerves were stretched to the breaking point. Grappling for something—anything—to keep from thinking about their dilemma, she glanced around.

She had only been to the Rainbow Bend Ranch once before and that had been several years ago when her father had coerced her into accompanying him on a horse-buying trip for the resort. It had been a lame attempt on his part to bridge the ever-widening gap between them. She hadn't wanted to be there and spent the time wishing she was anywhere else, instead of taking in the gorgeous scenery.

But as Shane drove the truck over the ridge and down the winding road leading into the picturesque valley, she couldn't get over the breathtaking view. "This is beautiful, Shane. You're so lucky that you got to grow up here."

"I like it," he said, stopping the truck beside a rustic two-story log ranch house. "But not everyone appreciates the isolation."

Melissa frowned. "You make it sound as if it's stuck out in the middle of nowhere. I wouldn't consider ten miles outside of Aspen all that far from civilization."

"That's because you haven't been here in the winter," he answered, shrugging one shoulder. "When we get a heavy snow, the road up on the ridge can be closed off for weeks at a time, making trips into town few and far between."

"How did you get back and forth to go to school when you were a child?" she asked, remembering that he had graduated with honors.

"When I was younger and winter hit, I stayed in Aspen with my dad's sister and her family until they moved to New Mexico." He got out of the truck and walked around to open the passenger door for her. "By the time they left Colorado, I was almost out of school and old enough to stay on my own."

"That's when you stayed at Jarrod Ridge, wasn't it?" she guessed. Required by her father to work at the resort after school and on weekends, she vaguely remembered seeing Shane working with the horses the few times she had escorted guests to the stables.

Nodding, he reached into the bed of the truck for her overnight case, then placed his hand on the small of her back as he guided her toward the house. "My dad and yours had an agreement that I could stay at Jarrod Ridge the winter of my senior year, in exchange for me wrangling on the weekends and acting as a guide on some of the trail rides."

"Considering how much you've always loved horses, you probably didn't have much of a problem with that," she said, smiling as they climbed the steps to the wraparound porch.

He shook his head, then reached around her to open the front door. "Since the resort buys all of its stock exclusively from Rainbow Bend, it was like taking care of my own horses."

When they entered the house, Melissa got her first glimpse of Shane's home and it came as no surprise that everything from the pieces of antique harness and tack decorating the walls to the foyer's chandelier made of elk antlers was rugged and thoroughly masculine. Just like the owner. There wasn't so much as a hint that a woman had ever lived there and she couldn't help but wonder what had happened to his mother.

Melissa tried to think if she had heard anything about the woman. Nothing came to mind. Had his mother passed away when Shane was a child like her mother had?

"Cactus left this morning for Denver, so we'll be on our own for meals," Shane said, interrupting her thoughts. He hung his wide-brimmed hat on a peg beside the door, set her small bag on the floor and reached to help her out of her jacket. "Just let me know when you get hungry and I'll throw a couple of steaks on the grill."

She frowned. "For the past couple of weeks, it seems that I'm hungry all of the time."

"Is that because of the pregnancy?" She watched his gaze zero in on her midsection as if he was looking for a significant change to have taken place in the past few days. Apparently finding none, he raised his gaze to meet hers. "I remember one of my hired men joking about his wife eating like a field hand when she was pregnant with their little boy."

"I wouldn't say I'm that bad yet, but I do think the pregnancy could be the cause for the increase in my appetite." She nibbled on her lower lip as she tried to remember what some of her friends had mentioned about the early stages of their pregnancies. Nothing came to mind about constantly being hungry. "Since I've never been pregnant before, I'm not really sure," she said, shrugging.

He stared at her for several long seconds before nodding. "We'll have to check with your doctor about that when you go for your first visit." Looking thoughtful, he added, "In fact, it would probably be a good idea to start making a list of the things we need to ask him."

"Whoa, there, Cowboy. What do you mean by 'we'?" She shook her head. "I don't remember inviting you to go along with me."

"Doesn't matter. I'm going," he stated, as if it were a foregone conclusion.

"Why?"

"We'll discuss my reasoning later, as well as make a few important decisions," he said, giving her the same charming grin that never failed to make her pulse race. He picked up her bag and ushered her toward the stairs. "Right now, I'll show you to the bedroom and let you freshen up while I put the steaks on to cook."

When he guided her up the steps and down the

hall, she was a bit surprised that he opened a door and showed her into one of the guest rooms. They'd never spent an entire night together and she had assumed when he asked her to spend the weekend with him, he had intended for her to sleep in his room. But after hearing the news of her pregnancy, she had no doubt that his previous insatiable desire for her had cooled considerably.

He set her bag on the bed, then turning to go, took her into his arms. "When you get ready, come down to the kitchen. I should have supper ready in about twenty minutes." Then, before she could react, he softly kissed her cheek and left the room.

As she unzipped her case and started to put her clothes away, a sadness she couldn't quite understand filled her. Why did Shane's diminishing interest in her bother her so much?

It wasn't as if they were in love. They had both agreed before beginning their affair that the time they spent together would be relaxed and casual with no emotional involvement getting in the way of their respective careers.

Now that she had been given the responsibilities of running the resort's world-class spa, she had her hands full. She would love to have a husband and family of her own one day, but now just wasn't a good time to do it. Besides, Shane wasn't the right man to make that dream come true. His reputation for moving from one woman to another was only slightly better than her brother Trevor's.

Along with raising championship quarter horses, Shane was a highly successful architect specializing in the design of exclusive stables. His client list included some of the richest, most famous people in the equine world and he simply didn't have time for more than a casual relationship, anyway.

Melissa bit her lower lip to keep it from trembling. It was times like this that she missed having a mother the most. She would love to be able to turn to her mother and ask for her advice. Unfortunately, Margaret Jarrod had died of cancer when Melissa was two and she had grown up without the love and nurturing guidance of a mother.

Shaking off her uncharacteristic gloominess, she finished unpacking, then took a deep breath and stepped out into the hallway as she headed for the stairs. She had known her time with Shane would end at some point. She just hadn't realized it would be so soon. Nor could she have anticipated that she would be pregnant with his baby when it happened.

"When do you intend to call the doctor's office for your first appointment?" Shane asked, reaching for his glass of iced tea. Lissa had been extremely quiet for most of the meal and it was past time they addressed the issue that had been on both of their minds since she made her announcement that afternoon.

When she looked up from the bite of steak she had been pushing around the plate with her fork, she shook her head. "I really haven't thought that far ahead. I only took the test this morning. Then, before I had the chance to recover from the shock of the results, I was called to take over the yoga class at the spa and later met Avery for lunch."

"Shortly after you finished that, I showed up at your door and here we are," he guessed.

She nodded. "I still haven't had time to fully comprehend the fact that I'm actually going to have a baby."

"It is pretty unreal, isn't it?" He was having a hard time wrapping his mind around that fact himself.

Her vivid blue gaze reflected some barely contained panic and he was fairly certain he had that deer-in-the-headlights look about him, as well.

"I knew it was possible," she said, finally laying her fork down. "But seriously, only one time unprotected and I get pregnant? The odds against that happening have to be pretty high."

"Looks like that's all it took for us." He reached across the table to cover her hand with his. "But I want you to know, you aren't going to have to go through this alone. We're in this together. I'll be there to support you every step of the way, Lissa."

"I appreciate that." She stared at him for several long moments before she finally sat back from the table. "But if you mean monetarily, I think we both know that isn't necessary. I'm financially independent and have more than enough to handle whatever expenses there are before and after the birth."

Given their initial agreement to keep things casual, he could understand her misinterpretation of his promise, as well as her reluctance to believe he would commit himself to anything more than monetary assistance. But the idea that she considered him so shallow and irresponsible that he would just walk away from her and the child they created still didn't sit well.

"I'm not talking about child support," he stated, doing his best to keep his tone even.

"What *are* you talking about, Shane?" she asked, looking confused.

Rising to place their plates on the kitchen counter, he turned to face her. "I'm telling you that I'll be with you for doctor appointments, the baby's birth and raising him."

"In other words, you're telling me you're going to want joint custody." She nodded. "I can understand that and I don't see a problem. I'm sure we can work something out."

"Custody is going to be a nonissue," he said, shaking his head. He walked over to squat down beside her chair, then reaching up to brush a strand of long blond hair from her cheek, he smiled. "I'm pretty sure that sharing the responsibility of a child is automatic when his parents are married."

Her eyes widened and her mouth opened and closed several times as she obviously tried to find her voice. "Married?" she finally gasped.

"Yes."

Her expression stated louder than words ever could that she didn't believe him. "*Married* as in the tiered cake, white dress and 'I do'?"

"Yup."

"No."

"Why not?"

She closed her eyes, then opening them, shook her head as she pinned him with her crystalline gaze. "Have you lost your mind, Shane? You can't possibly be serious."

"Angel, marriage is one subject I never joke about," he said, meaning it.

"We can't get married, Shane," she insisted. "Beyond the basics, we really don't know that much about each other."

"Sure we do." He stood up and, lifting her into his arms, sat down in the chair to settle her on his lap. "I know you like when I do this." Kissing the side of her neck, he was rewarded with her soft sigh. "And you really like this," he added, slipping his hand beneath the tail of her aqua T-shirt. He used his fingertip to trace the satiny skin covering her ribs. As he slowly lowered his head, he moved his hand. "But you love this."

His mouth covered hers at the same time his hand cupped her breast and to his immense satisfaction, Lissa didn't so much as put up a token protest. Encouraged by her response, Shane deepened the kiss and once again marveled at her sweetness and the feeling of completion he always experienced when he held her.

He had kissed a lot of women in his time, but not one of them made him feel the way Melissa Jarrod did. Her slender body fit perfectly against his and her passion never failed to excite him in ways he could have never imagined.

His lower body tightened predictably and he decided he had better break the kiss before things got out of hand. At the moment, Lissa needed his comfort far more than she did his lust.

Drawing in some much-needed air, he smiled. "I told you I knew a lot about you."

She shook her head as if to clear it. "I wasn't talking about pleasing each other sexually and you know it."

"Correct me if I'm wrong, but isn't that a huge part of marriage?" he asked, unable to keep from grinning.

"Maybe for a man, but a woman needs more from a relationship than just good sex," she insisted. "*I* need more."

He raised one eyebrow. "Would you care to enlighten me?"

Leaning back, she stared at him for a moment as if she thought he might be a little on the simple side. "Do you realize we've never spent more than a few hours together at any one time? I may know you intimately in bed, but I don't know anything about you otherwise. I don't know what you like to read, what kind of movies you prefer or even what your favorite color is."

He frowned. "I don't see how any of that would make or break a marriage."

She pulled from his arms and stood up. "Don't you see? Those are the kinds of things you know about the person you are committing to spend the rest of your life with." Sighing heavily, she turned to face him. "I don't even know what side of the bed you sleep on or if you snore."

"So you're telling me that knowing whether I snore or not is more important than a gratifying love life?" he asked, laughing.

If looks could kill, the one she sent his way would have him laid out in two shakes of a squirrel's tail. "Will you be serious, Shane? I'm trying to explain what constitutes a committed relationship."

Oh, he knew exactly what she was driving at. Lissa thought she needed to know what made him tick. But she was wanting more from him than he was comfortable giving. He had never been in the habit of sharing more than the surface details about himself with anyone and he wasn't inclined to do so now.

Unfortunately, if he wanted her to go along with his plan, he was going to have to give her something she considered relevant. "Nonfiction, action-adventure, red and left."

She looked confused.

"I mainly read nonfiction and my favorite movies are action-adventure. I like the color red and I prefer the middle of the bed. But if I had to choose a side, it would be the left." He grinned. "As for the snoring, you can let me know about that tomorrow morning."

"Those things are nice to know," she said, looking a little more satisfied with his answers. "But that's just the tip of the iceberg."

Before she could press him further and delve into areas he would rather not go into, he decided to turn the tables and ask a few questions of his own. "What about you? What is there about Lissa Jarrod that you think I need to know?"

He gave himself a mental pat on the back at her pleased expression. "Let's see. I like pizza, I hate Brussels sprouts—"

"Who doesn't?" he said, making a face.

She laughed. "And I adore romantic movies."

"What about horses?" he asked, wondering if they had that in common. "Do you like to ride?"

"I haven't ridden in several years, but I used to enjoy going on some of the trail rides offered at Jarrod Ridge." Smiling, she added, "I even had a favorite horse named Smoky Joe that I always rode."

Shane stood up and took her into his arms. "I don't remember you going on any of the rides I guided."

Loosely wrapping her arms around his waist, she gazed up at him. "That was because I was too young. When you were eighteen and leading those trail rides, I was only eleven."

"Now hold on just a minute," he said, frowning.

"Didn't you tell me one time that you worked at the resort when I did?"

"Yes." He felt her body tense. "Of course, I wasn't on the payroll. But I started doing simple things like delivering messages from one office to another. That was when I was eight."

"Ah, the pre-e-mail and text-messaging days."

She nodded. "By the time I turned ten I had graduated to showing guests how to find their way around the resort grounds. Then, at sixteen, I started working the front desk."

Shane wasn't opposed to a kid doing a few chores. Hell, his dad had him mucking out stalls and feeding horses from the time he was old enough to carry a feed bucket. But it sounded as if Donald Jarrod had his kids doing more than just simple chores.

"Whose idea was it for you to go to work at such an early age?" he asked, remembering that he had seen all of the Jarrod children working various jobs around the resort.

She shrugged one slender shoulder. "My father wanted all of us to know the business inside and out. I suppose he thought by starting us out young, we would learn what made Jarrod Ridge the premier resort in Aspen."

He could tell by the tensing of her muscles and the tight tone of her voice that they were skirting a touchy subject. "Do you think it would be all right for you to go riding tomorrow?" he asked, deciding to lighten the conversation. It was obvious she didn't care to talk about her father or the resort and he would have a much better chance of her agreeing to marry him if she were in a better mood. "I'd really like to show you the rest of the ranch. But if you think it would hurt you or the baby, we can wait," he hastened to add.

Her expression brightened. "I would really like that. I'm pretty sure it will be all right. I have a friend in California who rode her horses until she was six months pregnant and everything was fine."

"Great." He pressed a kiss to her forehead. "If you think what you saw of the ranch from the top of the ridge is beautiful, you'll really like seeing Rainbow Falls."

Her eyes twinkled with excitement, making him glad that he had thought of taking her to see it. "You have a waterfall on your property?"

"Yup."

"I love waterfalls. They're always so peaceful and relaxing. We even have the sound of a waterfall piped into the massage rooms at the spa."

"We'll have to get up early," he warned. "It will take us several hours to get there because of the terrain, but believe me, it's well worth it." For reasons he didn't understand and wasn't inclined to dwell on, he wanted to make the outing special for her. Thinking quickly, he added, "I thought we could pack a few sandwiches and have lunch by the falls."

"That sounds absolutely wonderful, Shane." She

covered her mouth with her hand to hide a yawn. "I can't wait."

"I think you'll have to." He chuckled. "Aside from the fact that it's already dark outside, you'd probably fall asleep in the saddle before we rode out of the ranch yard."

"You're probably right." She yawned again. "For the past few days, it seems that I can't get enough sleep."

"Is that because of the pregnancy, too?" He knew a whole lot more about pregnant mares than he did about pregnant women, but he figured it could be the reason behind her fatigue.

"I assume that's the reason," she said, resting her head against his chest.

Shane tightened his arms around her and lowering his head, covered her mouth with his for a quick kiss. Then, reluctantly stepping back, he turned toward the kitchen counter. "Why don't you go into the living room and put your feet up while I load the dishwasher and clean up?"

"Are you sure I can't help?" she asked, sounding tired.

"Positive. It won't take but a few minutes." He rinsed their plates and started stacking them in the dishwasher. "There is one thing you could do for me, though."

"What's that?"

"Turn on the sports channel and see if you can

catch who won the game this afternoon between the Rockies and the Cardinals."

"You're a baseball fan?"

Looking at her over his shoulder, he grinned. "I like baseball as much as the next guy. But this game is kind of special. I have a bet going with Cactus and I'd like to see who wins. He thinks the Cardinals will sweep the Rockies in this three-game series and I say they won't."

Laughing, she shook her head as she started toward the living room. "Men and their sports."

As he started the dishwasher, he couldn't help but think about how fast his plans had changed. When he had first come up with the idea of bringing Lissa to the ranch for the weekend, he had thought they would be spending the majority of their time within the confines of his bedroom. But that had changed in the blink of an eye with her announcement that she was going to have his baby.

Now, even though it made him as jumpy as a day-old colt, his main priority was convincing her to let him do the right thing by her and the baby. He wiped off the counter, then turning out the kitchen light, headed for the living room.

He had three days of uninterrupted time with her to figure out how to get her to say yes. Given her argument about their not knowing enough about each other, it probably wasn't going to be easy.

Smiling to himself as he walked down the hall, he decided he was more than ready for the challenge.

His personal code of honor demanded that he make her his wife and help her raise their child. And there wasn't a doubt in his mind that before he took her back to Aspen, she would agree to be just that.

Three

When Shane turned off the television, Melissa asked, "How much money did you win from your housekeeper?"

"None. If he had won, I was going to have to cook for the next month." Shane laughed. "But since he lost, the old boy is going to have to keep the driveway cleared of snow until spring."

"How old is Cactus?" she asked, hoping he was younger than Shane made him sound.

"I'm not sure," he said as he rose from the couch to take her hand in his. "He's a little sensitive about his age, but I'm pretty sure he's at least seventy and probably a few years older than that."

"He's that old and you're going to make him get

out in the cold to clear the snow?" she asked, allowing him to help her to her feet. She didn't like the idea of Shane taking advantage of the older gentleman. "Tell me you're going to take pity on him and let him out of this stupid bet."

"Not on your life." Grinning, he shook his head. "I don't feel the least bit sorry for him. He'll be on a tractor with a heated cab, a built-in CD player that he can crank up as loud as he wants with his favorite bluegrass music, and if I know Cactus, he'll have a Thermos of Irish coffee to keep him company."

"You make it sound like he was going to win either way."

Shane nodded as they climbed the stairs. "We go through this every fall. He'll come up with a bet he knows he can't win in order to do something he enjoys."

She didn't understand that kind of logic. "Then why doesn't he just volunteer for the job?"

"Because that's not how the old guy works," he explained. "When his arthritis started making it hard for him to do some of the ranch work, I knew he didn't want to leave the ranch. It's been his home for as long as I can remember. So I started complaining about needing someone to cook and take care of the house." Shane grinned. "I didn't really need anyone to do that, and he knew it. But he couldn't come right out and ask me for the job."

"So that's when the bets started?" she guessed.

Shane nodded. "He bet me that I couldn't beat his

time at saddling a horse. If he won, I had to buy him a new pair of boots and if I won, he would take the housekeeping job."

She liked that Shane would go to those lengths to preserve the older man's dignity. It told her a lot more about his character than he realized.

"You did it to save his pride."

"Exactly." Chuckling, Shane opened the door to the room he had shown her earlier. "So, with this latest bet, he not only gets to drive the tractor and pretend he's doing ranch work again, he has something to gripe about while he's doing it. And if there's anything he likes better than complaining, I don't know of it. He got his nickname because he's prickly as a cactus."

Melissa smiled as she entered the room. "He sounds like quite a colorful character."

"He is." Leaning one shoulder against the door-frame, Shane folded his arms across his wide chest. "He can be an ornery old cuss, but he's got a heart of solid gold. I'll make sure you get to meet him sometime."

"I'd like that." When he stood there as if he waited for something, she rose up on tiptoes to kiss his cheek. "Good night."

Before she could back away, he put his arms around her. "It will be once we go to my room."

"I don't understand." With his strong arms around her and the feel of his hard body pressed to hers, she suddenly felt winded. "If you wanted me to spend the night in your room…why did you put my case…in here?"

"I thought you might like to have the privacy this afternoon when you freshened up," he said, nuzzling the side of her neck. "I never intended for you to sleep here."

When his lips skimmed the hollow below her ear, a tingle raced up her spine. "Oh, I thought—"

"—I'd want you to leave my bed once we'd made love," he finished for her. "Not a chance, angel."

That wasn't what she had been thinking, but it was better than telling him that she thought he had lost interest in her now that she was pregnant. Some men couldn't get away from a woman fast enough when they learned of an unplanned pregnancy. Not knowing him any better than she did, what else was she to think?

But apparently she had been wrong about his desire waning. She sighed. It was just one more example of their lack of knowledge about each other, not to mention a serious breakdown in communication.

Before she could point that out, he asked, "Where's your bag? I'll take it to my room."

Taking a step back, she walked over to open one of the dresser drawers and removed her nightshirt. "After I unpacked, I put it in the closet."

He frowned as he pointed to the garment she held. "I've never known you to wear nightclothes."

"That's because you always left my place before I put them on," she shot back. "And since you seemed surprised to learn that I do wear a nightshirt, I assume you don't wear anything to bed."

"Nope," he said, grinning. "I don't like the encumbrance."

She shook her head. "This is what I was talking about earlier, Shane. If we had spent more time getting to know each other, we would know these things."

"You never wanted me to spend the night because you were afraid someone at the resort might find out and start gossiping about it," he pointed out.

She couldn't argue with him about that. It had been at her insistence that he leave Willow Lodge each night after they'd made love.

"But that's water under the bridge now," he said, shrugging.

Too tired to debate the issue any further, she nodded. "I suppose you're right."

He put his arm around her shoulders and steered her out into the hall. "I'll help you move your things to my room in the morning before we leave. Right now, we need to get to bed. We'll have to be up early if we're going to have lunch at the falls tomorrow."

When he led her into his bedroom and turned on the bedside lamp, she took a moment to look around. A lot could be learned from someone's personal space.

She wasn't at all surprised to see the large room was decorated in the same rustic, masculine style as the downstairs. A king-size log bed with a Native American–print comforter and pillows dominated the room. The bright colors of the matching drapes contrasted perfectly with the dark log walls and heavy, peeled-log dresser and chest of drawers.

If she had ever had any doubts about Shane being the quintessential cowboy, they were gone now. One look at his choice of decor was all it took to know that he was a lot like the land he loved—rugged and a little wild. The type of man that was dangerous to a woman's peace of mind. The very type women just couldn't seem to resist.

"How long has your family owned the ranch?" she asked.

"A little over a hundred and twenty-five years." He unbuttoned his shirt. "Hasn't your family owned Jarrod Ridge about as long?"

Fascinated by the play of his chest muscles when Shane shrugged out of the shirt, it took a moment for her to realize what he had asked. "Y-yes, my father's great great-grandfather started it and every generation since has expanded the business."

"What do you think your generation will add to the resort?" he asked, unbuckling his belt and reaching for the button at the waistband of his jeans.

"I don't know," she said absently. She was far too engrossed in watching him reveal his magnificent body to worry about what would happen at Jarrod Ridge.

When he pushed the denim down his thighs, her heart skipped a beat. She had watched him strip off his clothes many times since they began their affair.

She had even helped him take them off a few times, but the sight of his well-developed physique never failed to take her breath away.

"Aren't you going to change?" he asked as he reached for the waistband of his boxer briefs.

He either didn't know the effect he had on her or he was intentionally trying to drive her crazy. She suspected it was the latter.

Suddenly feeling as if she would burst into tears and not entirely certain why, Melissa quickly took off her clothes and pulled the nightshirt on. Walking around to the right side of the bed, she got in and closed her eyes. She was on Shane's ranch, in his bed and pregnant with his baby. It was all too much to comprehend.

Overwhelmed by the events of the day and completely exhausted, she couldn't stop a tear from slipping from beneath her lashes. She swiped it away with the back of her hand and turned onto her side in hopes that he hadn't noticed.

"Lissa, are you crying?"

"N-no."

She felt the other side of the bed dip as Shane stretched out beside her. A moment later, he wrapped her in his arms and turned her to face him.

"What's wrong, angel? Why are you crying?"

His concerned tone and the feel of him holding her so tenderly against him was all it took for the floodgates to open. Sobbing her heart out and unable to stop herself, she clung to him as the torrent of emotion ran its course.

"I—I don't know…why…that happened," she said when she was finally able to get her vocal cords to work. She had never been more embarrassed in her entire life.

"I think I do," he said as his hand continued to stroke her hair in a soothing manner. "You've had a hell of a day and you're so tired you can barely keep your eyes open."

His understanding words and the gentle tone of his deep voice helped ease some of her humiliation. "You're probably right. I think this has quite possibly been the most stressful day I have ever endured."

He reached over to switch off the lamp. Then, cradling her to him, he kissed her so tenderly another wave of tears threatened.

"Try to get some sleep, angel." His arms tightened around her. "It's all going to work out. I give you my word on that."

Too exhausted to think about everything that had happened since her return to Aspen two months ago for the reading of her father's will, Melissa snuggled against Shane and closed her eyes. Maybe with the morning light things would be clearer. Maybe then she would be able to cope with the fact that her life had spun completely out of control and there didn't seem to be a single thing she could do to stop it.

When Shane led the gelding out of the barn and over to the fence, he smiled. "Does this horse look familiar?"

Lissa's blue eyes twinkled with excitement. "He looks just like Smoky Joe."

"That's because he's old Smoky's little brother," he said, handing her the reins. After hearing that the blue roan had been her favorite at Jarrod Ridge, Shane purposely chose the horse for her to ride to Rainbow Falls.

"Thank you," she said as she softly stroked the horse's velvet muzzle. "What's his name?"

"He's registered with the American Quarter Horse Association as Smoke Storm, but we just call him Stormy." Walking back into the barn to get a saddle and blanket from the tack room, Shane returned to placed the saddle over the top fence rail. Then, smoothing the saddle blanket over the gelding's back, he added, "I don't want you to worry that he might be more than you can handle. In spite of his name, there's nothing stormy about him." He picked up the saddle and positioned it on the blanket. "I've seen kittens with more piss and vinegar than this guy."

Lissa smiled as she hugged the animal's neck. "Smoky Joe was that way, too. You could do just about anything with him."

Shane nodded. "That's why we bred the same mare and stallion several different times. The colts they foaled were all good-natured and perfect for people who aren't used to riding a lot."

"In other words, perfect for the inexperienced guests at Jarrod Ridge," she guessed.

He pulled the cinch tight. "That was the idea."

While Lissa and Stormy got to know each other, Shane quickly saddled his sorrel stallion. "Need a leg up?" he asked, turning to see if she needed help mounting the roan.

"I think I can get this," she said, slipping her booted foot into the stirrup.

He stepped behind her in case she had problems and immediately decided that he would have done well to take her at her word. When her perfect little blue-jeans-clad bottom bobbed in front of his face as she climbed onto the saddle, the air rushed out of his lungs like helium from an overinflated balloon.

Holding her soft body to his throughout the night, then waking up with her in his arms this morning without once making love to her, had been a true test of his control. But Lissa hadn't needed his lust. She had needed his comfort and he had been determined to give it to her or die trying.

Exhausted, emotionally spent and extremely vulnerable, she had tried to give the impression that she was fine. He knew differently and once he had taken her into his arms, she had finally let down her guard and accepted the support he had promised her. But not without considerable cost to his well-being.

With her breasts pressed to his chest and her delicate hand resting on his flank, he had spent the entire night aroused. And if that hadn't been enough to send him hovering on the brink of insanity, he had awakened this morning with one of her long, slender legs intimately lodged against his overly sensitive groin.

That had sent him straight into the bathroom for a cold shower. By the time he finally stepped from beneath the icy spray, his teeth had chattered uncontrollably and he would have bet everything he had that he could spit ice cubes on command.

Unfortunately, his gallantry was beginning to wear thin. He wasn't sure how much longer he would be able to play the consummate gentleman without going stark, raving mad.

"Earth to Shane. Come in please," Lissa said, bringing him back to the present.

"What?"

She laughed. "I asked if you are going to just stand there daydreaming or if we're going for a ride?"

"Uh, sorry," he muttered. He couldn't tell her that he had been thinking about how much he wanted to hold her, how much his body ached to be inside her. "There are a couple of different ways to get to the falls and I was trying to decide which would be the fastest," he said, thinking quickly. There was only one trail leading to the waterfall, but she didn't know that and he wasn't about to admit that he'd been fantasizing about stripping them both and making love to her until they both collapsed from exhaustion.

"How far is it to Rainbow Falls?" she asked as he mounted the stallion and they rode through the corral gate.

"It's only about three miles as the eagle flies, but having to skirt some of the steeper terrain and due to all of the bends in the river, it takes a few hours," he explained.

She gave him a wistful look. "I wish I had known about this trip before we left the lodge. I'd have brought my camera. I'm sure the scenery is going to be gorgeous."

He decided not to remind her that once he made her his wife, she would be able to take as many pictures of his ranch as she wanted, any time she wanted. But he wasn't a fool. If he did remind her of that fact, she would most likely come up with more ways they didn't know each other and be on the defensive.

That was the last thing he wanted. His plan hinged on the element of surprise. When he played his ace in the hole, he had no doubt he would have her agreeing to marry him faster than he could slap his own ass with both hands.

"Shane, this is absolutely breathtaking," Melissa said as they rode single file over the ridge and around a switchback into the upland valley.

"It isn't much good for pasturing the horses, but I like to camp out here occasionally," he said, leading the way down the slope.

"I love camping out," she said, remembering the wonderful time she'd had when her father allowed her to go on a couple of overnight trail rides with some of the resort's guests.

It had taken considerable thought on her part and several arguments with her father to convince him that she would be there to address any special needs of the Jarrod Ridge guests. He had finally relented, but only after she had pointed out that she would technically still be working for the resort and not just frittering away her time. God forbid that she did something with her time that she actually enjoyed, she thought, unable to keep from feeling resentful.

"What's wrong?" Shane called over his shoulder.

Jarred back to the present, she focused on the man riding the big red stallion ahead of her. "Nothing. Why do you ask?"

Stopping his horse, he turned in the saddle. "I've seen happier faces on condemned felons."

"The sun was in my eyes," she said, hoping he would drop the matter.

"If you say so." His expression told her that he wasn't buying her excuse, but to her relief, he let it go.

She didn't want to discuss the unreasonable demands Donald Jarrod had placed on his children. It was something she had spent her entire adult life trying to forget and she certainly didn't want to ruin an otherwise glorious day thinking about her childhood. Besides, she didn't know Shane well enough to share the dirt on a family that, up until her father's death and the subsequent discovery that she had an illegitimate half sister, had an impeccable reputation.

They rode in companionable silence for some time before he pointed to the river. "As soon as we go around this bend, you'll see Rainbow Falls just off to the right."

Riding side by side once they cleared the tree line, Melissa's attention once again turned to Shane. He was an expert horseman and handled the stallion with ease. But aside from admiring the way he sat the horse, she simply loved watching him.

With his black Resistol pulled down low on his brow to shade his eyes and a day-old growth of beard, he looked a little wild, possibly dangerous and totally delicious.

A tremor coursed through her and she had to remind herself that lusting after the man was not conducive to getting her life back under control. Not only had she become pregnant because of it, the physical attraction she had for him was in danger of transforming into something deeper, something more meaningful.

Even though what she felt for him was probably nothing more than a temporary infatuation, in the end it could still do a lot of emotional damage and leave behind some deep long-lasting scars.

As devastatingly handsome and charming as Shane was, he just wasn't the type of man for her. He had the reputation of moving from one woman to another, leaving a string of broken hearts in his wake. Given the circumstances they found themselves in now, that was one complication she could definitely do without.

He had made it clear right up front that he wasn't looking for a lasting commitment. Neither was she. She had her own business in California and she might be returning to her life there once the year required to obtain her inheritance was over. She'd reasoned that it was better not to look for anything deeper than a casual relationship until she had decided what she was going to do. After witnessing what some of her friends went through as they tried to maintain long-distance commitments, she had quickly decided it wasn't for her. Things never seemed to work out, and the hurt and disillusionment that went along with a breakup was something she definitely wanted to avoid.

Besides, she hadn't really taken Shane's proposal seriously. That's why she had dismissed outright his outrageous suggestion that they get married. It had to have been a knee-jerk reaction to the startling news, and once he had more time to think about it, she was certain he would see reason. He would probably even be relieved that she'd had the foresight to turn him down.

The sound of rushing water brought her out of her disturbing introspection and, looking up, Melissa realized they had ridden around the bend in the river and arrived at Rainbow Falls. It was everything Shane had told her and more.

Cascading from the ridge high above, the water fell a good seventy-five feet onto the massive boulders below, then slowing, it formed the lazy river that meandered across the valley floor. What caught and held her attention more than anything was the faint rainbow caused by the sun reflecting off the mist created by the falling water.

"It's absolutely beautiful," she said, understanding why it had been named Rainbow River.

"I was pretty sure you would like it." She could hear the satisfaction and pride in Shane's voice and knew he was pleased that she hadn't been disappointed.

They stopped the horses along the riverbank just out of the icy mist and dismounted. As soon as her feet hit the ground, her legs felt as if the tendons had been replaced with stretched-out rubber bands and her muscles had turned to Jell-O.

When she took a wobbly step, Shane was immediately at her side to support her. "Are you all right?"

Nodding, she took another tentative step. "I should go riding more often. Maybe then I would be in better condition."

Shane took her into his arms. "I think you're in great shape, angel." He laughed. "You'd have to be to twist yourself up like a Christmas bow in those yoga classes."

"Yoga is more about stretching and relaxing the muscles." Smiling, she enjoyed the feel of him holding her to him. "Horseback riding takes a certain amount of tensing the thigh muscles to help you stay balanced in the saddle."

"Your thigh muscles don't seem to be all that weak when you hold on to me," he said, nuzzling the side of her neck. His deep baritone sent shivers of excitement streaking up her spine and her legs threatened to fail her for an entirely different reason this time.

Before Melissa had the chance to respond to his suggestive words, his mouth came down on hers and she forgot all about her weak knees or the internal lecture she had given herself about lusting after the man. All she wanted, could even think about, was the feel of his lips moving over hers with such gentle care.

When he used his tongue to coax her to allow him entry to her tender inner recesses, she wrapped her arms around his waist and held on for dear life. As he teased and coaxed her to answer his exploration with one of her own, a lazy heat spread throughout her body and her lower stomach tightened with the ache of unfulfilled desire.

But the spell that seemed to hold her in its grip was broken when he moved his hands to lift the tail of her pink T-shirt and the icy mist coated her bare abdomen. The breeze had shifted, carrying the spray farther than when they first got off the horses and they were both getting wet.

Shane quickly moved them out of the way, but the mood was effectively shattered and not a moment too soon. What on earth had she been thinking?

She had forgotten all about why going blithely along as if nothing had happened wasn't going to solve her dilemma. They hadn't fully discussed or made any decisions about her being pregnant, and that was something they were going to have to address in the very near future. The pregnancy couldn't be hidden indefinitely. Once she started showing, people were going to start talking and asking questions. She wanted to be ready with some answers when they did.

Unfortunately, it was always this way when Shane held her, kissed her. Sound judgment and common sense seemed to take a backseat to the passion and desire he created within her.

"I think we'd better...break out those sandwiches we made...before we left your house," she said, trying to catch her breath. "I'm starting to...get hungry."

His mouth curved upward in a wicked grin. "To tell you the truth, Lissa, I am starved to death right now. But my hunger hasn't got a damned thing to do with food."

Doing her best to ignore the excitement that his candid comment evoked, she walked over to the roan and began unpacking one of the saddlebags. "You, Mr. McDermott, are incorrigible."

He laughed as he helped her spread a blanket for their picnic. "More like insatiable, angel."

"That may be, but do the best you can to contain yourself," she said, smiling as she carried their lunch to the blanket.

Kneeling at the edge of the fleece, she avoided his intense blue gaze as she placed the sandwiches on plates, then opened two small bottles of apple juice. If she looked at him, there was a very good chance she would abandon her resolve and that was something she couldn't afford to let happen.

"We have things to talk about and decisions to make," she said, taking a sip from her juice.

His expression turning serious, Shane lowered himself to sit on the blanket beside her. "Let's put a hold on that for right now. We'll have plenty of time to make our plans tomorrow." Smiling, he reached for a sandwich. "You need to take today to relax and regroup, anyway. Yesterday was a pretty rough day for you."

It was the first reference he had made to her meltdown the night before, and she was grateful that he didn't seem overly interested in pursuing it now. "Maybe you're right."

"I know I am," he said, sounding so darned sure of himself, she wasn't sure whether she should kiss him or take something and bop him with it.

Either way, she decided to take his advice. There would be plenty of time tomorrow to figure what to do about a carefree affair that had unexpectedly become a very serious issue.

Four

The first shadows of evening had just begun to stretch across the valley when Shane and Lissa rode back into the ranch yard. All in all, it had been a pretty good day, he decided as they dismounted. He had been more than a little pleased by her reaction to his ranch and looked forward to showing her more when they had time.

"I've been thinking that supper in front of the television would be nice tonight," he said, leading their horses into the stable. "We can watch a movie on one of the satellite channels or pop a DVD in the player." Unsaddling the stallion, he carried the tack and blanket into the tack room, then returned to the center aisle of the stable to do the same with the roan. "Although, I think I had better warn you. I don't have much in the way of romantic movies in my collection."

"Why doesn't that surprise me?" she asked, laughing as she reached for a brush to groom the gelding. "I have to admit though, a night of vegging out does sound nice. And whatever you choose to watch is fine with me. I'll probably fall asleep before the opening credits even get started."

Finished with brushing the stallion, Shane led the animal down to his stall, then returned for Stormy. "Why don't you go on to the house and take a hot shower? It will only take me another few minutes to feed and water the horses."

Without waiting to see if she took him up on his suggestion, Shane walked Stormy to his stall, then set about giving the animals oats and filling their water troughs. He was surprised when he turned around to find that Lissa had sat down on a bale of straw beside the tack room door to wait for him.

"I thought you were going to take a shower and change," he said, walking up beside her.

Shrugging, she smiled. "I thought we could go back to the house together."

He liked the sound of that and without hesitation, he picked her up and sat down to settle her on his lap. Her arms automatically circled his neck and she laid her head on his shoulder.

Damn, but he loved holding her like this. "Legs still a bit wobbly from riding so much?"

"A little. But not as bad as the first time I dismounted." She snuggled closer. "Thank you for today," she said softly. "I really enjoyed seeing your ranch and Rainbow Falls. It's all very beautiful."

Her warm breath whispering over his neck and the feel of her cradled against him sent his hormones racing. His arousal was not only immediate, it left him feeling light-headed from its intensity.

"I'm glad you had a good time," he said, shifting to a more comfortable position.

"I've been thinking, Shane."

He didn't like the sound of her tentative tone. "About what?"

"This weekend should probably be our last time seeing each other."

Her voice was so quiet he wasn't sure he had heard her correctly. But a bucket of ice water couldn't have been more effective at putting an end to his overly active libido.

Sitting her up on his lap, he met her gaze head-on. "You want to explain yourself? What do you mean this is our last time together?"

She sighed. "Jarrod Ridge is a family-oriented resort. Some of the older investors would likely take a dim view of our having an affair."

"What do you think is going to happen when they find out you're pregnant out of wedlock?" he shot back. The way he saw it, they'd take the news a whole lot better and be less likely to condemn if she had the baby's daddy standing beside her.

She nibbled on her lower lip a moment before shaking her head. "I've thought about that, too. I'm hoping they won't find out."

A chill raced up his spine. She wasn't talking about…

"I'll have to check with our attorney, Christian Hanford, to see if there's a way to keep from losing my inheritance if I move back to California. But having the baby out there would keep the talk down around the resort," she said, oblivious to the fact that she had damned near given him a coronary before she finished explaining. "You and my family will be the only ones who know that I've had a child. I know they'll keep that kind of news quiet in order to keep from jeopardizing our business."

Why did everyone's opinion matter so much to her? For that matter, why did the whole family protect the Jarrod Ridge reputation as if it were as valuable as the gold in Fort Knox?

"Why the hell are you protecting the resort above all else, Lissa?" he asked before he could stop himself. But once the words were out, he couldn't really say he regretted the question.

She looked stunned. "What do you mean?"

"Why are you scared to death about what everyone is going to say or think?"

Shane knew he was treading on dangerous ground, but he had a feeling that it had been drilled into her as a child that appearances were everything and the reputation of the resort came before anything else.

Even if it meant sacrificing her own happiness or well-being.

Her body stiffened and he knew he had hit the nail on the head. "My father's death caused enough upheaval. Jarrod Ridge doesn't need unrest among the people with a vested interest in its success," she insisted. "We need their funding to bring more events to the resort."

He could tell she was avoiding having to answer his questions. He decided to let that slide for now. But eventually she was going to have to stop putting that damned resort and its precious reputation ahead of her own wants and needs. And if it took him having to bring that to her attention, he was up for the challenge.

"I'm one of the investors in the resort and I couldn't care less what the majority of those old goats think."

He pulled her close and wondered what kind of childhood she'd had. If being put to work at the age of eight and her unrealistic concerns about gossip were any indication, it had to have been miserable.

"But we aren't going to talk about any of that now," he said, determined to change the subject. "This afternoon, we made an agreement to get this all straightened out tomorrow. I'm going to hold you to that."

Deciding not to give her the opportunity to argue the point further, he captured her mouth with his. Resistant at first, he felt her begin to relax against him as he traced her perfect coral lips with his tongue, then coaxed her to open for him. His blood heated and his body reacted as it always did when she was in his arms. When he stroked her tongue with his, he could tell from her soft moan that she was as turned on as he was.

Unfortunately, sitting on a bale of straw in a stable had to be one of the least sensual places on earth. Cursing himself as nine kinds of a fool for starting something he couldn't finish until they went to the house, he groaned and reluctantly broke the kiss.

"I think it's about time we took that hot shower," he said, setting her on her feet.

"We?" she asked as he rose to take her hand in his and hurry her toward the stable doors.

He didn't even try to stop his wicked grin. "I've decided it's about time for the ranch to 'go green.' We'll save water by showering together."

When they reached the house, Shane stopped only long enough to remove their boots, then led Melissa toward the stairs. No matter how foolish it might be, she willingly followed him straight into the master bathroom.

She was determined not to think about this weekend being the end of their affair or the loneliness she would suffer once it was over. It might not be smart, but she wanted to store up the memory of his tender touch and the strength of his lovemaking. She would need them on those lonely nights that lay ahead of her once they stopped seeing each other.

"You do realize you're way overdressed for a shower, don't you?" he asked, his blue eyes twinkling with mischief as he closed the door.

She smiled. "I could say the same thing about you, Cowboy."

"Really?" He reached for the snaps on his chambray shirt as he took a step toward her. "I'm pretty sure I can remedy that."

"Don't." She reached up to remove his hat, then hanging it on the doorknob, took his hands in hers and lowered them to his sides. "Let me see if I can take care of it for you."

Releasing the first closure, she kissed his tanned collarbone. "That wasn't too difficult," she said, lightly skimming her nails along his skin as her fingers traveled on to the next snap. She flicked it open, then pressed a kiss to the newly exposed skin. "Neither was that."

His abdominal muscles contracted when she continued on to the next one. She smiled as she slowly released each closure to nibble and kiss his perfect torso. "I think I'm starting to get the hang of this."

"Oh, I would say you've become quite proficient at it." His voice was husky and when she glanced up, the heated look in his blue gaze stole her breath.

As they continued to stare at each other, she finished unsnapping his shirt and tugged the tail of it from the waistband of his jeans. Parting the lapels,

Melissa moved to push the garment over his shoulders and down his arms.

Her heart skipped a beat as she gazed at his sculpted chest and abdomen. Unable to resist, she touched the hard ridges of his stomach with her fingertip, then traced the thin line of hair from his navel to where it disappeared into the waistband of his jeans. She was rewarded with his sharp intake of breath.

"You've got a good start there, angel," he encouraged. "Don't stop now."

"I don't intend to." Unbuckling his leather belt, she shook her head. "I was always taught not to quit until a job was finished." She released the button at the top of his jeans and toyed with the metal tab below. "And to make sure the job was done to the best of my ability."

Slowly, intentionally, she pulled the zipper downward. By the time she eased it over his persistent arousal to the bottom of his fly, Melissa wasn't certain which one of them was having more trouble drawing their next breath.

"Oh my, Mr. McDermott," she teased as she lightly touched the bulging cotton of his boxer briefs. "You seem to have a bit of a problem."

His big body jerked as if an electrical charge had coursed through it. "You caused my current dilemma. Now what are you going to do about it?" he asked through gritted teeth.

The feral light in his eyes caused a delicious

warmth to spread throughout her being. "What would you suggest I do?"

"Finish what you started."

Smiling, she put her hands on his sides, then slipping her fingers inside both waistbands slid his jeans and underwear over his hips and down his legs. He quickly stepped out of them, then kicked them to the side.

She took a moment to appreciate his perfection. Her heart skipped several beats as she let her gaze slide from his handsome face down his torso and beyond. Muscles developed by years of hard ranch work padded his shoulders and chest and his stomach was taut with ridges of toned sinew. Every cell in her body tingled as she took in the beauty of Shane's male body and his strong, proud arousal.

"I love your body," she found herself murmuring.

"It was made just for yours, angel." Lifting the hem of her T-shirt, his grin was filled with such promise it sent goose bumps shimmering over her skin. "Since you've been so nice and helped me out, I think it's only fair that I return the favor."

"I think so, too," she said.

As methodically as she had removed his clothing, Shane removed hers and tossed them into the growing pile on the bathroom floor. When he removed the last scrap of silk and lace, he stood back.

"You're absolutely gorgeous, Lissa." He pulled her into his arms, and the feel of hard masculine flesh touching her much softer feminine skin caused a need within her so deep it reached all the way to her soul.

"I think we'd better take that shower while we still have the strength," he said, his voice hoarse.

She waited until he adjusted the water, then stepped under the luxurious, multiheaded spray. When he joined her, Shane turned her away from him, then reached for a bottle of shampoo. As his large hands began to gently massage her scalp and work the shampoo down the long strands, Melissa didn't think she had ever felt anything more sensual than having him wash her hair.

Neither spoke as he rinsed away the last traces of shampoo, then reached for the soap. Working the herbal-scented bar into a rich lather, he held her gaze as he slowly smoothed his hands over every inch of her body and by the time he was finished she felt more cherished than she ever had in her entire life.

"My turn," she said, taking the soap from him.

Treating him to the same sensuous exploration, she took the time to commit to memory every muscle and cord of his perfect physique. When she finally touched him intimately, she watched him tightly close his eyes. His head fell back and a groan rumbled up from deep in his chest a moment before he took the soap from her, rinsed them both thoroughly, then gathered her to him.

He lowered his head and the moment his mouth came down to cover hers, she put her arms around his wide shoulders and her eyes drifted shut. She could feel herself being lifted and automatically brought her legs up to wrap them around his lean hips. They fit against each other perfectly, and when he entered her with one smooth stroke, Melissa reveled in the feeling of being one with him.

As water sprayed over them from all sides, their wet bodies moved together in perfect unison, and all too soon, she felt herself start to climb toward the peak of completion. Her muscles tensed as the need grew and intensified. Then, as if something inside of her broke free, pleasure filled every fiber of her being and stars danced behind her tightly closed eyes.

Almost immediately Shane's body surged within her a final time and he crushed her to him. She held him just as tightly as he rode out the storm and found his own shuddering release.

When she finally gained the strength to move, Melissa leaned back to look at his handsome face as he still held her to him. For the past couple of months, she had told herself their affair was strictly physical and she could walk away from it at any time with no regrets. She now realized that she had been deluding herself. From the moment he introduced himself at a meeting between her family and the Jarrod Ridge investors, she had not only been attracted to him physically, she had been drawn to his charming personality and easy sense of humor.

"You're amazing," he said, giving her a tender kiss as he lowered her to her feet. He turned off the shower, then helping her out of the enclosure, patted them both dry with a large, plush towel. "Why don't I pop a pizza in the oven and find something for us to watch on one of the movie channels, while you dry your hair and get dressed?" he asked as he wrapped the towel around her, then tucked it under her arms.

"That sounds wonderful," she said, realizing she was actually quite hungry.

He gave her a smile warm enough to melt the polar ice caps. "I'll meet you downstairs on the couch in about twenty minutes."

Feeling more relaxed than she had since taking the pregnancy test, Melissa picked up the hair dryer and turned it on. She wasn't going to think about their predicament, what they were going to do about it or that in less than two days she would no longer be enjoying a few stolen hours with Shane. Tonight she was going to concentrate on the moment and face tomorrow when it came.

"What's your life like out in California?" Shane asked as the movie he had selected for them ended.

The film's storyline had been about a woman returning to her hometown and the life she had left behind to do that. That got him to thinking. He knew what it had been like for Lissa since returning to Aspen for the reading of her father's will. She had to stay for at least one year and manage the Tranquility Spa in order to inherit her share of Jarrod Ridge. But her life in Los Angeles remained a complete mystery to him.

"Life in southern California is, in a word, hectic." She shrugged one slender shoulder. "I've been there since I started college and you would think I'd be used to the pace after all this time."

Her answer surprised him. "But you're not?"

"Not really." She shook her head and shifted on the couch to face him. "Everyone is always in such a hurry to get somewhere or to do something. Then, when they do accomplish whatever they set out to do, they are in a huge hurry to do something else."

"Life in the fast lane can be draining," he said, wondering why she had chosen to go to college so far from home. "But I think it's that way in most urban areas."

She nodded as she removed the fluffy tie holding her hair in a ponytail. "It's a little better in Malibu where I live now, but life still moves a lot faster than Aspen."

"That is a nice area." He had been to Malibu a few times and although it was way too crowded for his taste, Shane had found the view of the ocean to be beautiful. "Do you live near the beach?"

"I have a condo not too far from the Malibu Pier." She smiled. "I like living on the beach and my spa and yoga center, Serendipity, is only a couple of miles away. That's another plus for me."

"Who's running things while you're away?" he asked, reaching out to tuck a wayward strand of hair behind her ear. "I'm sure you left someone you could trust in charge."

He ran his index finger over her hair. He loved the feel of the silky golden threads against his skin. He drew in some much-needed air and forced himself to concentrate on what she was saying. Lissa felt it was important that they talk and learn about each other. Besides, if he was going to get her to go along with his plans of getting married, he was going to have to pay a little closer attention.

"I have two wonderful assistant managers." She smiled fondly. "Michael is very efficient at managerial duties and in the treatment room his hands are pure magic."

"Oh, really?" For reasons he didn't quite understand and wasn't ready to analyze, the only hands Shane wanted her to consider magical were his.

Her enthusiastic nod caused a slow burn to start in the pit of his stomach. "Michael warms the oil with his hands, then when he puts them on your body and starts kneading the muscles..." She closed her eyes and smiled as if imagining the man's hands on her. "...it's pure heaven."

The irritation in Shane's gut exploded into all-out anger and he couldn't figure out why. Maybe it had something to do with the fact that Lissa seemed to enjoy having the man's hands on her a little too much. It might even be the probability that she had been alone with the guy in a dimly lit room with nothing but a thin sheet draped over her nude body. Or more likely, it was a combination of all of it. Whatever the reason, he didn't like it one damned bit.

But Shane couldn't understand the proprietary feeling he had toward her. It wasn't as if he hadn't been with his share of women before Lissa returned to Aspen. It would be ridiculous of him to expect her to have gone without companionship before they started seeing each other. Yet he couldn't quite shake the territorial feeling that ran through him.

"Aren't some of the women who work for you just as good at giving massages?" he asked, wondering why she hadn't asked one of her female employees.

She nodded. "In their own way, yes, they are very good. But being a man, Michael naturally has more strength in his hands and gives a more thorough deep-tissue massage."

"How long has he worked for you?"

"Let's see, he and his life partner, Hector, moved from Florida into the condo below mine about three years ago, and I hired them both shortly after that," she said, looking pleased with herself. "I was really lucky to get them before another spa snapped them up. Besides Michael being the best masseuse I've ever seen, Hector is a master yoga instructor and conducts most of the yoga and meditation classes at Serendipity. He's my assistant manager for the yoga center."

Shane's anger cooled immediately when he realized neither of the men were interested in Lissa. The fact that he felt such relief was almost as disturbing to him as his possessiveness had been. He had never been the jealous type and couldn't imagine what the hell had gotten into him.

Deciding it was time for a change of topic, he asked, "Do you miss not living near the beach?"

"Absolutely," she said, nodding. "Listening to the waves is nice, especially at night when I'm ready to go to sleep. I like to sit on the beach sometimes and watch them roll in to shore. It reminds me of how small and insignificant my problems are compared to the big picture."

"Don't you miss watching the seasons change, angel?"

"They do change," she admitted. "But it's subtle and not nearly as big of a change as here. It's beautiful here in the fall." She grinned. "And I do love Aspen in the winter. There's nothing like flying down the mountain on a pair of skis after a new snow."

"You like the fresh powder?"

"Absolutely." She tilted her head. "What about you? Do you like to ski?"

He gave her a mischievous grin. "I have been known to tear it up on a few of the slopes around here. I've also done a little cross-country skiing."

Yawning, she leaned her head back against the couch. "I've missed being able to participate in the winter activities we have in the mountains."

"They have some nice skiing in California," he reminded her.

"Yes, but I would have to drive several hours to

get there." She smiled. "I like having a ski slope practically in my backyard."

"Then why did you go to college in California in the first place?" he asked before he could stop himself.

Shane had a feeling it had something to do with her getting away from home and the control of Donald Jarrod. But she'd shied away from discussing her relationship with her father, and from her expression, she wasn't interested in discussing it now.

She hesitated as if choosing a suitable answer. "I was young and wanted to spread my wings a bit." Hiding another yawn behind her hand, she gave him a sheepish grin. "I think I need to go up to bed before I fall asleep right here."

He knew she was making an excuse to escape before he had the opportunity to ask any more questions. "You're probably right." Turning off the television, he rose to his feet, then helped her to hers. "What do you say we go upstairs and see just how good I am at giving a massage?"

"But I don't have a problem with tightness in my shoulders or neck," she said as he led her toward the stairs.

"Angel, I wasn't talking about massaging your back." He couldn't stop his wicked grin. "The areas I had in mind are on the front side of your body and a whole lot more interesting."

Shane lay staring at the ceiling long after the woman in his arms drifted off to sleep. The evening had been perfect and given him a glimpse of what life could be like once he and Lissa were married.

Married. The word alone should have had him running for the hills, and he still couldn't quite believe that he was actually going to take the plunge.

Two days ago, the idea of marriage and having a child never crossed his mind. It was simply something he had never allowed himself to contemplate. He had witnessed the hell his father went through when his mother left and that was more than enough to convince Shane he wanted no part of the institution.

He could remember the nights he had lain in bed as a small boy listening to his mother and father argue about how unhappy she was living out in the middle of nowhere. Eventually her pleading for his father to sell the ranch and move them all to a metropolitan area had turned to threats of her leaving.

Then, one day when he was nine, Shane came home from school to find his mother gone and his father passed out with an empty whiskey bottle at his feet. Cactus had stepped in to watch over him and when his father finally sobered up after a two-month bender, Shane asked several times where his mother was. "Gone" was all he could get out of his father each time he asked. Shane finally gave up and stopped asking.

But Hank McDermott was never the same after that. Other than being there to raise his son and instill a strong set of values in him, it was as if his dad had quit caring about everything else and reminded

Shane of a horse that had its spirit broken. Once full of life, his father rarely left the ranch and removed everything in the house that hinted a woman had ever inhabited the place.

Shane had never wanted to give that kind of power over him to any woman. Never wanted a child of his to lie awake at night wondering where his mother was and why he never heard from her again. But with Lissa's announcement that she was pregnant, he suddenly found himself determined to do the very thing he had vowed never to do—get married.

Glancing at her head resting on his shoulder, he took a deep breath and tried to relax. As long as he kept everything in perspective and his feelings for her under control, everything should be fine.

He would be a good provider, a faithful husband to her and a loving father to their child. That's all any woman could ask of a man and all Shane was ready or willing to give.

Five

"It's about time you hauled your sorry butt out of bed."

At the sound of the elderly gentleman's comment, Melissa stopped abruptly just inside the kitchen doorway. Standing at the stove, wearing nothing but a pair of long underwear and boots that had seen better days, the man had his back to her and apparently only heard her approach. She assumed he was Shane's housekeeper, Cactus, and he obviously thought that Shane had come downstairs for breakfast.

How could she let him know that she wasn't who he thought she was without startling him?

When he suddenly turned around, they both jumped. "God's nightgown! Where in the name of Sam Hill did you come from?"

"You must be Cactus," she said, unsure of what else to say. "Shane's told me a lot about you."

"Well, he never told me a damn…danged thing about you," he stammered. "If he had, I sure wouldn't be standin' here in nothin' but my long johns." His wrinkled cheeks turned fiery red above his grizzled beard. "Excuse me, ma'am. I'll go get myself decent."

The man disappeared into a room off the kitchen as quickly as his arthritic legs would allow. A moment later, Shane walked up behind her to wrap his arms around her waist.

"How did you manage to get breakfast started so fast?" he asked, kissing her nape.

Her skin tingled from the contact. "I didn't. It appears that your housekeeper, Cactus, has arrived home a little earlier than expected."

He sighed as he rested his chin on her shoulder. "I'm sorry, Lissa. I should have known this would happen. Whenever he goes to see his sister they always get into an argument and he ends up coming home early about half the time."

"It doesn't matter." She turned within the circle of his arms to smile up at him. "Cactus probably doesn't know anyone affiliated with the resort. Besides, I seriously doubt that he would tell them I was here, even if he did."

Shane kissed the tip of her nose. "Why is that, angel?"

"Because he knows I could tell them I caught him

cooking breakfast in his long underwear," she said, laughing. "If his blush was any indication, I think I embarrassed him all the way to the roots of his snow-white hair."

Rolling his eyes, Shane shook his head. "He definitely marches to the beat of his own drum. But don't worry. He'll get over it."

"Boy, I got a bone to pick with you," Cactus groused as he limped back into the room. "Why didn't you tell me you were gonna have a lady friend comin' for a visit this weekend?"

"I didn't figure it would matter, since you weren't supposed to be here," Shane answered, unaffected by the older man's irritation. Releasing her, he walked over to the coffeemaker. "Have a seat at the table, Lissa, while I pour us a cup of coffee. Lissa, this is Cactus Parsons, my housekeeper and the orneriest old cuss you'd ever care to meet."

"It's nice to meet you, Cactus," she said, smiling.

He nodded. "Ma'am."

Remembering something one of her friends had mentioned about not drinking caffeinated beverages while pregnant, Lissa shook her head. "Thank you, but I think I'll pass on the coffee."

When Shane walked over to sit beside her at the table, Cactus asked, "How do you like your eggs, gal?"

"Say scrambled," Shane whispered. "That's the only way he knows how to cook them."

"I heard that, and it ain't true," the old gentleman retorted. "I know how to put cheese in 'em or if your lady friend would like onions and green peppers, I can make 'em that way, too."

Shane laughed. "But they're still scrambled."

"It don't matter," Cactus insisted, his toothless grin wide. "They're still different than just plain old eggs."

Having grown up in the house where teasing and good-natured banter hadn't existed, Lissa enjoyed listening to the exchange between the two men. It told her a lot about the kind of man Shane was.

Besides going out of his way to preserve an old man's dignity by making bets they both knew were a complete farce, Shane went along with and even encouraged the man's complaints because he knew it made Cactus happy.

That was something her father certainly would have never done for one of his employees. For that matter, he hadn't bothered to do anything even remotely similar to that for his own children.

There wasn't a single time in her life that she could remember her father teasing or playing with her or her brothers. He had reminded them on a daily basis from the time they were old enough to listen that if they weren't excelling academically or working to somehow improve Jarrod Ridge, they were letting themselves down and disappointing him.

"Here you go, gal," Cactus said, interrupting her

thoughts as he placed a plate of bacon and eggs in front of her.

As soon as the plate touched the table, the food that had smelled so delicious only a few moments before caused a terrible queasiness in the pit of her stomach. Glancing at Shane, she watched his easy expression turn to one of concern and she knew she must look as ill as she felt.

Unable to make an excuse for leaving the table, Melissa jumped from the chair and ran as fast as she could for the stairs. She barely managed to make it into the master bathroom and slam the door before falling to her knees.

She had never in all of her twenty-six years been as sick as she was at that moment. If the fact that she was pregnant hadn't sunk in before, it certainly had became very real now.

Feeling as if the blood in his veins had turned to ice water, Shane took the stairs two at a time as he chased Lissa. What the hell was wrong with her?

She had seemed fine when they got up and came downstairs for breakfast. Then, without warning, she'd turned ghostly pale and bolted from the room like a racehorse coming out of the starting gate.

As soon as he entered his bedroom he heard her and found the bathroom door locked. "Lissa, let me in," he demanded.

"Go…away…Shane." Her voice sounded weak and shaky.

"Not until I know you're going to be all right." If he had to, he would break the damned door down. But he wasn't going anywhere until he found out what was wrong with her.

"I think…I have…morning sickness," she said, sounding downright miserable. "Please leave…me… alone so I…can die…in peace."

Feeling completely useless, Shane drew in a deep breath and walked over to sit on the end of the bed while he waited for her nausea to run its course. He felt guilty. If not for one of his swimmers, she wouldn't be in there feeling as if death would be a blessing.

He rested his forearms on his knees and stared down at his loosely clasped hands. He wished there was something he could do for her, but he was at a total loss. Horses didn't suffer through morning sickness and, since he never intended to have a wife and kids, he had never bothered to learn more than the basics about human pregnancies. Now he was going to have to play catch-up and learn all he could on the subject.

Several minutes later as he sat there mentally compiling a list of things that he wanted to research, he heard the bathroom lock click open and Lissa slowly opened the door. His heart slammed against his ribs at her appearance.

She looked as though she had just been through hell. Her usual peaches-and-cream complexion was still a pasty white, perspiration dotted her forehead and her long blond hair hung limp around her shoulders.

"I asked for privacy," she said, sounding completely spent.

"I gave you as much as I thought you needed." He might fall short with his lack of knowledge, but there was no way he would have left her on her own and gone back downstairs. "Does morning sickness last the entire length of the pregnancy or is it a short-term thing?"

Walking over to sit down on the bed beside him, she shook her head. "Every pregnancy is different. Some women have it for the entire nine months and others aren't bothered by it at all. My friend in California only had a problem with morning sickness for a month or so before it disappeared."

Nine months of being sick every morning? Just the thought made his skin crawl. In his estimation even a day or two was way too much.

"Is there something the doctor can give you to keep it from happening?" he asked, hoping there was.

He put his arm around her shoulders and tucked her to his side. Surely in this day and age there had to be something to help a woman get through it.

"I think there is medication to help with the nausea, but since I haven't been to the doctor yet, it's irrelevant at the moment." She yawned. "Maybe it would be a good idea for you to take me back to the resort this afternoon."

Shane didn't have to think twice about his answer. "No way." Rising to his feet, he pulled her up with him, then walked her around to the side of the bed. "There's no one there to take care of you and as sick as you are, I don't want you being by yourself."

"If I need something or someone, I can call Erica," she said, referring to the half sister the Jarrod children had learned of during the reading of their father's will.

"We both know you wouldn't do that," he stated, pulling back the comforter. "Your sister would want an explanation, and you aren't ready to give her one." He motioned for her to lie down. "I told you that I was going to see you through all of this and that is exactly what I intend to do, angel. Now, stretch out and take a nap. Maybe you'll feel better when you wake up."

"You're not going to be a bully about this, are you?" she asked. He thought she might dig her heels in and try to resist him telling her what to do, but to his satisfaction she climbed into bed. "Because if you are, I'm not—"

"Only if I have to be, to make sure I keep you and the baby safe and well," he said, careful to keep his voice gentle. Pulling the cover up over her, he sat down on the side of the bed. "Now get some rest, Lissa." It was only after he kissed her smooth cheek that he realized she had already fallen asleep.

Shane wasn't certain when he had developed the fierce protectiveness that coursed through him now, but there was no denying its presence or its overwhelming strength. Staring down at the blond-haired woman in his bed, he silently made her a promise. No matter what it took, he would do everything in his power to keep her and their child safe and healthy.

"Where's Cactus?" Melissa asked when she came downstairs to find Shane sitting at the computer in his office.

"He and a couple of the men who stayed around for the weekend are playing poker down at the bunkhouse," Shane answered, looking up from the screen.

"What excuse did you give him about my…sudden exit from the room?" She could only imagine what the outspoken old man had to say about that.

"He didn't ask," Shane said, shaking his head. "He muttered something about it being my fault he burned the bacon as he scraped your plate into the garbage disposal." He shrugged. "I didn't bother to correct him." His expression changed to one of concern. "Are you feeling all right?"

His consideration touched her deeply. She had awakened to find a plate of crackers and a cup of weak tea on the bedside table, along with a note from him, telling her not to get up until she had consumed both. Apparently Shane had found the home remedy on the Internet, and whether it had been the nap or the crackers and tea, she did feel a lot better.

Nodding, she sat down in one of the two leather armchairs in front of his desk. "Right now I'm doing fine. I don't know for certain, but I assume since it's called 'morning sickness' that I won't be bothered again until tomorrow when I wake up."

"Good." He stood up and walked around the desk to sit in the chair beside her. "I've been checking the Web for information on pregnancy and doctors. If the tea and crackers work to help alleviate the worst of the nausea, it's best to stick with that, rather than a prescription medication. I'll set my alarm to get up earlier and have them waiting on you when you wake up tomorrow."

She smiled. "It sounds like you've done quite a bit of research."

"You wouldn't believe how much information there is on pregnancy." Clearly amazed, he shook his head. "The first thing we need to do is make an appointment with an obstetrician and get you on prenatal vitamins. Then, we'll have to review your diet to see where nutritional adjustments are needed."

Melissa stared at him a moment as she tried to assimilate Shane the ladies' man, with Shane the expectant father. "I intend to call for an appointment as soon as you take me back to Aspen," she assured him. "And I'm certain I'll be given instructions on what foods I should avoid and what I should add to my diet, when I see the doctor."

Nodding his obvious approval, he went on. "We'll also need to—"

She held up her hand to stop him. "Back up, Cowboy. Where is all this 'we' stuff coming from?"

"I told you, angel. I'm going to be with you every step of the way." He reached over to take her hand in his. "You're not going through this alone."

"I truly appreciate your willingness to help," she said slowly. "But if I'm in California and you're here in Colorado—"

"That's unacceptable," he interrupted, shaking his head. "I'm not going to let you risk losing your inheritance, Lissa."

"And I can't take the risk of having even one of the investors pull out of the upcoming projects planned for Jarrod Ridge."

Unable to sit still, Melissa rose to her feet to pace the floor in front of his drafting table. They had reached the moment she had been dreading. Decisions were going to be made that would affect the rest of their lives, as well as that of their child's. She just hoped with all of her heart they made the right choices.

"There are a lot of people dependent on the resort's success." She needed to make him understand. "Jarrod Ridge is the single largest employer in Aspen. If future projects like the Food and Wine Gala are canceled because the investment capital isn't there, people will start losing their jobs."

"None of that is going to happen," he said calmly.

Turning to face him, she couldn't believe his assertion. "You know Elmer Madison and Clara Buchanan. They are huge investors in Jarrod Ridge and two of the most puritanical members of the group, not to mention the most influential. We both know they'd disapprove of me becoming an unwed mother and convince several of the other investors to take their money elsewhere. I can't be responsible for—"

"The first thing I want you to do is calm down," he cut in. "Stress isn't good for you or the baby." His commanding tone indicated that the issue wasn't up for debate. "And the second is, you're worrying for nothing. Once they learn we're getting married, there's nothing they can say without looking like the pompous, judgmental asses they are."

"Shane—"

"Hear me out, Lissa." He rose to his feet, then walked over to loosely wrap his arms around her waist. "There's no way I'm going to allow you to go back to California to have our baby alone."

"You're starting to sound like a bully again," she warned. No one had told her what she was or wasn't going to do since she had left home after high-school graduation, and she wasn't inclined to let Shane pick up where her father had left off.

"I'm not being a bully. I'm trying to get you to see reason." His tone was less dictatorial and he had apparently gotten the message that she wasn't going to be ordered around. "This is my child, too, Lissa. We may not have planned on you becoming pregnant, but that doesn't mean I don't want to be just as much a part of his life as you do."

She had always wanted children some day and prayed that their father would be more interested and involved than her own father had been with his. That would be next to impossible with her living in one state and Shane in another.

Nibbling on her lower lip, she shook her head. "I'm sure we could work something out that gives us both equal time."

"Don't you see? Marrying me solves everything, angel." He drew her close to press a kiss to her temple. "You get to keep your inheritance, the resort keeps its investors and our baby gets a full-time momma and daddy to raise him."

Either her resistance was down or what he said was beginning to make sense to her. She did want to maintain her share of Jarrod Ridge and she could likely only do that by remaining in Aspen to manage Tranquility Spa. If she married Shane, some of the investors might grumble about her becoming pregnant before the marriage, but it should be enough to keep them from pulling their funding.

Leaning back, she gazed up at his handsome face. She had always hoped to have a husband and family, but in her dreams she had imagined marrying for love, not to save the resort's reputation and funding.

He must have sensed her resolve was weakening. "I give you my word that you won't regret becoming my wife, Lissa," he promised. "We can make this work. We already have a lot more going for us than other couples have."

His statement took her by surprise. "We do?"

He nodded. "We get along well, we enjoy and appreciate some of the same things, we have a fantastic love life and a baby on the way. The way I see it, that's a damned fine start."

"But there's still a lot we don't know about each other," she said, unwilling to give in so easily.

"We'll learn as we go," he said with a knowing grin.

The skunk knew she was going to agree with his plan. Was it too much to ask that he not gloat about it?

"How would we tell everyone the news?" she asked, wondering what her family would say.

Shane looked thoughtful for a moment. "I can make reservations to throw a dinner party in the Sky Lounge. I'm a Jarrod Ridge investor and given the way your family feels about losing its backers, I'm sure your brothers, sister and their significant others will feel compelled to attend."

If there was one thing she was certain of, it was the compliance of her family with one of the resort's investors. Shane and his father before him had contributed quite a lot of money to special events at

Jarrod Ridge. There was no way her brothers would risk losing that.

"I can't think of a single reason that anyone in my family would turn down your invitation."

"Good." His grin widened. "Now, can you think of anything else we should do before we tell your family?"

She shook her head. "Not at the moment."

"Then there's only one thing left to do." He dropped to one knee and taking her hand in his, smiled up at her. "Melissa Jarrod, would you do me the honor of becoming my wife?"

Staring down at Shane, she couldn't help but wonder what she was getting herself into. "I can't believe I'm about to say this," she murmured. Closing her eyes, she took a deep breath. Then, straightening her shoulders, she opened her eyes and nodded. "Yes, Shane, I'll marry you."

Six

The following week as he sat thumbing through a magazine in the obstetrician's waiting room, Shane took note of the pregnant women around him. Their stomachs were various sizes, and he couldn't help but wonder what Lissa would look like in the months to come.

Tossing the magazine on a table beside his chair, he glanced over at her, sitting beside him. He tried to envision her slender figure growing large with his child. From his research, he had learned that some women didn't start showing their condition until late in the pregnancy, while others blossomed early. He wondered which way Lissa would carry their baby.

His speculation was cut short when a nurse called

their names. "Melissa and Shane, if you'll follow me, we'll get your blood work taken care of and weigh you before the doctor does your examination."

Once the woman had drawn Lissa's blood and collected what she needed for a variety of other tests, they were ushered into a small room at the end of the hall. Taking both of their health histories, the nurse finally gave Lissa instructions on preparing for the examination and left the room.

"I think they know more about me now than I do," Lissa said as he helped her lay back on the uncomfortable-looking table.

"If you stick with the same doctor, they'll have all the information on record and it won't take as long the next time," he said, seating himself in a chair beside her.

Raising up on one elbow, she looked at him as if he had sprouted horns and a tail and carried a pitchfork. "Next time?"

"Well, I assumed you'd want more than one child," he said, wondering what the hell had gotten into him. They were just at the beginning of one pregnancy and he was talking about another?

If someone had told him a week ago that he would be sitting in a doctor's office, waiting to find out when his baby was due, he would have laughed them into the next state. Now, he found himself looking forward to learning the approximate time he would become a daddy and discussing the possibility of even more children.

Unreal.

"Let's get me through this pregnancy first," she advised, lying back down against a pillow. "Then we'll discuss our options."

He was saved from opening his mouth and making things worse with her when an attractive middle-aged woman, wearing a set of scrubs and a lab coat, walked into the room. "I'm Dr. Fowler," she said, smiling.

For the next half hour, the doctor examined Lissa, told them what to expect during the first trimester and answered their questions. Then, giving them an approximate date in April for the birth, she handed them a list of do's and don'ts and told them to make an appointment to see her in a month.

"I think I'm on information overload," Shane said as he escorted Lissa across the clinic parking lot to his truck. He helped her up into the cab, then walked around to the driver's side and slid in behind the steering wheel. "What do you say we go to the ranch and chill out until the dinner party tomorrow night?"

"That sounds good," she said, buckling the shoulder belt. "I don't particularly want to run into any of my family until after we tell them our news."

"Why not?" he asked, starting the truck. Never having had a brother or sister, sibling dynamics were something of a mystery to him.

"My brothers probably haven't noticed my frequent absences from the spa this week, but I know my sister, Erica, and my brother's fiancée, Avery, have." She shook her head. "They're sure to ask why I canceled our lunch date today, and I don't want to lie to them."

"I don't blame you." He liked that she was honest and preferred not to say anything, rather than tell a lie.

"Have you told Cactus anything about all of this?" she asked, hiding a yawn behind her delicate hand. "I'm sure he's curious."

Shaking his head, Shane turned the truck onto the road heading west out of Aspen. "No, but he has to know something is up."

"Has he said anything?"

"Not a word."

"Then how do you know he's aware there's something going on?" She looked bewildered and so darned cute, it was all he could do to keep from stopping the truck in the middle of the road and kissing her senseless.

"I've never brought a woman to the ranch before," he answered.

"Never?"

Shane shook his head. "Nope."

"So that's why Cactus was so surprised to see me that morning," she said, sounding sleepy.

"Yup. He hadn't seen a woman in that house since my aunt and her family left Aspen to move to Santa Fe."

He wasn't sure why, but he had never before felt

compelled to bring a woman home with him. Nor had he ever been tempted to take a woman to see Rainbow Falls. At least he hadn't until he met Lissa.

Glancing over at her, he realized she had fallen asleep. What was it about her that was different from other women he had been involved with?

As he steered the truck onto the private road leading over the ridge to the ranch, Shane decided that he was probably better off not knowing. There were some questions that were better left unanswered and he had a feeling this was one of them.

"Melissa, you look amazing," Avery Lancaster said, when she and Melissa's brother Guy walked up to her outside of the doors to the Sky Lounge. "Is there a new facial treatment in the spa I haven't heard about?"

Hugging her brother's fiancée, Melissa smiled as she shook her head. "I've just been getting more rest and eating a bit healthier."

It wasn't a lie. Of late, all she wanted to do was sleep and she had added an extra serving of fruits and vegetables to her diet each day.

"Well, whatever you're doing is working," Avery said, laughing. "You're positively glowing."

"You do look different," Guy agreed, frowning.

The fact that her brother thought he noticed a change in her was a bit of a shock. Since meeting the beautiful wine expert at his side, he was barely aware of anything else around him.

Melissa's brother Trevor chose that moment to stroll over to them. "Do any of you know what this party is all about? I've never known McDermott to be overly social. Usually the guest lists for his get-togethers consist of himself and the lady of the moment."

"Are you sure you aren't talking about yourself?" Guy asked, grinning.

Unrepentant, Trevor laughed. "I never said I thought McDermott was in the wrong on that."

"To answer your question, I have no idea what this dinner is about," Guy said, opening the door to the lounge. When the three went inside, he held the door for Melissa. "Are you coming?"

"I'll be there in a minute," she said, spotting her half sister, Erica, and her fiancé, Christian Hanford, as they got off the elevator.

Listening to her family speculate about Shane's invitation was the last thing she needed. Her nerves were already as tight as a bowstring. Once they made their announcement about getting married and having a baby, the course would be set. She just prayed with everything that was in her it was the right one.

"Avery and I missed you at lunch yesterday," Erica said, hugging Melissa close. "Are you all right?"

Feeling guilty for avoiding her newfound sister for the past week, she nodded. "I'm fine. I've just been preoccupied lately with…a new project."

Melissa truly liked her half sister and regretted that her father hadn't let them all know about her.

But whatever Donald Jarrod's reasoning had been, the family hadn't learned of her existence until the reading of their father's will two months earlier.

"Let's go in and see what McDermott has up his sleeve," Guy's twin, Blake, suggested as he joined them. As usual Blake had his trusted secretary, Samantha Thompson, at his side, and Melissa wondered for at least the hundredth time since meeting her how long it would take for Blake to realize what a beautiful woman Samantha was.

As the five of them entered the Sky Lounge, Melissa immediately spotted Shane at the doorway of one of the private gathering rooms, greeting her family as they arrived. He always looked good to her, but tonight he looked positively devastating in his black suit and tie. Very few men could look at ease in business suits as well as jeans and a work shirt. Shane managed to do it effortlessly.

"Where's Gavin?" he asked when they reached him.

"He should be here shortly," Blake answered, shrugging. "As we were getting on the elevator, I saw him in the lobby, talking to an old friend of his."

Motioning toward a large round table in the center of the room, Shane smiled congenially. "Have a seat and we'll get started as soon as he gets here." Trailing behind the two couples, Melissa stopped when Shane touched her arm. "I want you to sit in one of the two chairs tipped up against the table," he whispered close to her ear.

Seeing the chairs with their backs leaning against the table's edge, she nodded. Walking over, she set the chair upright and seated herself. She knew from the look on Erica's face that her sister expected Melissa to sit in the empty chair beside her. She hated that she might have hurt Erica's feelings, but she was sure her sister would understand once she and Shane explained the purpose of the party.

"Sorry I'm late," Gavin apologized as he and Shane approached the table together. "I ran into one of the guys we graduated high school with and stopped to say hello."

Once her brother was seated with the rest of her family, Shane straightened the chair beside her, but instead of seating himself, he remained standing. "I know you're all wondering why I invited you here tonight," he said, making eye contact and smiling at each individual at the table.

"Well, now that you mention it, we did—" When his oldest brother elbowed him, Trevor stopped short to glare at Blake.

Shane smiled. "I don't blame you. I would have been curious, too, Trevor."

Melissa tightly clenched her hands, resting in her lap. He was about to reveal the secret they'd kept for the past two months, and although it would be a relief to have their affair out in the open, she just hoped they were doing the right thing.

Lost in thought, she was surprised when Shane reached down to take her hand in his and pull her up to stand beside him. "Since your sister's return to Aspen a few months ago, we've been seeing each other and our relationship—"

"I knew it!" Trevor said triumphantly. Obviously proud of himself for noticing what the others had missed, he added, "When I saw the two of you together back in July, I knew something was going on."

"Don't break your arm patting yourself on the back there, Trevor," Gavin said drily. "I suspected Melissa was hiding something, too. I just didn't know what it was."

When the laughter at the table died down, Shane put his arm around Melissa's shoulders and gazing into her eyes, announced, "Lissa and I wanted all of you to be the first to know, we're getting married and will be welcoming our first child next spring."

Before anyone could react, Shane lowered his head and gave her a kiss that caused her head to spin and her toes to curl inside her sensible black pumps. When he finally raised his head, there was a hushed silence. Then, everyone started talking at once.

"Congratulations you two," Guy said, grinning from ear to ear. "It looks like my pastry chef is going to be busy for quite some time making nothing but wedding cakes."

"That's great," Trevor said happily. "Now that McDermott is off the market, I won't have as much competition with the ladies."

"I'm so happy for you," Erica said, rushing around the table to hug Melissa.

Avery was right behind Erica to wrap her arms around Melissa. "I never suspected a thing. I don't know how you managed to keep quiet about a relationship as serious as this." Giving her a watery smile, Avery added, "I think it's wonderful."

As her brothers and Christian took turns shaking Shane's hand, Melissa noticed that although Blake's secretary, Samantha, added her congratulations, the woman seemed uncharacteristically quiet and subdued. What could possibly have the vibrant brunette so down in the dumps?

Before she had a chance to speak to the woman and ask if everything was all right, Gavin wrapped Melissa in a brotherly bear hug. "I wish you every happiness, little sister."

Tapping on his water glass with the edge of his knife, Blake drew everyone's attention. "I'd like to make a toast."

To her surprise, one of her brothers had ordered a bottle of champagne and the waiter had just poured them all a glass of the sparkling pink wine. All except for her and Avery. Their glasses held sparkling white grape juice.

"I'm pregnant," Melissa said, pointing to Avery's glass. "What's your excuse?"

Her friend made a face. "Remember, champagne makes me sneeze."

Melissa didn't have time to dwell on the matter when Blake raised his glass.

"To Melissa and Shane," he said, smiling. "May you have a long and happy life together."

Everyone raised their glass in agreement, then taking a sip of wine, settled down to dinner and conversation. As it always did, talk turned to plans for expanding the resort's services and special promotions. Melissa tuned most of it out as she watched her family.

Apparently so did Erica and Avery. They'd been huddled together since finishing their desserts and she wondered what the two of them were up to.

All in all, the evening had gone quite well, she decided, feeling more at ease than she had in several days. It was a huge relief to have her and Shane's relationship out in the open.

As the evening drew to a close and everyone gathered their things to leave, Erica and Avery pulled Melissa aside. "Let's get together for lunch on Wednesday," Avery said, her eyes twinkling.

"We want to start making plans for a baby shower," Erica added, just as excited.

Melissa was touched by their enthusiasm and happiness for her. "I'd like that, but don't you think it's a bit early to start planning something like that? I'm only a couple of months along."

"You can never start planning the perfect party too early," Avery said, laughing.

"Besides, from everything I've been told, it will

start getting extremely busy in a couple of months when the ski season starts," Erica agreed. "If we get most of the details worked out now, we won't be so rushed later on."

Agreeing on a time for their lunch, Melissa watched her sister and future sister-in-law leave the restaurant. She loved finally having female family members. After growing up as the only girl in a house full of boys, it was definitely a welcome change.

"I think everything went pretty well tonight," Shane said, walking up to put his arm around her. "At least, none of your brothers threatened to grab their shotguns and run me out of town."

She laughed. "I doubt that any of them own a shotgun." As they walked from the Sky Lounge, she added, "I'm just glad everything is out in the open and we don't have to sneak around anymore."

"Yeah, I'm not going to miss those midnight treks from the stables through the woods to Willow Lodge one damned bit. It's a wonder someone hadn't noticed and thought I was a Peeping Tom." Waiting for the elevator, his laughter turned into a grin that held such promise it stole her breath. "From now on, I'll just roll over and turn out the light."

"Really?" she asked, laughing at his lascivious grin.

"Most definitely." He leaned close to whisper, "And just in case you have any doubts about that, I intend to give you a demonstration as soon as we get back to the lodge."

* * *

Using Lissa's key, Shane let them into Willow Lodge, then closing and locking the door behind them, took her into his arms. He nibbled kisses from her neck up to her delicate earlobe.

"I've been wanting to have you all to myself all evening." Used to being alone with her, he'd had the devil of a time keeping his hands to himself.

"The dinner party did seem to drag on, didn't it?" She put her arms around his waist and snuggled close. "Thank you, Shane."

He leaned back to gaze down at her. "For what?"

"For taking charge tonight when we told my family about us." She kissed his chin. "I wasn't quite sure how to go about it."

"I never said I hadn't rehearsed a few dozen different speeches before I settled on one." He grinned. "When you're in a room full of men who just might take your head off and shout down your neck because you got their little sister pregnant, it inspires you to think things through."

"You did just fine," she said, unknotting his necktie. He loved the feel of her fingers brushing his throat as she removed the silk tie.

Placing his hands on her shoulders, he turned her around. "As good as you look in this dress, I think you'll look much better out of it."

Slowly sliding the zipper down from her neck to her lower back, he sucked in a sharp breath. "Good thing I didn't know earlier that you weren't wearing a bra," he said, kissing the back of her neck. "I'd have never made it through the evening."

When he started to slide the black dress from her shoulders, she caught the front to her and shaking her head, stepped away from him. "Why don't you build a fire in the fireplace while I change?"

As she walked from the room, Shane blew out a frustrated breath and slipping off his suit coat, unbuttoned and rolled up the sleeves of his dress shirt. Building a fire hadn't been high on the list of things he'd had planned for the evening. In fact, it hadn't been anywhere on it. But it was something Lissa wanted, and he was finding more and more that he was willing to do whatever it took to make her happy and see her pretty smile.

A nice fire had just started crackling in the stone fireplace when the lights in the great room went out. A moment later, Lissa walked up and knelt down beside him in front of the hearth.

"I thought these might be nice to snuggle up with," she said, setting a stack of pillows and a couple of fluffy blankets on the floor beside him.

Glancing over at her, he did a double take. She was wearing the sexiest black satin robe he had ever seen. One side of the slinky little number had slipped down over her bare shoulder and he knew as surely as he knew his own name, she didn't have a stitch of clothes on beneath it.

"Do you want me to make some hot cocoa?" she asked before he could find his voice.

Shane swallowed hard and shook his head. The shimmering light cast by the fire seemed to bathe her in gold, and he knew for certain he had never seen her look more beautiful.

"The only thing I want is right here beside me," he said, pulling her to him. He brushed his mouth over hers. "Do you have any idea how sexy and desirable you are?"

"I haven't really thought about it," she said, toying with the top button of his shirt. "I've been too busy thinking about how much I think you deserve a good, relaxing massage."

His mouth went as dry as a desert in a drought. What man in his right mind would turn down having a beautiful woman run her hands over every inch of his body?

Without a word he stood up, and while she arranged the blankets and pillows on the hardwood floor in front of the fireplace, he made short work of taking off his clothes. It was only after he lay facedown on the soft blankets that she slipped the robe off. Dropping it beside him, she picked up a bottle of oil that he hadn't noticed before. He felt her pour several drops of the warm liquid onto the middle of his back.

At the first touch of Lissa's palms on his bare skin, Shane felt as if he had died and gone to heaven. Her gentle, soothing touch was driving him crazy and his reaction was not only completely predictable, it was immediate.

By the time she worked her way down the back of his thighs and calves, then told him to turn over, he felt as if the temperature in the room had gone up several degrees. Never in his entire life had he experienced anything as exciting and arousing as having Lissa's hands gliding over his body.

Their eyes met and, holding his gaze with hers, she drizzled a small amount of the oil onto the middle of his abdomen. As she caressed his shoulders and pectoral muscles, Shane ached with the need to hold her, to touch and excite her as she was doing to him.

"Enough," he said, catching her hands in his to pull her down beside him.

Covering her mouth with his, he traced her soft lips with his tongue. He didn't think he had ever tasted anything sweeter. When he coaxed her to open for him and the tip of her tongue touched his, he felt as if a charge of electric current coursed from the top of his head all the way to his feet.

He broke the kiss and turned her to her back. Deciding to treat her to a little of the same sweet torture she had put him through, he picked up the bottle of oil. Smoothing the slick liquid over her satiny skin, he paid special attention to her breasts and tightly puckered nipples. By the time he moved down to her flat stomach, he wasn't certain which one of them was suffering more.

The blood rushing through his veins caused his ears to ring as he stared down at her. Her expressive blue eyes reflected the same hunger that filled him and her porcelain cheeks wore the blush of intense passion. Shane knew for certain he would remember her this way for the rest of his life.

The evidence of her desire fueled his own and the need to once again make her his was overwhelming. Using his knee to part her thighs, he settled himself over her.

"P-please," she murmured.

"What do you want, angel?"

"You." She reached to put her arms around him. "I want you, Shane."

His breath lodged in his lungs as he pressed himself forward and her supple body accepted him. Closing his eyes for a moment in a desperate attempt to hang on to his rapidly slipping control, he held himself completely still. He wanted to make this last, to love her slowly and thoroughly. But when she wrapped her long legs around his hips to hold him to her, Shane knew he had lost the battle.

With his pulse pounding in his ears like a sultry jungle drum, he slowly began to rock against her. The way she met him stroke for stroke, their bodies perfectly in tune, sent a flash fire to every fiber of his being and clouded his mind to anything but the mind-blowing pleasure surrounding them.

All too quickly, he felt her body tighten around his. Her feminine muscles clung to him, driving Shane

over the edge, and he felt as if he had found the other
half of himself when together they found the release
they both sought.

Melissa couldn't help but smile when she snuggled
against the man sleeping next to her. After they made
love in front of the fireplace, he had carried her into
the bedroom to make love to her again. Then, true
to his word, he had rolled over and turning off the
bedside lamp, pulled her close and gone to sleep.

As she studied his handsome face, she thought
about how wonderful he had been at dinner. He had
seemed genuinely happy when he told her family
about their upcoming marriage and the baby they'd
have in the spring.

Placing her hand on her still-flat stomach, she
couldn't help but marvel at the fact that she was going
to be a mother. For as long as she could remember,
she had hoped to one day have a precious little mir-
acle of her own to hold and love. She reached out to
touch Shane's strong jaw with her fingertip. He had
made that happen and she couldn't help but love him
for it.

Her heart skipped a beat. She had known from the
beginning of their affair that she was in danger of
getting in over her head. He had been clear that their
involvement was temporary and she had wanted that,
too. But the attraction she had felt for him was too
strong, had been too immediate not to pose a serious
threat to her peace of mind.

She had told herself she could control her infatuation and avoid falling in love with him as long as she kept things in perspective. She knew now that she had been lying to herself all along.

If the truth was known, she had fallen in love with him the moment they laid eyes on each other two months ago. He was the most charming, considerate man she had ever met and the longer she was around him the deeper her feelings had grown.

Her chest tightened and a tear slid down her cheek. She quickly swiped it away with the back of her hand. In the coming months, she was going to have almost everything she had always hoped for. She was going to marry the man she loved, have a home in one of the most beautiful places on earth and start the family she had always longed for.

So why couldn't she be happy and content with that?

Melissa knew exactly what was keeping her picture-perfect fantasy from becoming reality. She wanted it all. She wanted the home, the family and the one thing she wasn't sure Shane would ever be able to give her…his love.

Seven

"It looks like I'll just have to take a couple of the appointments myself," Melissa said as she and Rita went over the afternoon reservations.

"I'm so sorry, Ms. Jarrod," Rita apologized for at least the tenth time. "I don't know how I could have made that kind of mistake."

"It's all right, Rita. These kinds of things happen from time to time," Melissa assured her. "Just look a little closer next time to make sure there's an opening at the time requested by the guest."

Rita was beginning to gain more confidence and improve her managerial skills, and Melissa was hopeful that would continue. She knew the woman was a single mother and needed the job to support herself and her son. She certainly didn't want to cause Rita any more stress by having to replace her.

"Ready to go?"

Looking up, Melissa smiled at Avery as she entered the Tranquility Spa's reception area. "Would you mind if we have lunch in the Sky Lounge today?" she asked. "I only have an hour or so before I have to be back."

"Problems?" Avery asked.

Giving Rita an encouraging smile, Melissa shook her head. "Not really. I'm afraid there was a mix-up and we're overbooked this afternoon. It seems all of the Jarrod Ridge guests want a spa treatment before this weekend's dinner honoring the investors. I'm going to have to do a couple of the massages and at least one of the facials myself."

"Wow! You are busy," Avery said, her eyes widening. "But that actually works out better for me, too." She grinned. "In fact, I was going to ask you if the Sky Lounge would be okay. I wanted to stop by and talk to Guy for a few minutes after we eat."

"What about Erica?" Melissa asked, grabbing her purse. "Is she going to be able to meet us?"

Avery nodded. "I called her this morning and asked her to get a table by one of the windows and that we'd meet her in—" she looked at her watch "—oops. Five minutes ago."

"Then I suppose we'd better get going," Melissa said, laughing. She loved that in the past couple of months she had gained a sister and a future sister-in-law that were also quickly becoming her best friends.

A few minutes later, as they got off the elevator and entered the Sky Lounge, they immediately spotted Erica and hurried over to the table she had been saving.

"I'm sorry we're running late," Melissa apologized as she slid into one of the empty chairs.

"You can blame me for that," Avery said, seating herself. "Guy was running late leaving to go to the restaurant this morning because I...that is we...I mean—"

Grinning as they watched Avery squirm, Melissa and Erica both propped one elbow on the table, cupped their chins in their hands and asked in unison, "Yes?"

"Uh, never mind." Avery's cheeks were pink as she shook her head and quickly picked up a menu. "I think I'm going to have the tuna melt."

"Nice save," Melissa said, laughing as she picked up her menu.

After they placed their order, the conversation turned to plans for the baby shower. "I won't know for a few more months whether to decorate in pink or blue," Melissa said, shrugging.

Erica smiled. "What are you hoping for? A boy or a girl?"

"I haven't really given it much thought," Melissa admitted. "But it doesn't matter to me as long as the baby is healthy."

"That's all that's important," Avery said, nodding.

Choosing a date in February for the shower, they discussed nursery themes and shops where Melissa should register. By the time they finished lunch and left the restaurant, she had only a few minutes to get back to the spa.

"I suppose I'll see you both on Saturday evening at the dinner?" she asked as they got off the elevator in the lobby.

"Christian and I wouldn't miss it," Erica said.

"We'll be there." Avery grinned. "I'll probably have a hard time keeping Guy out of the kitchen, though. You know how he is about wanting every dish to be perfect."

"Since Guy took over managing the resort's restaurants and brought in Louis Leclere as chef, the efficiency of the kitchen staff has improved greatly," Melissa said.

"The new items they've added to the menu seem to be a big hit, too," Erica added.

Melissa checked her watch. She had only a few minutes to make it to the first massage appointment. "I'm really sorry, but I have to run. See you on Saturday."

As she hugged them both and headed down the hall toward the spa entrance, something Erica asked her at lunch kept running through her mind. It didn't matter to her whether their baby was a boy or a girl.

But did it matter to Shane whether they had a son or a daughter?

Like most men, he would probably prefer to have a boy. But she didn't think he would be disappointed either way. Unfortunately, it was hard for some men to hide their feelings. She had always suspected that her father had been disappointed she was female.

Of course, she couldn't say he had treated her brothers much better. He had driven all of his children to be overachievers and in the process alienated them from the very thing he had wanted them to embrace—Jarrod Ridge.

Shaking her head, she relegated thoughts of her late father to the back of her mind as she walked through the reception area of Tranquility Spa and prepared to go back to work. The sooner she finished for the day, the sooner she and Shane could leave for the ranch.

For some reason he had insisted they have dinner at Rainbow Bend, which was fine with her. She loved the peace and quiet of the remote ranch and after a day filled with booking mix-ups, Melissa couldn't wait to get there.

"Dinner was delicious, Cactus," Lissa said as she helped clear the table. "How did you know I love country-fried steak smothered in milk gravy?"

The elderly man beamed. "I didn't, but I sure am glad you liked it, gal."

Shane sat back and watched the exchange with

interest. Cactus didn't care for most people and the fact that he was falling all over himself to please Lissa said a lot. If Shane didn't know better, he would swear the old boy was completely smitten.

Of course, he couldn't blame Cactus. With each passing day, Shane found himself thinking about her more often, wondering what she was doing and counting the hours until they could be together again. It was something he wasn't sure he was comfortable with, but there didn't seem to be anything he could do to stop it, either.

Deciding that it would be better for his peace of mind to simply not think about it, he left the table. "Lissa, I have something that I'd like for you to take a look at."

"Can it wait?" she asked, handing Cactus a plate to rinse. "After that wonderful meal, the least I can do is help Cactus with the cleanup."

"Don't you worry about it, gal," Cactus said, shaking his head. "Since Shane got me this here dishwasher, I don't mind doin' kitchen chores near like I used to."

"Are you sure?" When Cactus nodded, she surprised the old man by kissing his wrinkled cheek. "Thank you for dinner. It was wonderful."

Shane had known Cactus all of his life and he'd never known the man to be at a loss for words. He always had something to say, whether it was to give his unwavering opinion or complain—which was usually the case. But the old geezer couldn't seem to find his voice. He just stood there wearing the sappiest expression Shane had ever seen.

"You wanted to show me something?" Lissa asked, drawing Shane's attention. She had walked over to him and he had been so astounded by Cactus's atypical behavior, he hadn't noticed.

Smiling at her, Shane nodded. "But there is something I think we need to do first."

"What's that?"

"We are going to make Cactus's day," he whispered close to her ear. Shane put his arm around her shoulders and tucked her to his side. "Cactus, what would you say if I told you that pretty soon you'll be able to cook for Lissa a lot more?"

"That'd suit me just fine," Cactus said, nodding his approval. "She's a danged sight more appreciative 'bout my cookin' than you are."

Shane laughed. "So you want me to start kissing you now after every meal?"

"Try it and you'll be missin' your front teeth," Cactus warned, turning back to the dishes in the sink.

"Then I guess after we get married, I'll just have to leave the kissing up to Lissa," he said, anticipating the old gent's reaction. Shane didn't have long to wait.

He hadn't seen Cactus move as fast in years as when he spun around to face them. "Well, I'll be damned." If he'd had teeth, his ear-to-ear grin would have lit a city block. "Married, you say?"

Shane glanced down at Lissa and winked. "Do you think I should tell him the rest?"

"You might as well," she said, smiling.

"There's going to be a baby joining us in the spring." A sudden, unfamiliar feeling settled in his chest and Shane realized that he was actually beginning to get excited by the prospect of becoming a daddy.

"I guess now that there's gonna be a woman and youngin' underfoot, you're gonna expect me to stop my cussin', scratchin' and spittin'," Cactus said, his grin belying his complaint.

"It probably wouldn't be a bad idea." Laughing, Shane turned Lissa toward the hall, then called over his shoulder, "You'll have to give up cooking breakfast in your long johns, too."

As they walked down the hall to his study, he chuckled. He could still hear Cactus grumbling about kids, women and bone-headed ranchers who expected him to give up everything worth doing.

"What did you want to show me?" Lissa asked, when they entered the study and he closed the door.

She looked so sweet and desirable, he didn't think twice about taking her into his arms and kissing her until they both gasped for breath. When he finally raised his head, Shane drew in some much-needed air.

"I've been wanting to do that all day."

Her smile sent his temperature skyrocketing. "I've missed you, too."

"How was your day at the spa?" he asked, a bit surprised that something so mundane suddenly felt important to him.

She shook her head. "Don't ask. You really don't want to know."

Leaning back, he frowned. "That bad, huh?"

"Just tiring." She explained about the booking mix-up, then smiling, asked, "How about you? Anything interesting happen?"

"I got a call from Sheik Al Kahara." He shrugged. "He wants to hire me to design all new stables for the Thoroughbred farm he just bought in Kentucky."

"That sounds like a challenge," she said, sounding genuinely interested. "Do you have to do a lot of traveling with jobs like that?"

"I have to travel occasionally, but not more than once or twice a year." He shook his head. "Most of my clients e-mail the size of stable they want and what they want included in the design. I send them a quote and then once we sign the contracts, I go to work on the design. But the sheik's is going to be a piece of cake. He basically wants the same setup I designed for the stables at his palace in Almarif."

Her eyes widened. "Do you have a lot of foreign clients?"

"I have quite a few."

"Are they all royalty?"

Her curiosity about his career pleased him more

than he would have thought. "Not all of them are royalty, but I have designed stables for several members of this or that monarchy." Taking her hand, he led her over to the other side of the room. "But I don't want to talk about sheiks or stable designs right now." He motioned for her to sit in one of the chairs in front of the fireplace. "I want your opinion on something."

"I can't guarantee how much help I'll be, but I'll try," she said, smiling as she settled into the high-backed leather armchair.

"Oh, I think your opinion on this counts for a lot more than you think." He turned to remove the small, black velvet box he had placed on the fireplace mantel before leaving to pick her up after she got off work. Flipping the box open, he turned to hold it out to her as he watched for her reaction to the pear-shaped diamond solitaire in a white-gold setting that he had bought for her the day before. "Do you think you would be interested in wearing this to the investors' dinner on Saturday evening?"

If the look on her face was any indication, he had hit a home run. "My God, Shane, it's beautiful."

Removing the sparkling jewelry from the box, he took her left hand in his to slip the ring on her third finger. To her delight and his relief, it fit perfectly.

"How did you know my ring size?" she asked, jumping from the chair to throw her arms around his neck.

"I guesstimated," he said, catching her to him. "So you like it?"

"I love it." She leaned back to stare down at her hand. "It's exactly what I would have chosen." Then, looking up, the smile she gave him lit the darkest corners of his soul. "Thank you."

"Are you ready for my other surprise?" he asked, kissing the tip of her nose. He decided there wasn't anything he wouldn't do just to see her smile at him like she was at that very moment.

Her eyes widened. "There's something else?"

He took her by the hand and led her out of the study to the front door. "I want you to close your eyes and keep them closed until I tell you to open them."

"What are you up to now?" she asked, laughing.

"If I told you it wouldn't be a surprise." Shane grinned. "Would you rather I blindfold you?"

She shook her head. "No, I promise I'll keep my eyes closed."

Once she did as he asked, he helped her down the porch steps and across the yard. "Don't peek," he warned, releasing her hand to untie a set of reins from the corral fence.

"Shane, what on earth—"

Placing the leather straps in her hand, he said, "Okay, you can open your eyes."

When she did, she looked puzzled. "I don't understand."

"Stormy is yours now, angel." The look on her face was everything he had hoped for.

"He's mine?" Her eyes sparkled as she stared at the blue roan, standing saddled in front of her.

"Yup." Shane grinned. "I've already sent in the paperwork to transfer his registration to you."

She glanced at the sun sinking low in the Western sky. "Do you think we have enough time to take a short ride?"

Grinning, Shane nodded. "I thought you might want to do that. That's why I had one of my men saddle Stormy and have him ready." As Lissa mounted her horse, Shane walked into the stable. He returned with his stallion and swung up onto the saddle. "We should have time to ride to the trailhead that leads to Rainbow Falls and make it back before dark."

"Thank you for everything." Riding the roan up beside his sorrel, Lissa leaned over to kiss his cheek. "This is the nicest, most thoughtful thing anyone has ever done for me." Her delighted expression suddenly turned to a teasing grin. "You are going to get so lucky tonight."

"Then let's get the hell out of here," he said, nudging his stallion into a lope.

"What's your hurry, Cowboy?" she asked, laughing as she urged Stormy to follow.

"I want to get back." When she caught up to him, he grinned. "I could really use some…luck."

* * *

As they rode across the valley back to the stable, Melissa couldn't keep from smiling. "I love it here."

"Really?" It sounded as if Shane had a hard time believing she meant what she said.

"Who wouldn't love this?" Twisting around in the saddle, she took in the majestic beauty of the surrounding snowcapped mountains. "This has to be the quietest, most peaceful place on earth."

"Some people would rather live where there are people around and things to do besides sit and listen to the grass grow," he said, staring straight ahead.

She shook her head. "I'm not one of them."

"That reminds me. There's something else we need to discuss before we get married," he said slowly. "Where do you want to live?"

Confused, she stopped her horse. "This is your home. I assumed you'd want us to live here."

Reining in the stallion, Shane turned to meet her questioning gaze. "I do want to live here. It's home. But I also know and accept that once the snows start, I may only get out of the valley a handful of times until the spring thaw. I accept the fact that there isn't a convenience store just around the corner. It's a good ten-mile drive if you forget to buy something while you're in town."

It was almost as if he was trying to talk her out of living on the ranch. Once they were married, didn't he want her to live with him?

"I remember you telling me the first day you brought me here that the road leading into the valley sometimes gets closed off for several weeks."

His intense gaze caught and held hers. "Do you think you can stand being snowbound for that long?"

She stared at him for several moments before she spoke. "I can't answer that right now because I've never been in that situation, Shane." She flicked the reins to urge Stormy into a slow walk. "What I can tell you is this. I understand all the drawbacks of living here and I'm still more than willing to give it a try."

Each lost in thought, neither had much to say as they rode into the ranch yard. Dismounting the horses, by the time they had the animals groomed and turned into their stalls, Lissa had started yawning.

"I have to send an e-mail to a potential client. Why don't you go on upstairs and take a hot shower?" Shane asked, when they entered the house. He caught her to him for a quick kiss. "I promise I won't be long."

"I think I'll do that," she said, hiding another yawn. She smiled apologetically. "I'm beat."

"I know, angel." Kissing her again, he released her and took a step back. "I'll be up in a few minutes."

Shane watched her climb the stairs before he went into his study and opened his e-mail. Quickly composing a message with a quote for his architectural services, he pressed the send button, then turning off the computer, sat back in his desk chair.

The evening couldn't have gone more perfectly. Lissa had loved the engagement ring he'd bought her and couldn't have been happier when he gave her the roan gelding. The ride to the trailhead had gone well, too—right up until she mentioned how much she enjoyed the peace and quiet of his ranch.

What had gotten into him anyway? Why couldn't he have taken her at her word that she wanted to live on the ranch? Why had he felt compelled to point out all the drawbacks of living on the Rainbow Bend?

Something he had overheard his father tell Cactus right after Shane's mother left kept running through his mind. At first, Carolyn McDermott had loved living on the ranch and hadn't minded the isolation. But as the years went by, being snowbound for weeks on end and having no neighbors close by had taken its toll and she had come to hate the picturesque valley.

After living on the ranch for a while, would Lissa end up feeling the same way? Would her resentment grow to the point that she left and never looked back?

Unlike his mother, Lissa was from Aspen and well aware of what the weather was like in the Rocky Mountains. But she had lived in California for the past eight years and although she said she missed the winter activities, she also liked living on the beach. After being snowbound a few times, what if she decided she preferred the more temperate climate of Malibu? And what if instead of leaving her child behind as his mother had done, Lissa took their son with her?

Staring at the dark computer screen, Shane drew in a deep breath. He didn't think Lissa would do that to him. Even before he'd convinced her to let him do the honorable thing and make her his wife, she had told him that arrangements could be made for him to be part of their child's life.

Rising from the chair, he turned off the desk lamp and left the study to head upstairs. Lissa had told him she wanted to try living on the ranch and that was really all he could ask of her. Only time would tell if her enthusiasm would turn to loathing. As long as he kept that possibility in mind and didn't allow his fondness for her to develop into a deeper emotion, he should be fine.

Unfortunately, he was finding that harder to keep in check with each passing day. Lissa was quickly becoming an addiction, and one that he wasn't sure he would ever be able to live without.

Eight

"How was your meeting with the other Jarrod Ridge investors this afternoon?" Melissa asked when Shane stopped by the spa the following afternoon.

"Long and boring as hell." He chuckled. "At least it was right up until I made my little announcement about our engagement." Laughing out loud, he shook his head. "You should have seen Elmer Madison's and Clara Buchanan's faces."

"Let's go into my office and you can tell me all about it," she suggested, not wanting to talk in front of the spa staff and resort guests.

They had agreed that he would tell the other members of the investment group they were getting married, but decided to wait until after the wedding to let them know about the pregnancy.

Once they entered her office and closed the door, she turned to face him. "Tell me what happened."

"When Elmer asked if there was any more business we needed to discuss, I stood up and announced that I'd asked you to marry me and that you had said yes."

He took off his cowboy hat and sailed it over to land on the couch. Then, pulling her against him, he kissed her until she saw stars.

"I—I want…details," she said, trying to catch her breath when he finally lifted his head. "What could they possibly find wrong with our getting married? You didn't mention the baby, did you?"

"No, that would have probably sent both of them into outer space." Shane shook his head. "I think they are both scared to death that, by marrying you, I'll get in on an investment they won't."

"That's ridiculous." She frowned. "All investments for special events are done through the group. They can pull out of the group at any time or choose not to support a project, but we offer all investment promotions to the group as a whole, not to individuals."

"I know, angel." He shrugged. "It might be they are afraid that once I'm married to you, I'll start contributing more and end up getting a bigger return on my money. Either that or they're both a few cards shy of a full deck." He grinned. "My guess is it's a little of both."

"Did they say anything?" She couldn't imagine what it would be if they had.

"Nope. They didn't say a word."

"Then how do you know they had a problem with our getting married?" Maybe Shane had misinterpreted their reaction.

His blue eyes twinkled with humor. "When I said that you and I were getting married, old Elmer turned so red in the face, I thought he might bust that blood vessel that stands out on his forehead whenever he gets upset."

"What about Clara?" Melissa asked, trying not to laugh at the visual picture Shane was painting. "What was her reaction?"

"She was taking a drink of water and got so choked, I thought I was going to have to perform CPR on her." He made a face. "I'd rather climb a barbed-wire fence buck naked than put my mouth on hers."

"And all this time, I thought you had a secret crush on Clara," she teased.

His exaggerated shudder and horrified expression had her laughing so hard, she found it hard to breathe. "Not in this lifetime. Just the thought of getting 'cozy' with that old bat is enough to make a man swear off women for good."

She couldn't stop laughing. Clara was at least twice Shane's age and always looked as if she had just sucked on a lemon.

His expression suddenly turned serious. "Lissa,

I want you to know that although the pregnancy brought about our decision to get married, you don't have to worry. I give you my word that I'll always be a good provider and a faithful husband."

Taken aback by his unexpected proclamation, she stared at him. "I'll be a good, faithful wife to you. But what brought this on?"

"I know that my reputation of moving from one woman to the next is only slightly better than Trevor's," he explained. "I just wanted you to know that I honor my commitments. You never have to worry about me going out and finding someone else."

After spending so much time with him in the past couple of weeks and seeing him interact with Cactus, she knew for certain Shane wasn't that kind of man. "It never crossed my mind that you wouldn't be anything but faithful to our marriage."

The sudden knock on the door came as no surprise. The spa had been extremely busy all day with guests getting ready for the dinner tomorrow night.

Reluctantly leaving Shane's arms, Lissa walked over to open the door. "Is there a problem, Rita?"

"I hate to bother you, but Joanie just got sick and had to go home," her assistant manager explained. "She has two half-hour facials booked and I'm afraid all of the other girls' schedules are full. Will you be available to take her place or should I cancel the appointments?"

"I'll be right there, Rita." When the woman went

back to the reception desk, Melissa closed the door and turned to Shane. "I'm really sorry, but I have to get back to work. We've really been slammed today. It looks as if I'm not going to get out of here for at least another couple of hours."

He picked up his hat from the couch and walked over to where she stood by the door. "I need to go anyway." He gave her a tender kiss, then reached for the doorknob. "I have to pick up my tux at the cleaners and then I have a couple of things Cactus wanted me to get before we go back to the ranch for dinner." Shane grinned. "He's planning on making you his world-class beef stew and sour-dough biscuits."

Just the thought made her mouth water. "That sounds scrumptious."

Nodding, Shane opened the door. "I'll be back to pick you up this evening around five."

Walking out into the reception area, Melissa sighed as she watched Shane leave. She loved him and if she hadn't known that before, she would have after his reassurance that he would be a good husband.

Cowboys had a reputation for their word being their bond. If it was important enough for him to tell her he would be committed to their marriage, then he fully intended for it to work out between them.

It hadn't been the declaration of love she would have preferred, but it was enough to give her hope. Maybe one day he would say the three words she longed to hear.

* * *

"When would you like to get married? Shane asked as he and Lissa sat in front of the Willow Lodge fireplace. After having dinner with Cactus, he had driven them back to the cabin for a nice quiet evening alone in front of a crackling fire.

"So much has happened over the past couple of weeks, I haven't had time to give it a lot of thought," she said, snuggling against him. "But I'd like to wait until after Erica and Christian's wedding. I don't want to take anything away from their special day."

He nodded. "I can understand that. When is it?"

"Christmas Eve." She looked thoughtful for a moment. "What would you think of a New Year's Eve wedding?"

"Sounds good to me," he said, kissing the top of her head. "Do you want a big wedding?"

"Not really." She sat forward and reached for her mug of hot cocoa. "I think I'd like something small with just family and close friends."

"Whatever you want, angel." He grinned as he leaned over to kiss away a smudge of melted marshmallow from the corner of her mouth. "I guess the next question would be where do you want the ceremony?"

He watched her look around the great room of the lodge. "I think right here would be nice."

"You don't want to get married at Jarrod Manor?" He'd thought she would want to have it at the family mansion.

"No." Her emphatic answer surprised him.

They stared at each other for several silent moments before he asked, "Why not, Lissa?"

She hesitated, then just when he thought she was going to avoid answering his question, she shook her head. "I don't have a lot of pleasant memories there."

"But that's where you grew up." He reached for her cup of cocoa to set it on the coffee table, then took her hands in his. "What was there about it that made you unhappy, angel?"

"There wasn't any one thing," she said, sighing. "It just never felt like much of a home to me."

"Why is that?"

He watched her shrug one slender shoulder before she met his questioning gaze. "I think you've probably figured out by now that I wasn't overly close with my father."

Shane nodded. From what she'd said about her dad wanting his children to start learning about the resort at such an early age and her obsession with how other people's opinions of her could reflect badly on Jarrod Ridge, he'd come to the conclusion that Donald Jarrod had placed his business above all else and taught his children to do the same.

"I've been told that when my mother was alive my father wasn't as focused on Jarrod Ridge as he became after her passing," she said quietly. "But for as long as I can remember, he never had time for us. He was always too busy either working or traveling to promote the resort." Her expression turned resentful. "And he expected us to make Jarrod Ridge our number-one priority, as well."

He had dealt with Donald Jarrod on several occasions through the investors group, as well as when the man bought horses for the resort stables, and he didn't think he'd ever met a bigger workaholic. But surely Jarrod had realized his family was more important than business.

"Maybe he was unaware—"

"Oh, I think he knew." She rose from the couch to walk over to the floor-to-ceiling windows of the great room. "Unfortunately, it's too late now to do anything about repairing our relationship."

Shane got up from the couch to walk up behind her. Wrapping his arms around her, he pulled her back against him. "I'm sure your dad was just trying to be a good provider for you and your brothers, angel."

She sighed. "That might be, but tell that to a child wanting nothing more from her father than his love and attention."

Although Shane's dad had lost interest in almost everything in life after his wife left, he'd still been there to raise his son. And, in his own way, Shane was certain his father had loved him. But apparently Lissa hadn't had that assurance.

"You at least had your brothers," he said, tightening his arms around her.

Nodding, she rested the back of her head against his shoulder. "I did, but they were all older. Besides, they were boys and didn't want to play with dolls or have tea parties."

Shane chuckled. "No, I can't imagine any of your brothers wanting to do that."

She turned within the circle of his arms to face him. "Just the thought is pretty amusing, isn't it?" she asked, the ghost of a smile curving her coral lips.

He nodded. "Blake would have probably shown up in a suit and tie and Trevor would have invariably brought a date."

Her smile broke through. "Of course."

Happy to see that her mood had lightened considerably, Shane pressed his lips to hers. "So it's decided, then. We'll get married here on New Year's Eve with family and close friends."

Resting her head against his chest, she nodded. "I think I'm going to invite Hector and Michael. They're two of my closest friends in Malibu, and besides, I'd like to talk to them about running the spa for me with the option to buy after a specified length of time."

"Are you sure you want to get rid of your business?" It pleased him that she intended to make her move to Colorado permanent, but he hated to see her give up a business she'd built from the ground up and was obviously quite proud of.

"It's not so much that I want to get rid of it," she admitted, yawning. "But I grew up with a father who was more absent than not and I don't want that for our child from either of his parents. Besides, I'll have

Tranquility Spa, and if we stay as busy as we are now, I'm going to talk to Blake about expanding."

"Uh-oh. It looks like the sandman is about to pay you a visit," he said, chuckling when she yawned again. "We had better get you to bed."

"I hope I can stay awake during the investors' dinner tomorrow evening," she said when he rose and guided her toward the hall.

"Yeah, it would be a shame to fall asleep during one of the speeches." Shane laughed.

"Maybe I better plan on taking a nap tomorrow afternoon," she said as they entered the bedroom.

"I'll plan to take one with you," he said, giving her a wicked grin.

"You're insatiable, Mr. McDermott," she said, shaking her head.

He took a step toward her. "And I intend to show you just how ravenous I am as soon as we get into bed."

As he and Lissa walked into the Jarrod Ridge Grand Ballroom for the festivities, Shane knew beyond a shadow of doubt that he was with the sexiest, most beautiful woman in attendance. Lissa had put her long blond hair up in some kind of soft, feminine twist, exposing her slender neck. He would like nothing more than to kiss every inch of it.

But the long, shimmery black evening dress she wore was what had his libido shifting into high gear. Slinky and form-fitting, it emphasized every one of her delightful curves and each time she moved it reminded him of a sleek jungle cat's elegance and grace.

Remembering where they were, he tried to rein in his unruly hormones. If he didn't get things under control soon, everyone in the whole damned place would know exactly what he had on his mind.

He spotted Clara Buchanan on the other side of the room and concentrated on how she would react to the evidence of his wayward thoughts. That was enough to take the wind out of any man's sails.

"There's Blake and his secretary, Samantha," Lissa said, bringing him back to reality. "They'll be seated at the head table with Erica and the rest of my brothers."

"What about us?" he asked. "Is that where we're sitting?"

"No. As an investor, you'll have your own table and I told Guy to have the kitchen staff put my place card next to yours."

"You're both looking very nice tonight," Trevor said, walking up to them. Lissa's brother had a pretty, young brunette clinging to his arm.

"Good to see you again," Shane said, shaking Trevor's hand.

After a few minutes of exchanging small talk, Trevor and his date moved on. "I wish he would settle down a bit," Lissa said quietly. "I've seen Elmer and Clara watching him, and they don't look all that pleased."

Putting his arm around her bare shoulders, Shane kissed her temple. "I agree that your brother is known to play it pretty fast and loose with the ladies, but it's really none of Elmer's or Clara's business what he does or how he chooses to conduct his life."

Before Lissa could respond, several of the regular resort guests came over to greet them and pay their compliments to Lissa's family on another spectacular event.

"The food in past years has been very good, but the cuisine this year is outstanding," George Sanders, a food critic from Los Angeles, said enthusiastically. "As soon as I find him, I intend to let Guy know the resort's pursuit of culinary excellence will be the focus of my next column. The crème brûlée is to die for."

"I'm sure Guy will be very pleased to hear that," Lissa said, smiling.

Once the portly gentleman stopped gushing about the food and moved on, Shane placed his hand on Lissa's back. "Why don't we find our table and see who our dinner partners are?"

He could use a reprieve and he was sure Lissa felt the same way. Besides, hearing himself repeat the same greeting at least twenty times, his face felt as if it had frozen in a permanent grin.

When they found their table close to the main table at the front of the room, Shane held Lissa's chair, then settled himself onto the one beside her. "It looks like we're hosting the politicians," he said, glancing at the place cards on the elegantly set table.

She nodded. "I just hope they put their political differences on hold for the evening."

"I'll see what I can do about that," Shane offered. "I happen to know that Senator Kurk and Representative Delacorte are both into fly-fishing. If it looks like the conversation is going to turn into a debate, I'll invite them both to go fishing next spring on the Rainbow."

"Thank you," she said, looking grateful. "I would really like for the evening to remain free of controversy."

"Shane, my boy, I hoped I would see you here this evening," Senator Kurk said, approaching their table. "I think you know my wife, Beatrice?"

Shane stood up while the older woman sat down. "It's nice seeing you again, Mrs. Kurk," he said nodding. He shook the senator's hand, then sat back down. "I'm glad you could join us."

"The way I hear it, congratulations are in order. A little bird told me you're planning on taking a trip down the aisle," the man said, smiling at Lissa. "Is this lovely girl your bride-to-be?"

"Senator Kurk, Mrs. Kurk, I would like for you to meet my fiancée, Melissa Jarrod," Shane introduced them.

"Melissa?" Beatrice Kurk exclaimed, disbelievingly. "I didn't recognize you, dear. You're all grown up. I think the last time we saw you, you were getting ready to leave for college."

As Lissa and the senator's wife exchanged pleasantries and caught up, Representative Delacorte and his wife arrived. Dinner was served shortly afterward and to Shane's immense relief, the two politicians seemed to have put their opposing political views aside for the evening.

While the women asked Lissa about new services at the spa and plans for their upcoming wedding, Shane found himself enjoying the men's stories of fishing for trout in the various rivers and streams in the Rocky Mountains. He was even surprised to learn the men were pretty good friends when they weren't at loggerheads over political issues.

As they waited for dessert to be served, the two men and their wives politely excused themselves. Shane knew they were going to work the room and try to secure votes for the upcoming elections before the event's closing speeches began.

Relieved to once again be alone with her, Shane turned to Lissa. But her attention was trained on her brother Trevor seated at the head table with her other siblings and their respective dinner companions.

"I can't believe what he's doing," she said, shaking her head. Seated beside a shapely redhead, the brunette that had been clinging to Trevor earlier was nowhere in sight. "I can only imagine what Elmer and Clara are thinking right now."

Watching his future brother-in-law whisper something to the redhead, then while her head was turned, wink at a blonde seated a few tables to the left of the head table, Shane had to admit the man was asking for a boatload of trouble. He saw nothing wrong with a single man playing the field. Hell, he'd had his own share of women before he met Lissa. But Shane had at least had the good sense to limit himself to being with one woman a night.

If Trevor wasn't careful, he was going to set himself up to be right in the middle of a class-A catfight. And once the women figured out he'd been playing all of them, they would stop blaming each other and turn on him with claws bared.

"Shane, could I speak with you in private for a moment?" Senator Kurk asked, standing at Shane's shoulder. Engrossed in the show at the head table, he hadn't seen the man approach.

"Of course," Shane answered, somewhat puzzled by the senator's serious demeanor. Rising from the table, he kissed Lissa's cheek. "I'll only be a few minutes."

He hated leaving her alone, but relieved to see Avery Lancaster heading toward their table, Shane turned his full attention to the man walking beside him. He had never seen Patrick Kurk look as serious or as determined as he did at that moment.

When Avery sat down in the chair next to her, Melissa couldn't help noticing the scene playing out just beyond her friend's shoulder. Her brothers Guy and Gavin had walked up behind Trevor at the head table. One of them spoke to him, then all three men left the room.

"What's going on?" she asked, turning to her friend.

"Guy and Gavin are going to strongly suggest that Trevor use a little more discretion with the female guests here tonight," Avery answered quietly.

"I'm glad," Melissa said, meaning it. "He's not doing the resort's reputation any favors."

"You mean 'come to Jarrod Ridge and get your heart broken by one of its handsome owners' isn't going to be the resort's new slogan?" Avery asked sardonically.

Melissa loved Avery's quick wit. "I somehow doubt that would help business," she said, laughing.

"Where's Shane?" Avery asked, looking around.

"Senator Kurk wanted to speak to him in private about something." Unconcerned, Melissa took a sip of her water. "He's probably hitting Shane up for a campaign donation or wants him to volunteer to hold some kind of fundraiser."

Avery nodded. "It's not enough that politicians want our vote, they also want our money."

"Are Guy and Gavin having their talk with Trevor?" Erica asked as she joined them.

Melissa smiled at her sister. "I'd say it's hitting the fan, even as we speak."

Erica winced. "I'd hate to be in poor Trevor's shoes right now."

"Me, too," Melissa and Avery both spoke at the same time.

"I'm glad I have you two together," Melissa said, deciding it was time for a change of subject. Even though Trevor deserved getting the warning about his notorious behavior, she took no pleasure in it having to be done. "One of the guests at the spa left a magazine in the reception area and it had pictures of a nursery decorated with an 'under the sea' theme," she explained. "I really liked it and I think that's what I want to use for the nursery. It incorporated all of the pastel colors and had the cutest baby sea creatures."

"I looked at that just the other day," Avery said, nodding. "It's adorable."

Melissa briefly wondered why Avery had been looking at nursery themes, but dismissed the thought. Her friend had probably been looking for ideas to use for the baby shower.

"I love the little pink sea horse and blue octopus," Melissa added, knowing she had settled on the theme she wanted for the nursery.

"It would be perfect for a boy or girl, too," Erica agreed enthusiastically. "And we can use all of the colors when we decorate for the shower."

Melissa hugged both women. "You two are the best. Thank you for planning this baby shower for me."

"Uh-oh. It looks like I'm going to have to go soothe the savage beast," Avery said suddenly, pointing toward Guy as he walked back into the ballroom.

"He doesn't look as if the encounter with Trevor was pleasant."

"I doubt that it was," Melissa said, hating that her family had to deal with yet another conflict.

"I'm afraid I need to get back to Christian," Erica apologized, rising to her feet. "I see he's been cornered by someone, no doubt looking for free legal advice."

As she watched her two best friends walk back to their fiancés, Melissa wondered where Shane was. She checked her watch. He had told her he would only be a few minutes and that had been a half hour ago.

Deciding he would probably be back soon, she left the table to freshen up before the closing speech began. As she started down the hall toward the ladies' powder room, she couldn't help but recognize Shane's voice coming from just around the corner.

"I'm flattered that you asked me to help with the investigation, Senator," Shane said. Melissa started to join him and the senator, but his next words stopped her in her tracks. "I have a couple of stables to design, but after I send the blueprints to the contractors, I'll have all the time in the world to devote to the investigation."

"There could be times when you'll have to do some frequent traveling," Senator Kurk warned.

There wasn't even so much as a moment's hesitation before Shane answered the man. "That won't be a problem. There's nothing keeping me from spending all the time needed on the job sites and giving them my undivided attention."

Lissa couldn't stand to hear any more. She and their child were nothing? Hadn't he listened to what she'd told him just the night before?

Feeling as if her heart had shattered into a million pieces, she turned and walked straight to the resort's lobby. Shane was no different than her father had been. He intended to put work ahead of his family, and that was something she just couldn't accept.

At the front desk, she asked for a piece of the resort's letterhead and an envelope. When she finished scribbling the note, she sealed it in the envelope and handed it to one of the clerks working the reservations desk.

"I want this delivered to Erica Prentice at the head table in the Grand Ballroom," she said, surprised that her voice sounded so steady. "Take it now before the closing speech starts."

"Yes, Ms. Jarrod," the young woman behind the counter said. "I'll take it to her right away."

As the woman hurried down the corridor leading to the ballroom, Melissa thought about walking to the lodge, but decided against it. She had left her light wrap at the table and the temperature outside had already dropped considerably. Besides, she didn't relish the idea of walking that distance in three-inch heels.

She turned to the concierge. "I want someone to drive me to Willow Lodge."

The man nodded. "It may take a few minutes to—"

"Now!" If she didn't get back to the lodge soon, there was a very real danger of her falling apart right there in the middle of the lobby.

Never having heard her bark orders at anyone, the man moved faster than she had ever seen him and in no time Melissa found herself seated in the back of one of the resort's courtesy limousines. She forced herself to remain stoic on the short ride up the road to Willow Lodge. She knew that she had already caused enough gossip and speculation among the employees with her outburst at the concierge. She didn't want to add more by dissolving into a sobbing heap in the back of the limo.

When the driver stopped in front of the lodge, she got out and hurriedly let herself inside. Only after she had closed and locked the door did she give in to the emotions that she had held in check since overhearing Shane and Senator Kurk.

First one tear and then another slipped down her cheeks and Melissa rushed into the bedroom to collapse on the bed. As she stared at the diamond ring on her left hand the loneliness of a lifetime came crashing down on top of her. She had never been able to live up to her father's expectations and it appeared that she wasn't enough for Shane now.

Nine

When Shane and the senator returned to the ballroom the closing speech had just begun and all eyes were focused on Blake Jarrod, Lissa's brother, the new CEO of Jarrod Ridge. As he thanked the guests and investors, Shane looked around for Lissa.

Where the hell had she gone? Had she become ill and had to leave? If so, why hadn't she found him to take her back to Willow Lodge?

As he scanned the crowd to see if she might be sitting at another table, he glanced at the head table. Lissa's sister, Erica, was staring at him and he could tell from her expression that she knew something about where Lissa might be.

Frustrated by the fact that he couldn't get to

Erica to ask where Lissa had gone until after Blake concluded his speech, Shane barely heard his name being called when the investors were asked to stand and be recognized. By the time Blake gave his closing remarks, Shane was already on his feet and threading his way through the crowd to the head table.

"Where did Lissa go?" he demanded when he reached Erica.

"Just before Blake's speech she sent me a message that she was having someone take her back to Willow Lodge," Erica said, looking worried. "Do you think she's not feeling well?"

"I don't know, but I'm sure as hell going to find out," he said, already turning toward the door. "Thanks."

"Please let me know if she's all right," Erica called after him.

Nodding that he would, Shane impatiently made his way through the crush of people leaving the ballroom. Was there something wrong with her or the baby?

As all of the things that could go wrong during the first trimester ran through his mind, he quickly decided that he'd done a little too much research about pregnancy. Apparently, ignorance really was bliss. It had to be better than the hell his imagination was putting him through now.

It seemed as if it took an eternity to make his way across the crowded lobby and out the resort's main doors. Unwilling to wait for the valet to bring his truck around, Shane broke into a run as he headed for the lane leading up to the private lodges.

Why had Lissa sent her sister the message saying she was leaving instead of him? What had happened between the time he and the senator stepped out into the corridor and the time they reentered the ballroom?

As he sprinted up the steps and across the deck of Willow Lodge, he fished for the key Lissa had given him from his pocket. His fingers felt clumsy as he rushed to unlock the door and let himself in.

"Lissa?" he called when he finally opened the door.

The silence was deafening. He glanced around the room. Her handbag was lying on the couch as if she'd tossed it aside so he knew she was there.

"Lissa, where are you?" he called, his heart thumping against his ribs as his fear increased. When he found her in the bedroom, she was lying on the bed, sobbing uncontrollably. "Lissa, angel, what's wrong?"

Before he could sit on the side of the bed and take her into his arms, she raised her face from the pillow she clutched. "D-don't, Shane." Shaking her head, she scooted to the opposite side of the mattress. "P-please just…go home."

What had gotten into her? When he left the table at the dinner, she had been fine.

"What's wrong?" he demanded.

"I want you...to leave," she sobbed. "Just go... back to your ranch...and leave me alone."

"Angel, you're not making sense," he said, trying to maintain a patient tone. "Calm down and tell me what happened to make you so upset."

Pushing herself to a sitting position, she swiped at her eyes with the back of her hand, then shook her head. "I overheard you and Senator Kurk."

"And?" He couldn't think of a single thing they had discussed that would send her into such an emotional meltdown.

"There's nothing to keep you from traveling extensively?" She shook her head. "What about me? What about our baby? Are we always going to come in a distant second to whatever project you're working on? Aren't we important enough to you that you want to be with us?"

"Calm down, Lissa."

"Don't tell me what to do, Shane. All my life I've come in last place behind a man's work and I won't do it again." Her eyes flashed with a mixture of hurt and anger. "Answer my question. Do you or do you not want to be here with me to make a marriage between us work?"

He had told the senator he was free to travel and devote his time to investigating design flaws in several federal and military buildings. But he couldn't tell her the reason he'd agreed, because he didn't like admitting—even to himself—that he needed distance to regain his perspective.

When he remained silent, Lissa's crushed expression caused his gut to twist into a painful knot. "I think your silence is answer enough, Shane." Removing the engagement ring he had given her, she reached across the bed to place it in his hand. "I'm just glad we discovered that it wouldn't work out between us before we actually got married."

"Lissa—"

"Don't, Shane," she said, sounding completely defeated. "There's really nothing left to say."

Staring at her for several long moments as he tried to put his tangled thoughts into some semblance of order, he shook his head. "This isn't over, Lissa."

Silent tears slid down her smooth cheeks. "Yes, it is, Shane."

He could tell from the look on her face she wouldn't listen to anything he had to say, even if he had been able to explain himself. "What about the investors and your family? What are you going to tell them?"

"That's really no longer any of your concern," she said flatly. "I'll handle whatever announcement I need to make regarding our breakup."

Suddenly angry, he asked, "What about the baby? I want to know—"

"From now on, anything you have to say to me can be done through Christian Hanford. Closer to the baby's birth, I'll have him contact your attorney to work out a custody agreement." She took a deep breath and pointed toward the door. "I'd really like to be alone now, Shane. Please lock the door as you leave."

He stared at her for a moment longer before turning to walk out of the bedroom. Placing the door key she'd given him on the kitchen counter, he let himself out of the house and descended the porch steps.

As he slowly walked down the lane toward the resort's main building, the engagement ring he still held felt as if it burned a hole in his palm. When he'd given it to her, he could tell it meant the world to her and he'd suspected then that she'd fallen in love with him.

He knew now that his instincts had been right on the mark. Lissa did love him and he could tell that it had broken her heart when she'd taken off the ring and handed it back to him only minutes ago.

His anger escalated, but it wasn't directed at anyone but himself. What the hell was wrong with him? How had he let things get so out of control?

He'd known for the past couple of weeks that he was walking a fine line, and keeping his feelings for Lissa in check was going to take monumental effort on his part. That's why he'd eagerly agreed to accept Senator Kurk's offer. He'd suddenly needed the distance between them to pull back before he found himself in far deeper than he'd ever intended to go.

But was it already too late? Had he done the unthinkable and fallen in love with her?

Shaking his head, Shane wasn't sure. And until he

got it all figured out, it would be best to leave things as they were between them. He'd already hurt her terribly. He'd rather give up his own life than do it again.

Standing on the deck at Willow Lodge, Melissa stared at the mountains beyond. How could her life have changed so dramatically, yet everything around her stayed the same? She had never experienced such emotional pain, never felt so alone as she did at that moment, yet the birds still sang and the sun still shone on the golden aspens whispering in the crisp mountain breeze.

Why had she deluded herself into thinking that Shane would be as committed to making their marriage work as she intended to be? How was it possible that she had missed seeing he was as driven by ambition and work as her father had been?

Shane had told her he would be faithful, and she had no doubt he'd meant what he said. But fidelity was one thing. Spending the time together that a couple needed to make a marriage work was something else entirely.

She had been willing to give up the life she'd built for herself in Malibu to remain in Colorado so that they could be a family. Was it too much to ask that he make a few concessions, as well?

The night he'd given her the engagement ring, he'd told her that his career required only occasional travel. But at the first opportunity that had come along for him to spend more time away from her and their child, he hadn't been able to agree fast enough.

All her life she'd come in a distant second to her father's ambition to make Jarrod Ridge the number-one resort in the Rockies. She refused to settle for second place with her husband.

"Melissa, is everything okay?" Turning at the sound of her sister's voice, Melissa watched Erica climb the steps and walk across the deck toward her. "You left the dinner so suddenly yesterday evening, I was afraid you might not be feeling well. Are you all right?"

"No, and I'm not sure I ever will be again," she said honestly. "But I'll survive. I always do."

"What's wrong?" Erica asked, clearly alarmed. "Are you feeling ill? It isn't anything with the baby, is it?"

Melissa shook her head. "As far as I know the baby is fine."

Erica looked around. "Where's Shane?"

"I don't know. Probably at his ranch." Since learning she had a half sister and welcoming Erica to the family, the two of them had grown fairly close and Melissa did need to talk to someone. "I broke off our engagement last night."

"Oh, no!" Erica immediately wrapped her arms around Melissa. "I'm so sorry. You both seemed so happy."

Melissa shrugged one shoulder. "It's probably

better that it happened now instead of after we got married."

"That's true," Erica agreed. "But it's still so sad." When the breeze picked up, she suggested, "Why don't we go inside and I'll make us both a cup of herbal tea?"

A few minutes later Melissa sat at the table, staring at the steam rising from the mug Erica had placed in front of her.

"Are you sure the two of you can't work things out?" Erica asked quietly.

"I don't see how." Over the course of the longest, loneliest night of her life, she had asked herself a thousand times if she'd made the right decision. Each time the answer had been that she had. "We both saw our relationship differently and I'm not sure that could ever change."

They were silent for several minutes before Erica asked, "Is there anything I can do?"

Melissa nodded. "You can be there for me when I let the rest of the family know the marriage is off."

"You know that Avery and I will both be there to support you no matter what," her sister said without hesitation. "For that matter, I can't imagine any of our brothers being anything but supportive."

"I hope so." Erica hadn't grown up in the same house with their father and therefore had no way of knowing how much emphasis had been placed on appearances and the family's reputation. "I've decided that I'll be going back to California soon.

I can have the baby out there without causing any disruption with the investors."

"Melissa, you can't do that. You'll lose your share of the resort." Erica shook her head. "No one wants to see that happen."

"If I don't, we could lose a considerable amount of funding for highly successful events like the Food and Wine Gala." She rubbed the tension building at her temples. "We've probably already lost one of our biggest investors."

Erica frowned. "Who's that?"

Melissa gave her sister a sad smile. "Shane."

"Do you really think he'll stop funding special promotions because the two of you are no longer involved?" Erica looked doubtful. "I'm sure he's made a lot of money from helping fund Jarrod Ridge projects. I wouldn't think he'd want to give that up."

"I don't know. It could be a bit uncomfortable for both of us." She took a sip of her tea. "But aside from Shane pulling out of upcoming projects, some of the others aren't going to look kindly on me being pregnant and single."

Erica touched Melissa's hand. "I think you're giving those people too much power over you. It's none of their concern what you do in your personal life."

"Shane said virtually the same thing," she admitted.

Maybe she was giving too much credence to what others thought of her family. But it was hard to cast aside a lifetime of instruction on the importance of others' opinions of her. For as long as she could remember her father had lectured his children on how their actions directly affected the resort and how important it was to protect Jarrod Ridge's reputation above all else.

"The main thing is you don't have to make a decision about any of this right away," Erica said, rising to place her cup in the sink. "You have plenty of time to weigh your options, then you can decide what *you* want to do."

After Erica left, Melissa sat at the table contemplating their conversation. In this day and age, many women chose to be single mothers and no one thought anything about it. So why was she afraid of what two busybodies had to say about her? And why was she willing to lose her inheritance because of it?

She wasn't. The only opinions that really mattered were those of her family. They loved each other and since their father's death the bonds between them were strengthening. Maybe her brothers would stand behind her and her decisions if she stayed in Aspen.

Sitting up straight, she came to a decision. She didn't care anymore what people like Elmer Madison and Clara Buchanan had to say about her becoming a single mother. They weren't living her life. She was.

If they pulled out of the investment group because of her pregnancy, it would be their loss. There were probably several other townspeople who would readily take their place and reap the rewards of investing in Jarrod Ridge. And if not, the family could pick up the slack themselves.

Feeling slightly better, she sighed. If only she could resolve her feelings for Shane that easily. But making a rational choice to change your attitude about something was far easier than trying to change how you felt about a person.

There was no way around it and no way to stop it. She loved Shane with every fiber of her being and always would.

"Cactus, this is the worst meat loaf I've ever tasted," Shane complained, pushing his plate away.

The truth was, the meal could have been prepared by a gourmet chef and the results would have been the same. Everything he'd tried to eat for the past few days had tasted like an old piece of harness.

"It's been three days since you and that little gal parted ways and I swear you're in a worse mood now than you was when you first told me she wouldn't be around no more," Cactus grumbled as he cleared the dinner table.

Shane sighed and tuned Cactus out as the old man continued his rant. He knew he was being unreasonable about everything with everybody. But he couldn't seem to stop himself. He couldn't eat, couldn't sleep and nothing he did seemed to relieve the hollow ache that had settled in his chest when he walked away from Willow Lodge the other night.

"I'm sorry if I've been a little irritable," he said, knowing there was no excuse for taking out his bad mood on Cactus.

"A little irritable?" The old man looked disgusted. "Boy, I've seen pissed-off grizzly bears with better attitudes than yours."

Rubbing the tension at the base of his neck, Shane nodded. "I know. And I'm really sorry about that."

"Well, knowin' and doin' somethin' about it are two different things." Dishes clattered as Cactus dumped them into the sink. When he turned to face Shane, he pointed a wooden spoon at him. "Seems to me that if you're that miserable, you'd get your sorry hide back to town and see what you could do to patch things up with that gal."

"It's not that easy."

"Why ain't it?"

Shane wasn't surprised that Cactus thought it could be that easy. The old man saw things as black and white, right and wrong. If something went wrong, a person fixed it and moved forward. But some things just weren't that easy to repair.

"For one thing, I doubt that Lissa would open the door if I did go by her place."

"Then you catch her out somewhere and talk to her," Cactus shot back. "And if you have to get down on your hands and knees to tell her how sorry you are, then do it."

"How do you know I'm in the wrong?" Shane asked, feeling a bit affronted. He hadn't told the old man anything more than the wedding was off and Lissa wouldn't be visiting Rainbow Bend anymore.

"Far as women are concerned, it don't make no never mind who started it or what it's about," Cactus said sagely. "To their way of thinkin' it's always a man's fault."

"I'll take that under advisement," Shane said, starting down the hall. He didn't need to hear more of Cactus's advice on relationships. He already knew who was to blame for his and Lissa's breakup.

Once inside his study, Shane closed the door and walked over to his drafting table to sit down. He'd tried for the past couple of days to work on the plans for the sheik's stable, but hadn't accomplished a damned thing. For a man accused of being ambitious and driven, he certainly wasn't living up to expectations.

Staring off into space, he couldn't stop thinking about Lissa and the shattered look on her pretty face when he hadn't been able to answer her questions. He had a good idea he knew exactly why he had agreed to the senator's request to help with the investigation and it wasn't something he was proud of. Accepting the job had been his way of running, of trying to escape what he knew now to be inevitable.

He took a deep breath. A man never liked admitting, even to himself, that he was a coward. But the truth of the matter was, he was just plain scared.

Lissa made him feel too much. She made him want to reach out for the things that he had told himself he would never have.

Propping his elbows on the drafting table, Shane buried his head in his hands. Somehow when he wasn't looking, Lissa had gotten past his defenses and he'd done the unthinkable. He'd fallen in love with her.

His heart pounding in his chest like a jackhammer, he rose from the drafting table to walk over and stare out the window at Rainbow Valley. He hadn't wanted history to repeat itself, hadn't wanted to go through the same hell his father had by loving a woman.

But with the exception of trying to drink her memory away, Shane found himself in the same position. He loved Lissa and was finding it damned near impossible to live without her.

As he watched an eagle make a soaring sweep of the valley, he thought about something Lissa had said when she broke off their engagement. She felt she'd taken a backseat to a man's work all of her life. Now he was doing the same thing her father had done. From what he could remember, Donald Jarrod spent every waking minute overseeing every aspect of the thriving enterprise. And instead of the preferential treatment some men would have shown their own kids, Jarrod had seemed to expect his children to work harder and do more than anyone else.

It was no wonder when Lissa heard his conversation with Senator Kurk that she had assumed he was as driven and ambitious as her father. She had no way of knowing that he'd been running from himself and not striving to build his career.

He shook his head. Although he wanted to excel in his field, Shane had no intention of ever letting it take over his life. But he hadn't told her that the other night. Now, he wasn't sure she'd give him the chance.

But he had to try and he knew exactly where to start to make things right between them. Turning to walk over to his desk, Shane picked up the phone.

"Senator Kurk? This is Shane McDermott."

Ten

"Blake, is this a good time?" Melissa asked from the door of her brother's private office.

"What's up?" he asked, looking up from the papers on his desk that he and his assistant had been going over.

"There's something I need to tell you," she said, walking into the room.

"I'll leave the two of you alone," Samantha said as if sensing that Melissa's business with Blake was of a personal nature.

Of all of her brothers, Blake had turned out to be the most like their father. He was the consummate business man and had been the best choice to step in as CEO of Jarrod Ridge. He was also a bit intimidating.

Settling herself into the chair in front of his desk, she took a deep breath. "I wanted to let you know that I've ended my engagement to Shane."

His concerned expression when he got up and walked around the desk encouraged her. "I'm sorry to hear that, Melissa," he said, sitting down in the chair beside her. "Are you all right?"

The genuine concern she heard in his voice had her fighting back tears. "It's been a rough few days," she admitted. "But I'm doing okay."

"Is there anything I can do?" he asked.

"Not really." She shrugged one shoulder. "Although I'm sure once the word gets out around the resort there will be a lot of talk and speculation. I just thought you needed to know before that happens."

Blake nodded. "I appreciate that, but I'm more concerned about your welfare than I am the rumor mill."

"I hope you mean that, because I've made a decision I'm not entirely certain you'll be happy with." She met his puzzled gaze. "I'm staying here in Aspen."

His complete confusion was written all over his face. "Where else would you go?"

"At first I thought it might be best if I went back to California to have the baby." She stared down at her hands clasped tightly in her lap. Making the decision to place herself ahead of the resort was new to her and she only hoped her brother understood. "I know some of the investors aren't going to look favorably on my being a single mother, but—"

"I couldn't care less if those people contribute another penny to Jarrod Ridge," he interrupted.

Shocked at her brother's statement, she stared at him. "Really?"

He nodded. "They knew Dad would sell his own soul for this resort and its reputation. For years they've used that to hold us all hostage with the threat of withdrawing from the investors group. That ends now."

His decisive tone left no doubt in her mind that Blake meant what he said. "It won't make a difference if they do stop investing in special events, will it?" She didn't think it would, but she wanted to be sure.

Blake laughed. "Not hardly. Our great great-great-grandfather started the investors group when he needed capital to build Jarrod Ridge. We've grown way beyond needing anyone else's money to do whatever we want with the place."

"Then why hasn't the group been dissolved?" she asked, unable to understand why her father hadn't done so years ago.

"The same reason you were willing to give up your share of Jarrod Ridge and go back to California," Blake said. "Dad was afraid of what disgruntled investors like Clara and Elmer might say against the resort."

For the first time since walking into her brother's

office, Melissa felt some of her tension ease. "I take it you don't care what they say?"

"The locals aren't the ones keeping Jarrod Ridge going, nor do they make or break our reputation," he said, grinning as he shook his head. "The tourists do that. We keep the townspeople afloat with the clientele we bring in. I seriously doubt they're so vindictive they would bite the hand that feeds them."

"I hadn't thought of it like that." Rising, Melissa hugged her brother. "Thank you, Blake. Our talk has helped me more than you can imagine."

"That's what family is for, Melissa," he said, returning to sit at his desk. "And I'm sorry things didn't work out with you and McDermott."

"Me, too," she said sadly as she left his office.

As she walked back to the spa, Melissa wondered why her father hadn't seen what Blake pointed out about the resort's importance to the town. Or maybe he had and used the fear of ruining the resort's reputation to manipulate and control his children. Either way, the next generation of Jarrods weren't going to have to live under the threat of other people's opinions.

But the resolution to that problem brought little relief. In fact, it only gave her more time to think about Shane and the incredible loneliness and heartache she'd felt since breaking off their engagement.

Lost in thought, she was halfway across the reception area when she realized her assistant manager had called her name. "Is something wrong, Rita?" she asked, turning to face the woman.

"Ms. Jarrod, I'm afraid I've made another mistake with this afternoon's schedule," Rita said, looking as if she might burst into tears. "I don't know how it happened, but we have a guest in the Green Room, waiting for a massage and there isn't a masseuse available. Could you take the appointment?"

Sighing, Melissa nodded as she headed for the Green Room at the back of the spa. "Not a problem, Rita. Just double-check before you book next time."

In truth, she was glad to have something to take her mind off of how much she missed Shane. Anything was better than sitting in her office, thinking about all the things that could never be.

As soon as she opened the door to the dimly lit therapy room, the piped-in sound of a waterfall seemed to wash over her and caused her to catch her breath. She'd probably never be able to hear the sound again without thinking of Shane and the afternoon they'd spent together at Rainbow Falls.

Glancing at the massage table, she did a double take. There wasn't anyone there. The sound of the door being closed and the lock being secured had her spinning around to face whoever was in the room with her.

"Hello, Lissa." The male voice was so low, so warm and intimate, it felt as if he caressed her, and it caused her heart to skitter to a complete halt.

"Shane, what on earth do you think you're doing here?"

The sight of him was both heaven and hell rolled into one. She'd missed him so much, but the thought that they'd never be together caused such emotional pain, it was all she could do to keep from crying out from its intensity.

"I told you the other night that our discussion wasn't over," he said, advancing on her.

She quickly skirted the massage table to put it between them. "And I told you there wasn't anything left to say."

Wearing nothing but a towel wrapped around his waist, he folded his arms across his wide chest and shook his head. "Maybe you don't have anything more to add, but I have plenty."

Melissa closed her eyes and tried not to think about how wonderful it felt to be wrapped in those arms, to lay her head on that bare chest and have him hold her throughout the night. Opening her eyes, she shook her head. "Please, don't do this, Shane."

"Don't do what, Lissa?" he asked calmly. "Explain why I agreed to help Senator Kurk with the investigation? Or don't tell you about the war I've been waging with myself about why I hesitated to answer your questions?"

Why was he doing this to her? Couldn't he see it was tearing her apart just being in the same room with him and knowing they could never have a future together?

"None of it matters, Shane," she said, trying desperately to keep her voice from cracking. "You can't change, and I won't settle."

"Yes, it does matter, angel," he said, his deep baritone wrapping around her like a warm cloak.

Knowing that he wasn't going to leave her alone until she heard what he had to say, she pointed to his towel. "Do you really think this is the kind of conversation we should be having with you wearing nothing but that?"

"I don't have a problem with it." He moved his hand to release the terry cloth where it was tucked at his waist, causing her to go weak in the knees. "But I can take it off if you want me to."

"N-no," she said hastily, holding her hand up to stop him. "The towel will be fine. Just tell me what you came here to say, then leave."

He motioned toward the lounge chair in the corner. "This might take a while. Why don't you sit down?"

With her legs feeling as if they might not support her much longer, she conceded and walked over to lower herself onto the lounger. When he started to walk over to her, she shook her head. "You can say what you need to from over there."

If he got any closer there was a good chance he would reach out and touch her. That was something she couldn't allow to happen. If he did, she knew for certain she'd lose every ounce of her resolve.

She watched him take a deep breath. The movement of his rippling abdominal muscles sent a shaft of longing straight through her. Quickly averting her eyes, she concentrated on his suddenly serious expression.

"First of all, I want you to know that I'm not like your father, Lissa. I'm not driven to work every waking minute." He shook his head. "Don't get me wrong, I enjoy my career and I'm good at what I do, but that's just a part of my life. It's not all that I am."

"That isn't the message you were sending the other night," she interjected. "The way it sounded when you agreed to help with the congressional investigation, you couldn't wait to get started."

He nodded. "I know that's the way it seemed, but I wasn't taking the job because I couldn't resist the chance to work. I took the job because I felt the need to run."

It felt as if her heart shattered all over again and Melissa wondered how he thought his explanation was better than her assumption. "Y-you didn't have to…go to those lengths to get away from me," she said, hating that she could no longer keep her voice steady. "All you had to do was tell me you'd changed your mind."

"No, Lissa, I wasn't wanting to run from you," he said softly. "I wanted to run from myself."

Confused, she frowned. "I don't understand."

"Let me tell you a story that might help clear things up," he said. She didn't understand how that was going to make his explanation any clearer, but she could see from his expression that he thought it was very relevant. "When my mom and dad got married and he brought her to Rainbow Bend, she told him she loved living there. And who knows? Maybe she did for a while."

"Who wouldn't love living there?" she found herself asking.

"After a few winters of being stuck in the house with no way to get out of the valley for several weeks at a time, my mom found it intolerable." He gave her a sad smile. "You know, I can't remember a night when she was still with us that I didn't lie awake listening to her beg my dad to sell the ranch or, later on, threaten to leave if he didn't."

"Oh, Shane, I'm sorry," Melissa said. "That's why you kept warning me about being snowbound, isn't it?"

He nodded. "I wanted you to know up front what you were getting yourself into."

"Your mother wasn't from around here, was she?" she asked suddenly.

"No, she was from somewhere in Florida," he said, looking puzzled. "But why does that matter?"

"Because she wasn't used to the type of weather we have here." Melissa wasn't excusing the woman's behavior, but she was certain the differences in climates had to have come as quite a shock. "I grew up here. I'm used to deep snows and the difficulties that poses to traveling. She wasn't."

Shane seemed to mull that over a moment before he nodded. "You might be right about that. But it doesn't excuse her from leaving her husband and son and never looking back."

"You never saw her again?"

"No. I was notified a few years ago that she had been killed in a car accident."

Melissa could understand a child not seeing their mother due to death. Her own mother had died of cancer when she was two and she'd known Margaret Jarrod only through the pictures her father had kept. But how could a mother willingly walk away from her child and never contact him again?

"How old were you the last time you saw her?" she asked.

"Nine." He met her gaze head-on, and she could tell that he was still haunted by the abandonment. "But I actually lost two parents that day."

"But I thought your dad didn't pass away until your last year of college," she said, confused.

"His spirit was gone long before that," Shane said, sighing heavily. "After he finally crawled out of the whiskey bottle and burned everything that hinted at a woman ever living in the house, he did two things for the rest of his life. He worked and slept. Beyond that, he didn't have a lot of interest in life."

With sudden clarity Melissa knew exactly why her father had turned into a workaholic. He'd been trying to fill the void left by his wife.

"Did your father leave a picture of her for you?"

Her father hadn't been able to get rid of anything that had belonged to her mother.

"No, I barely remember what she even looked like." Shane shrugged. "But I made a vow that I'd never put myself in the position for the same thing to happen to me. I wasn't going to give that kind of power over me to any woman."

Afraid that his next revelation would be that he could never give her what she needed most—his love—she bit her lower lip to keep it from trembling a moment before she asked, "W-what does that have to do with you helping the senator?"

Shane walked over to kneel in front of her. "I was trying to run from the fact that I'd done the very thing I'd swore never to do, angel."

Melissa closed her eyes and tried not to read anything into what he had just said. She couldn't bear it if it turned out she was wrong.

"What were you trying to run from, Shane?" she finally found the courage to ask.

"I was trying to run from loving you, Lissa," he said, taking her hands in his. "There isn't much of anything in this life that I can honestly say I'm afraid of. But the thought of loving you the way I do and having you leave me one day, scares the living hell out of me."

Tears filled her eyes. "You love me?"

Nodding, he took her into his arms and crushed her to his broad chest. "I love and need you more than I need my next breath."

Before she could tell him that she loved him, too, he covered her mouth with his. Heat streaked throughout her entire body when he traced her lips with his tongue and she readily opened to grant him the access he sought. As he tasted and teased, her heart filled with the knowledge that Shane loved her. She'd never felt more complete than she did at that moment.

When he finally broke the kiss, Melissa leaned back to cup his face with both hands. "Shane McDermott, I love you with all my heart and soul."

"And I love you, angel." He gave her a quick kiss, then lifted her left hand to slip her engagement ring back onto her finger. "Promise me you won't give this back to me ever again."

Throwing her arms around his neck, she shook her head. "Never." It suddenly occurred to her that he had been wearing nothing but a towel from the moment she walked into the room. "Where did you keep the ring while you were telling me about your parents?"

He laughed. "You didn't notice that I kept my left hand closed?"

"I…well…not really." She smiled. "I was too busy looking at your…um, heart."

"Like that, do you?" he asked, grinning. He took her hand to place it on his chest. "It belongs to you now, Lissa. My heart, my soul, all of me belongs to you for the rest of our lives."

"And I'm yours, Shane," she promised. "I have been from the moment we met."

Lifting her, he sat down and settled her on his lap. "We have a few more things we need to discuss."

"What would that be?" she asked, laying her head on his shoulder.

"I believe you when you say that you love the ranch," he said slowly. "But I think we'll build a house here in Aspen to live in during the snow season."

Sitting up, she frowned. "But I won't mind being snowed in as long as it's with you."

He laughed. "I know, but I'm thinking down the line." He placed his hand on her still-flat stomach. "When our baby is old enough, I don't want to have him or her living with relatives to attend school like I had to do."

"I hadn't thought of that," she said, liking the idea that he wanted them to all be together.

"I also think it would be a good idea for us to spend this winter at Willow Lodge." He kissed her nose. "That way we won't miss any doctor appointments because of weather."

"You're just full of good ideas, aren't you," she said, unable to stop smiling. "That way while you're traveling for the congressional investigation, I'll at least have Erica and Avery over from time to time."

"You can have your family over as much as you like, but I'll be there, too," he said, pressing his cheek to her temple.

"You will?"

Grinning, he nodded. "I called Senator Kurk this afternoon and told him that after careful thought, I wouldn't be available for the job after all."

"Did he understand?" she asked, wondering if he'd made an enemy out of an old family friend.

"He told me he was disappointed, but he understood that being a newlywed I wouldn't want to be away from you." Shane kissed her temple, her cheek and the tip of her nose. "And that brings me to the last thing we need to talk over."

"A wedding date?" she guessed.

He nodded. "Are we still good for New Year's Eve, angel?"

"Absolutely."

He nibbled kisses along the side of her neck. "Why don't I get dressed and you take off the rest of the afternoon. I'd like to take you back to Willow Lodge and catch up on the three days we've been apart."

"That sounds like your best idea yet, Cowboy," she said, loving him more with each passing second.

He was her heart, her soul, her very life. She couldn't wait to be back in his arms again, celebrating the happiness of finding each other, the life they had created and the love she knew for certain they would share for the rest of their lives.

* * * * *

"You're being very contradictory tonight, Samantha. They'd eat you alive in the boardroom with that attitude," he mocked.

She stiffened. "Listen, Blake, I'll sleep with any man I want when I'm good and ready. Tonight I just wasn't ready. And in case you didn't notice, this isn't the boardroom."

No, but he did want to eat her alive right now.

Adrenaline pumping through him, he knew it was time to take action.

"Blake?" she croaked as he brought her into the circle of his arms, leaving only sheer inches between them. He'd never been this close to her before. Not close enough to see the rush of desire in her blue eyes. It knocked the breath from his body.

As hard as it was, he let her go. He knew all he needed to know for the moment. She wanted him. And he wasn't giving up. His plans for seduction were still very much alive.

Dear Reader,

I was thrilled when my editor invited me to write the fourth book in the DYNASTIES: THE JARRODS series. Better yet that the setting was Aspen, Colorado. What a gorgeous place for my hero and heroine to fall in love.

Being a writer is like being an actor who needs to get into character, and that made it such fun to write this book. I especially enjoyed writing a heroine who decides she has nothing to lose by instigating a brief affair with her handsome boss, before she walks away forever. Samantha turned into such a tease. As for my hero, Blake didn't know what hit him. He'd been forced to return home to take charge of the luxurious resort, determined to remain indifferent to the place and the people. He hadn't counted on the majestic mountains, renewed family ties, and the love of a beautiful woman like Samantha, to show him what really mattered most.

Like the beautiful Colorado scenery, I hope Samantha and Blake's love story takes your breath away.

Happy reading!

Maxine

TAMING HER
BILLIONAIRE BOSS

BY
MAXINE SULLIVAN

Published in Great Britain 2011
by Mills & Boon, an imprint of Harlequin (UK) Limited,
Eton House, 18-24 Paradise Road, Richmond, Surrey TW9 1SR

© Harlequin Books S.A. 2010

Special thanks and acknowledgement to Maxine Sullivan for her contribution to the Dynasties: The Jarrods series.

ISBN: 978 0 263 88320 6

51-1011

Harlequin (UK) policy is to use papers that are natural, renewable and recyclable products and made from wood grown in sustainable forests. The logging and manufacturing processes conform to the legal environmental regulations of the country of origin.

Printed and bound in Spain
by Blackprint CPI, Barcelona

Maxine Sullivan credits her mother for her lifelong love of romance novels, so it was a natural extension for Maxine to want to write her own romances. She thinks there's nothing better than being a writer and is thrilled to be one of the few Australians to write for the Desire™ line.

Maxine lives in Melbourne, Australia, but over the years has travelled to New Zealand, the UK and the USA. In her own backyard, her husband's job ensured they saw the diversity of the countryside, from the tropics to the Outback, country towns to the cities. She is married to Geoff, who has proven his hero status many times over the years. They have two handsome sons and an assortment of much-loved, previously abandoned animals.

Maxine would love to hear from you. She can be contacted through her website at www.maxinesullivan.com.

With thanks to the fabulous Desire™ editors, Krista Stroever and Charles Griemsman, who worked so hard to make this series special.

And to friend and Harlequin American author, C.C. Coburn, for her helpful advice on everything Aspen

From the Last Will and Testament of Don Jarrod

…and to my beloved son Blake I leave the grand piano that was your mother's pride and joy. Some of my fondest memories are of you, lying beneath that piano, listening to your mother play. I hope you will find room in your home for this beautiful piece and enjoy not just the beautiful music it puts forth, but the true love it represents.

One

"What are you doing in here?"

Samantha Thompson almost dropped her pen as her head snapped up, the desk lamp shedding enough light for her to see the handsome man standing in the doorway. "Blake, you scared me!"

Her heart didn't settle down once she knew who it was, it only increased pace as she looked at him in a dinner suit that fitted his well-toned body flawlessly. His commanding presence was of a man born to lead. This was Blake Jarrod, owner of Blake Jarrod Enterprises' Las Vegas hotels, and now the new CEO of Jarrod Ridge, his family's renowned resort in Aspen, Colorado.

And as his assistant of two years there was nothing unusual about her being in his office at ten at night. Just because they were now in Aspen at the Jarrod Manor and she was using the desk in his late father's office didn't change a thing. She had her reasons for being here.

And they concerned her boss.

Or soon-to-be-ex boss.

"It's late," he said, cutting across her thoughts in the way he usually did.

She took a steadying breath and looked down at the letter in front of her, giving herself one last chance to change her mind. Then she remembered this evening. The final straw had been watching a famous blonde actress flirt outrageously with Blake, and him sitting there enjoying it, taking it as his due.

Samantha couldn't blame him for wanting to sample what was on offer if he so chose. It was just that *she* wanted a little taste of him herself. She usually dressed sedately in finely tailored clothes whether she was in Vegas with Blake or here in Aspen, but tonight she'd outdone herself. She'd worn this slinky cream evening dress designed to grab his attention, putting her long, brunette hair up in a chignon when she usually wore it pulled back at the nape with a barrette, but it was clear now that nothing was going to happen between her and Blake.

It was *never* going to happen.

She'd realized that when he'd caught her eye and she'd smiled for all she was worth, looked the best she could be, and he'd turned back to the actress without a second glance, rejecting her just like Carl had rejected her. Her moment of epiphany had been that simple. She'd come to a decision then. The right decision for her. The *only* one for her.

She lifted her gaze. "Yes, it's late, Blake."

Too late.

He walked toward the desk, almost as if he sensed

something wasn't quite right. "I thought you said you were going back to Pine Lodge."

That had been her intention. She'd even stood in the lobby of the manor, her coat resting on her shoulders, waiting beside the doorman for the valet to bring the SUV around. She'd been determined to go back to their private lodge at the resort—she in her own room and Blake in the master suite.

Then someone had entered the hotel and the doors had slid open, and the cold night breeze from a midfall wind had slapped her in the face and chilled her to the bone, reminding her that it didn't matter what she wore or what she did, her boss would never take any notice of her except as his assistant. She'd spun around and headed for the private elevator, coming up here to the office in the family section of the manor.

"I needed to do something first," she said now.

There was an alert look to his eyes. "It's Friday night. Work can wait until tomorrow."

They'd been working every Saturday, trying to keep on top of things until they moved here permanently. And now that wasn't going to happen. Not for her anyway. "This can't wait."

He paused, those blue eyes narrowing in on her. "What can't?"

She swallowed hard. "My resignation."

Shock flashed in his eyes then went out like it had never been. "What are you talking about?" he said, his voice quiet. In control. He was *always* in control, especially where she was concerned.

"It's time for me to move on, Blake. That's all."

"Why?"

The question shot at her like a pellet but she managed to shrug. "It just is."

He put his hands on the desk and leaned toward her. "What's this about, Samantha? What's the real reason you want to leave?"

She'd faced him down over business issues occasionally but this...*this* was personal. Cautiously, she pushed the leather chair back and rose on her stilettos, then went to look out the large arched window behind her.

The scene below at the luxurious resort was surprisingly charming in October. Tonight, pocketed in amongst the tall peaks, the sleepy hamlet twinkled like fairy lights in the alpine breeze, a tapestry of winding streets, lodges, and village square. To a southern California girl who now lived in Vegas, this place had something nowhere else seemed to have.

It had heart.

"It's time for me to go," she said, keeping her back to him.

"You're unhappy here?"

"No!" she blurted out, swinging around, then winced inwardly, knowing she sounded contradictory and that he'd have to wonder why.

To be truthful, she'd been feeling slightly down ever since Blake's sister Melissa had announced her pregnancy a few weeks ago. She'd been happy for Melissa, so why it had bothered her she didn't know. Yet since then she hadn't been able to shake a feeling of being slightly depressed.

He'd straightened away from the desk. "So what's the problem?"

You are.

I want you to notice me.

Dammit, I just want *you*.

But how did you say that to a man who didn't even notice you as a woman? She was his trusted assistant and that was about it. She'd never acted overtly female around him. She kept everything businesslike between them. Looking back, perhaps occasionally she should have let her feminine side show. If she had, then perhaps now she might not be in this predicament.

Yet it wasn't that she was in love with him either. She was intensely attracted to him. He was an exciting, charismatic man who effortlessly charmed women like they were going out of fashion, but he was still discerning in whom he took to his bed.

She wanted to be charmed by him.

She wanted to be in his bed and in his arms.

Oh, God, it truly was hitting home that she'd never be in his spotlight. Until now a glimmer of hope had kept her going, but after his subconscious rejection of her tonight, she'd realized that if he knew her feelings about wanting him, then everything would change. She'd be totally embarrassed and so would he. She couldn't work like that. She'd be humiliated just like she'd been with Carl. It was better to leave with some dignity.

"Samantha?"

Hearing her name on his lips struck her like never before. She tilted her head at him. "Do you know something, Blake? You've never called me Sam. Not once. It's always Samantha."

His brows drew together. "What's that got to do with it?"

Everything.

She wanted to be Sam once in a while. Sam the

woman who'd left her ordinary upbringing in Pasadena to embrace the excitement of Vegas after a one-sided love affair gone wrong. The woman who wanted to have a purely physical affair with a man she admired, without ever risking her heart again. Not Samantha the personal assistant who helped run his office and his life and who kept the whole lot in check for him, all nice and neat and tidy, just the way he liked it. She couldn't believe she'd actually thought she'd had a chance with him.

And he was waiting for an answer.

"I have my reasons for resigning and I think that's all you need to know."

"Is someone giving you a hard time?" he asked sharply. "Someone from my family? I'll talk to them if they are. Tell me."

She shook her head. "Your family's great. It's…" She hesitated, wishing she'd given herself time to come up with a suitable explanation. Needless to say, she hadn't expected to be here tonight writing out her resignation, or that he'd even come upon her. She'd assumed he'd probably go off nightclubbing with Miss Hollywood. "I simply want something more, okay? It's nothing against you or your family. This is about me."

One eyebrow rose. "You want something *more* than first-class travel and a world-class place to live?"

"Yes." She had to tread carefully. "Actually I'm thinking of going home to Pasadena for a little while," she fibbed, then realized that wasn't such a bad idea after all. "Just until I decide what I want to do next."

"And that will give you more of what you want? I seem to remember you saying you'd left Pasadena *because* you'd been looking for more excitement."

She'd definitely said that—and she *had* been looking

for more than weekly piano lessons and weekend shopping with her girlfriends—but it had been so much more four years ago. Having fallen in love with a young architect who'd gone off to travel the world after she'd told him she loved him, she'd decided to find her own excitement. Her job with Blake had provided that excitement without any emotional involvement. Until now. And even now it was about lust, not love.

His eyes pierced the distance between them. "You seemed happy enough before to move to Aspen."

"I was... I am... I mean..." Oh, heck. She was getting herself tied up in knots. When Blake said he was moving back home and she should come with him, she'd been delighted. His estranged father's will had stated all the Jarrod offspring had to return to Jarrod Ridge for a year or lose their inheritance. Blake, being the eldest—only by a few minutes ahead of his fraternal and more laidback twin, Guy—had taken up the challenge of running the resort.

She'd looked forward to it, too, and they'd been traveling back and forth between Aspen and Vegas a couple of times these past four months, getting everything sorted. Blake would keep his hotels but would spend most of his time in Aspen. She'd been very happy with that. Until tonight.

She cleared her throat. "All my family and friends are back in Pasadena. I miss them."

"I didn't know you *had* any friends."

She pulled a face. "Thanks very much."

There was a flicker of impatience. "You know what I mean. You're always working or traveling with me and rarely go home except for the holidays. Your friends have never been a priority before."

"I guess that's changed." Thankfully Carl had never returned and she'd heard he'd married an English girl. Of course, time and distance had only shown her that she hadn't really been in love with him at all. She'd been in love with the *idea* of being in love with a man who'd talked of adventure in far-off places. She'd thought they'd do that together. God, what was wrong with her that she kept wanting men who *didn't* want her?

He held her gaze. "What are you going to do after Pasadena, then?"

"I'm not sure. I'll find something. Perhaps even one of those rare friends of mine might help me get a job," she mocked. All she knew was that she wouldn't continue working for Blake, not in Aspen nor in Vegas. A clean break was needed.

He eyed her. "You have plenty of connections. You could use them."

All at once she had an ache in her throat. It sounded like he was beginning to accept her decision. And *that* more than anything showed he really didn't care about her. She was just another employee to him. Nothing more.

"I'm thinking I might get right away from this type of work."

"And do what?"

"I don't know." She took a breath. "In any case, I'd really like to leave Aspen as soon as possible, so that I can wrap up things in Vegas before going home. It shouldn't take more than a couple of days." She'd make sure it didn't.

He scanned her face. "You're not telling me everything," he said, sending her heart bumping against her ribs.

"There's nothing else to tell. I do have a life and a family away from you, Blake, as hard as that may be for you to believe." She couldn't take much more of this. Going over to the desk, she picked up the letter. "So I'd appreciate it if you would accept my resignation." She walked toward him. "Ideally I'd like to leave here as soon as possible. Tomorrow even." Reaching him, she held out the letter.

He didn't take it.

There was a measured silence, then, "No."

The breath stalled in her throat. "Wh-what?"

"No, I won't accept your letter of resignation and certainly not on such short notice. I need you here with me."

His words sent a jet of warmth through her until she remembered this evening. It had been torturous watching him and that actress flirt with each other. How could she stay and keep up the pretence that she didn't want Blake for herself?

She continued to hold the letter out to him. "I can't stay, Blake. I really need to leave."

Now.

Tomorrow.

Certainly no later than that.

He ignored the sheet of paper until she lowered her hand. "I'm the new CEO here, Samantha. It wouldn't be professional of you to leave me in the lurch like this."

She felt bad but it came down to emotional survival. "I know, but there are others quite capable of replacing me. Just contact a high-end employment agency. I'll even do it for you before I go. Someone else would love to work here in Jarrod Ridge. They could be here by Monday."

His mouth tightened. "No."

She lifted her chin. "I'm afraid you have no choice."

"I don't?" he said silkily, inching closer. "You can't quit without a month's notice. It's in your contract."

She sucked in a sharp breath. "Surely you could waive that for me? I've given you two years of my life, Blake, and I've done the job exceptionally well. I've been at your beck and call 24/7. I think you owe me this."

"If you insist on leaving before your contract is up then I'll see you in court." He gave a significant pause. "I don't think that would look good on your résumé, do you?"

"You wouldn't!"

"Wouldn't I?

"This is business," he continued. "Don't take it personally."

She almost choked then. That was the problem. Everything was business between them. *Nothing* was personal.

Her hands shook with anger as she began folding the letter in four. Then she leaned forward and tucked it into his jacket pocket. "Fine. You've got your month. Two weeks here and then two weeks back in Vegas to finish up. After that I'm leaving for Pasadena." She went to step past him.

In a flash he grabbed her arm and stopped her, looking down into her eyes. It was the first time he'd ever touched her *with meaning* and something passed between them. She saw his spark of surprise before he dropped her arm. It surprised her, too.

"I never take no for an answer, Samantha. Remember that."

"There's always the exception to every rule. And I'm it, *Mr. Jarrod.*"

* * *

She was still shaking when she got out of the SUV and back to her room at Pine Lodge. She was angry at Blake's refusal to let her go without giving a month's notice, and excited by the awareness in his eyes when he'd touched her. Was she crazy to look more into this than she should?

Her heartbeat stretched into a gallop at the thought that he was attracted to her. A split second was all it had taken and she'd known what it was like to have this man want her. Would he let himself take it further? Remembering the way he'd immediately dropped his hand and withdrawn, she knew he wouldn't.

Yet he'd wanted to, and that was the difference between him and Carl. Oh, she'd had a physical relationship many years ago as a teenager, but looking back, that had been so adolescent. Since then it had only been Carl, and he hadn't wanted her beyond a kiss or two.

But with Blake tonight, she'd known for a moment what it was like for a *man* to really desire her. And that gave her hope that with a bit of encouragement he might make her his. What did she have to lose now? If she went home without taking this opportunity to become Blake's lover she'd always wonder what it would have been like to be kissed by him, to be held by him, to have their bodies joined. And she'd always ache inside for what might have been.

She frowned. How could she capture his attention again and keep it? So far she'd tried everything and nothing had worked. She'd made herself as attractive as possible for him, to no avail. She'd even tried flirting over dinner earlier, but it had fallen faster than a lead balloon. Instead she'd ended up jealous of that actress's ability to flirt so naturally. If only *she* could act like…

Just then a thought clicked in her mind. She couldn't believe she hadn't thought of this before now, but if flirting with Blake hadn't made him sit up and take notice of her, maybe he needed to be stirred up. Maybe he needed an award-winning performance. And a little taste of jealousy.

Yet Blake wasn't the type of man who wanted things made easy for him. Making it appear at least a little difficult to catch her had to be the way to go. He wouldn't be interested otherwise.

And what better way to get his attention than letting him see that other men wanted her? Blake wouldn't be able to resist the challenge. This past week at least two good-looking men had asked her out to dinner but she'd turned them down. She hadn't wanted to be with any man but Blake. She still didn't, but he didn't need to know that.

Starting tomorrow, she'd let herself be wined and dined by men who desired her. She wasn't about to take it any further than that, but she wasn't going to sit around any longer and be uptight Samantha for the rest of her time here either. Sam Thompson was about to break out of her shell.

After Samantha left his office, Blake stood there for a minute, stunned by his encounter with his assistant, and not only because she'd wanted to resign. When he'd touched her he'd had the strongest urge to pull her into his arms and make love to her. She'd felt it, too. He'd seen an acknowledgement in her blue eyes she hadn't been able to hide. Strangely, it excited him. He wasn't used to beautiful women holding themselves back. Women usually *gave* themselves to him.

Clearly it had taken Samantha by surprise as much as it had him. Equally as clearly, she wasn't about to act on it. She probably didn't know *how* to act on it. Over the two years that she'd worked for him he'd rarely seen her date. She was a beautiful woman who socialized with grace and class at functions they both attended, but there had never seemed to be a permanent man in her life. Admittedly *he* kept her busy, but he'd often wondered if she'd had a bad relationship somewhere along the way.

None of that mattered right now, he told himself as he strode over to the window, catching sight of the SUV taking Samantha back the short distance to their private lodge. He waited until the car drove past the cabins and lodges then weaved around a corner and out of sight before letting his thoughts break free.

Damn her.

He didn't often feel thunderstruck, but she'd dropped a bombshell on him tonight. How could she think of leaving him at a time like this? She was his right-hand man. His assistant who made sure everything ran like clockwork. He couldn't do without her and certainly not after coming home to run the resort. He and his younger brother Gavin had already talked about building a new high-security bungalow for their most elite guests in a separate area of the resort.

So why, right when he needed her the most, did Samantha want to bail out on him? He'd expected better of her than desertion. Her excuse that she wanted to go home for a while hadn't made sense. She wasn't one to let her emotions get the best of her anyway and neither was he. That was what he'd liked about her from the start. Now his instincts told him she wasn't telling him the full truth.

Yet if she couldn't be truthful after working closely together, then something was definitely wrong. It just went to remind him to never trust anyone. A person thought they had everything, and in an instant it was gone. Hadn't that been the way since his mother had died from cancer when he was six and his father had withdrawn and blocked everyone out emotionally? It was like both his parents had died at the same time. He'd grown up determined to be totally independent from any emotional entanglements.

Okay, so Donald Jarrod had enough of himself left over to push his five children to be achievers, but at what cost? Four of Donald's offspring had departed years ago to make their mark in other parts of the country. Guy owned a famous French restaurant in Manhattan and ran another business venture. Gavin was a construction engineer. And Melissa was a licensed masseuse who had run a spa and massage-therapy retreat in L.A. Trevor was the only one who'd stayed in Aspen, but had chosen to have nothing to do with the resort, and instead built up his own successful marketing business.

Hell, Blake hadn't seen much of his four younger brothers and sister these past ten years. As his fraternal twin, he was closest to Guy, but he'd still kept a close eye on all his siblings. If they'd needed him, he would have been there. Of course his mind was still out on his half sister, Erica, who'd only recently shown up to become part of the family.

Unfortunately now he needed to rely on *all* of them to make sure the place continued to be a success. It wasn't a feeling he enjoyed. He didn't like relying on anyone, but he'd thought he could count on Samantha.

Obviously he couldn't.

Feeling restless, he looked out over the renowned ski resort that had always been the one place he called home. No matter how much he'd tried to forget it, Jarrod Ridge was in his blood.

He was now the CEO of Jarrod Ridge, for God's sake. His ancestor, Eli Jarrod, had started up the silver mine during the mining boom of 1879, and built himself one of the biggest houses in Colorado. Then "The Panic" of 1893 had closed many of Aspen's mines, and Eli had added to his house and made it bigger, turning it into a grand hotel that was now Jarrod Manor. This place had been through a lot, surviving right through to 1946 when the ski resort idea was born. Jarrod Ridge hadn't looked back since. It was a powerful feeling being in charge of all he surveyed.

And a big responsibility.

And dammit, he wasn't about to let Samantha walk out on him when he needed her most. Even in a month's time he would still need her by his side. It was important to the resort to make sure the changeover went as smoothly as possible, and only Samantha could help him do that. She was the best assistant he'd ever had and he wasn't about to lose her. He would find a way to make her stay, at least until the new bungalow was up and running.

He expelled a breath as he went over to his desk, where he sat down on the leather chair and took the resignation letter out from his jacket pocket. Under the lamplight, he read it, hoping to glean some hint on what was going on inside his assistant's mind. The letter was as professional as expected. No surprises there.

Frowning, he dropped the letter and picked up the pen, rolling it between his fingers as he tried to think. He didn't understand. Surprise appeared to be the name of the game with Samantha right now.

Why?

All at once the metal in his hand went from cool to warm in a matter of seconds, reminding him of his cool and remote assistant who'd soon warmed up at his touch. His heart took a sudden and extra beat. Would Samantha warm up for him if he touched her again? Remembering the electricity between them when he'd grabbed her arm, a surge of need raced through him. Samantha didn't seem to know what she wanted, but he *did* know women. She had wanted him. She had reacted to his touch.

And if that were the case, then perhaps he'd touch her some more and keep her around as long as necessary. He was sure he could persuade her to stay at least another six months. By then they'd both be ready to end the relationship. Sometime in the new year he'd more than likely be over needing her help anyway, and by then he would have someone to replace her, both in the office and the bedroom. No other woman had lasted longer than that. He wouldn't let them. Having affairs was the best he could offer.

As for Samantha, she was independent. She'd have no difficulty moving on when the time came. Hell, she'd probably even instigate it.

For now, it would be his pleasure to awaken the woman in her. Seducing Samantha was definitely going to be a priority task.

Two

Samantha felt more than a few moments of trepidation when she woke to the early morning light and remembered what she'd done. She'd actually handed Blake her resignation. She would be out of his life in a month's time. She tried to picture being apart from him for the rest of her life, but the thought brought silly tears to her eyes that she quickly blinked back.

Taking a shuddering breath, she tried to put all this in perspective. She'd moved on before, hadn't she? It wasn't so hard. Of course leaving Pasadena had been an adventure as much as an escape. It would be a long time before she escaped wanting Blake Jarrod.

Oh, God.

Then she remembered the plan she'd come up with last night. At the time she'd thought it was brilliant, but now she wasn't so sure she should go out with other men to try and make Blake jealous. It didn't seem right to manipulate the situation like that.

And that left her exactly…nowhere.

Remembering the sizzle of Blake's touch, she wondered if she really wanted to leave without giving them a chance. It was comforting to know that he would not want to get emotionally involved, but to become his lover, to be forever warmed by the memory of being in his arms, didn't she have to do this for herself?

She could do it. This was a goal that was achievable. She may not be a femme fatale but she was considered attractive and she knew how to flirt. And while it may not have worked with Blake at the dinner last night, she knew she could interest other men here in Aspen. Hopefully she'd grab his attention that way.

Tossing back the covers like she was tossing away her shackles, she jumped out of bed. She felt more lighthearted by the minute.

After her shower, Samantha figured it would be prudent to distance herself from Blake as much as possible from now on. She wouldn't capture any man's attention if she was with him all the time.

First things first.

Apart from the maids from the hotel who tidied up Pine Lodge each day, she and Blake had decided to be mostly self-sufficient. The refrigerator was usually stocked with food or they could eat at Jarrod Manor, the main lodge on the resort where some of the family chose to live.

Usually they ate a light breakfast together—surprisingly Blake hadn't brought any women back to the lodge while she'd been here—before they walked the short distance to his father's old office at the Manor. Anything to do with his hotels in Vegas was kept separate and done here in the office they'd set up in a corner of the large living room. That work was mostly done after dinner each evening. There was a lot to do with running both businesses, especially now that it was pre-ski season here. Samantha didn't mind keeping so busy. Besides, it kept Blake close.

But today was different. Fifteen minutes later, she quietly closed the lodge door behind her and left without waiting for him. The Colorado sun was making a shy return as she breathed in crystal air and walked the winding streets in picture-perfect surroundings. As she approached this grandest of hotels, a thrill went through her. With its main stone building complemented by guest wings on both sides, its peaked roofs and balconies with iron railings and its frosted windowpanes, it looked like an enchanted castle.

The doorman greeted her as she entered the hotel from under the stone arch leading off the driveway. She smiled and walked through the wide lobby dotted with tables and chairs. Being the off-season, it was quiet at this time of the morning with only a few guests up and about. A young couple stood viewing photographs of the mountains displayed along the wood walls. Older couples looked ready to go sightseeing the many popular tourist attractions, than pamper themselves in the spa.

It was no better in the casual eatery off the lobby, and Samantha sighed as she scooped scrambled eggs onto a plate from the buffet. Couldn't there have been one measly attractive man in sight this morning? So much for her plans to make Blake jealous. It wouldn't happen if she couldn't even find a man to flirt with.

She lifted her head and saw Blake's half sister, Erica Prentice, come out of the kitchen area and walk through the room with Joel Remy, the resort doctor. Joel was tall, blond and good-looking and he'd asked her out only last week and she'd refused, not giving it any consideration. Things had changed.

Erica saw her and blinked in surprise as she came over to her table. "Samantha, what are you doing here eating breakfast by yourself?"

Samantha liked Erica, who hadn't known she was a member of the Jarrod family until a few months ago. Since then, Erica had become engaged to the Jarrod family attorney, Christian Hanford, and everyone was happy about it. Everyone except Blake, that is, though Guy had taken a while to come round. Erica was a PR specialist who had thrown herself into the running of the resort, willingly giving a hand wherever it was needed, just like the other family members. Samantha didn't understand Blake's attitude toward her.

She smiled at the other woman. "I was up early so I thought I'd get a head start on the boss."

Erica laughed. "Yes, I think as Blake's assistant you'd need to do that occasionally."

Samantha let her eyes slide to the man beside Erica. "Good morning, Joel. You're here early, as well."

The doctor smiled. "One of the kitchen staff burned her hand, but thankfully it was only minor."

Samantha nodded, then, "Where are my manners? Would you like to join me for breakfast? Erica, you, too, of course."

As if she was getting a vibe, Erica glanced from one to the other and went to speak, but Joel got in before her. "I can't, I'm afraid, Sam," the doctor said. "I have to go

out on another call. But how about I make it up to you?
It's Saturday and my night off. If you're free I'd love to
take you to dinner."

Samantha could have kissed him, but she managed
to restrain herself. If Blake didn't get jealous over this,
then at least she'd have some fun, right?

Thinking of Blake must have made him appear. He
was at this moment striding through the lobby with a
scowl on his face, heading for the private elevator. Her
heart jumped in her throat when he glanced over toward
them and saw her in the eatery. He changed direction
and advanced toward her.

She turned back to Joel, waiting a few moments
more for Blake to get closer. "Dinner tonight?" she said,
raising her voice just a little. "Yes, I'd like that very
much, Joel."

He grinned at her. "Great. How about I pick you up
at seven-thirty?"

"Perfect."

Blake was almost at the table.

"I'd better go see my next patient," Joel said, then
inclined his head as he passed by. "Good morning,
Blake."

Blake nodded, then stopped at the table and practically
glared down at Samantha. "You didn't wait for me."

She reminded herself how this man didn't like things
made easy for him. "I slipped a note under your door.
Besides, I do believe I start work at nine and until
then my time is my own," she said, aware of Erica's
speculative gaze.

Blake must have been, too. He darted an irritated look
at his half sister, then away, jerking his head at Joel's
retreating back. "What did the doctor want?"

Was he jealous already? She felt a thrill of excitement but before she could answer, Erica said, "Joel's taking Samantha out to dinner tonight."

Blake blinked in shock, but he recovered quickly, his blue eyes narrowing in on Samantha. "You can't go. I need you to work for a couple of hours tonight. I'm expecting an important call."

"I'm sorry, Blake, but I'm entitled to some time off."

He shook his head. "Not tonight, I'm afraid. I'd do it myself but as you know, I have a function to attend in town." He regarded her with a hint of smugness in his eyes. "That's why I pay you the big bucks."

Samantha's stomach started to churn. For all that she had wanted him jealous…for all that she anticipated him being difficult with the job…she still hadn't expected he would be quite so obstructive. It was obvious he was going to be exactly that from now on.

Well, she didn't like being told what to do, especially when it was out of spite. Oh, boy, she was going to really enjoy *not* making this easy for him now.

Her chin angled up at him. "Only for the next month," she pointed out smoothly, suddenly wanting to throttle him.

His mouth tightened. "Listen—"

"Blake," Erica's voice cut across him soothingly. "I really think you're being unfair here. If necessary, one of the staff can—"

"Mind your own business, Erica," he snapped, making both Samantha and Erica gasp. He grimaced, a pulse beating in his cheekbone. "Sorry. I shouldn't have said that." Then he looked at Samantha. "Go if you must," he said, then twisted on his heels and stormed off.

"Oh, my God, that was terrible, Erica," Samantha muttered. "I don't know what came over him."

Erica stood watching her half brother storm into the elevator. "I do."

Samantha sighed. "Yes, he seems to have a problem with you, doesn't he? I'm sure he'll be fine once he gets used to having a new sister."

"Half sister," Erica corrected with a wry smile, then sat down on the chair opposite. "Samantha, I don't think it's me who's upset him. What's going on between you two?"

Samantha was unsure how much she should confide in the other woman. When it came down to it, Erica was a Jarrod. Still, the others would have to know sometime. "I've given him my resignation. I finish up in a month's time."

"What! But why?" Erica cried. "I thought you loved your job." She reached across the table and squeezed Samantha's hand. "Please don't leave. I love you being here. You're part of the family."

Samantha felt her heart lift, then take a dive as fast. She'd only just begun to know Blake's family and now she had to leave. "It's time for me to make a change."

Erica gave her a penetrating look. "There's been something bothering you lately." She paused. "Blake needs you, Samantha."

For the job, that was all.

"Yes, he's made it quite clear that's why he's making me work out my contract for the next month." She couldn't stop her lips from twisting. "He told me it's nothing personal."

There was another pause, then, "I see."

Samantha realized she may have said too much. The other woman probably saw more than she should.

All at once Erica gave a disarming smile. "You know what I do when I'm feeling down? I go shopping. How about I take you into town after lunch and we buy you a new dress for tonight?"

Samantha knew Erica was trying to make her feel better. "It's a lovely thought, but I've already got enough dresses. And anyway, I have to work. Blake's going to make sure he gets his money's worth from me from now on."

Erica waved that aside. "I bet most of your clothes are suitable for Vegas, not here. And please...no woman ever has enough dresses," she teased, looking beautiful and happy but still slightly concerned. "Besides, I think it will do Blake good to do without you for a couple of hours." She winked. "He owes me now for being such a jerk."

Samantha appreciated it and she tried to smile but couldn't. "Erica, it's not a good idea." Despite being angry with Blake, she realized she'd probably pushed him a bit too much already today. She'd wanted to shock him into being jealous. Not give him a heart attack!

"Phooey! You want to look good for Joel tonight, don't you?"

Samantha thought about why she'd accepted the invitation to dinner with Joel in the first place. This was about making Blake jealous, she reminded herself, so she still had to keep trying. She couldn't give up after the first try.

She nodded. "Yes, I do."

"Then let's light a fire under him, honey, if that's what he needs."

Samantha did her best not to give anything away, but they both knew Erica was talking about Blake, not Joel. And seeing that this might be her one and only chance...

"Okay then, Erica. I'm in your hands. I have nothing to lose."

"Good girl! I'll come by the office after lunch." Erica got to her feet. "I'd better go and check on the staff member who burned her hand." She smiled and headed back the way she'd come.

As Erica left, Samantha sat for a few moments then looked down at the remains of her scrambled eggs. She just hoped she didn't end up like her breakfast—out in the cold and barely touched.

After lunch Blake's bad mood increased as he watched Erica leave his office, taking his assistant with her for the afternoon. They were going shopping, for Christ's sake! For a dress for Samantha's date tonight!

Damn Erica. His half sister was beautiful and smart, but, unlike his brothers and Melissa, he didn't totally trust her. After listening to her for the last five minutes, he hadn't changed his mind. She was unmistakably adroit at getting her own way, using his outburst this morning against him to make him feel guilty. It had worked like a charm, as she'd known it would.

But it was Samantha he really needed to fathom, he decided, leaning back in the leather chair. He'd woken up thinking he'd go after her with an enthusiasm he rarely felt for a woman these days.

And then it had all gone wrong. First, there had been the note slipped under his door that she'd already gone to breakfast and hadn't waited for him. She'd *never* done that before, not here in Aspen or anywhere else they'd stayed throughout the world.

Then he'd found her accepting a date with that gigolo doctor, Joel Remy. That was like going out with one of the ski instructors. Didn't Samantha know women were lined up to sleep with these guys? He'd seen it all his life.

Take a number, Samantha.

What the hell was going on here? She suddenly seemed a different person. It was like she'd decided to place being a woman first, his assistant second.

What had got into her? Was she trying to pay him back for not letting her walk out on the job early? Would she really *do* that? He grimaced. She was a woman, wasn't she? She'd probably decided to have a farewell fling just to rub his nose in it.

Thoughts of Samantha in bed with another man were suddenly anathema to him. He couldn't let her do it. He *knew* her and he knew she'd regret it.

And surely if she was going to make love to anyone, then she could damn well choose *him*. *He* was the one who'd worked closely with her for two years. *He* was the one who would appreciate her in bed. *He* was the one who had to save her from herself.

Three

As she descended the stairs that evening, carrying her clutch bag in one hand and her cashmere evening coat over her arm, Samantha's foot faltered on the next step. She'd been hoping to show herself off to Blake before he left for his business dinner, and now her heart began knocking against her ribs when she saw the man in question look up from the corner bar in their lodge and catch sight of her. His glass stopped halfway to his mouth and he stared…just stared…as she slowly came the rest of the way down.

Thanks to Erica, she knew she looked fantastic. She'd always taken pride in her appearance and in making sure she looked right for her position, but this long-sleeved dress—this piece of hot-pink knit material that stretched over her body like it had been lovingly cling-wrapped to every curve—made her feel a little naughty.

Without taking his eyes off her, Blake put his drink on

the bar and watched her walk toward him. "I'm stunned," he said in a deep, husky voice that held true admiration and sent her pulse skipping with delight. "I've never seen you look so…"

"Nice?" she gently teased as her confidence soared. She would forgive him anything right at this moment.

"Sexy."

The word took her breath away. She moistened her lips and saw his blue eyes dart to her mouth. "Thank you, Blake."

Then his gaze rolled down her, before slowly coming up again, his eyelids flicking briefly when he passed over her breasts both times. She had the feeling her nipples may have beaded with sexual excitement and one part of her wanted to hunch over and say "don't look," while another forced her to hold her shoulders back proudly.

His eyes—dark with a desire she'd never seen before—finally stopped at her head. "What have you done to your hair?"

She swallowed. It hadn't taken much to style the silky brown strands into bouncing curls around her shoulders. "I had a couple of inches cut off it."

"It looks terrific."

This was the reaction she'd been hoping for from him. "Thank you again."

He picked up his drink and took a sip. Then, "I have to ask you something."

Her heart took a leap. "What is it, Blake?"

"Are you sure you want to do this?"

She blinked. "Do what?"

Resign?

"Go out with Joel Remy."

His voice gave nothing away but her pulse started

to race even more. Dear God, could Blake be a little jealous? Had she actually managed to get through to him so quickly that she was a woman? A woman who needed him like she'd never needed any man before?

His eyes slammed into her. "He's not your style, Samantha."

Her heart almost burst through her chest. Blake *was* jealous. She tried to act nonchalant. She couldn't succumb and throw herself at him the minute he decided he wanted her for five minutes.

"How do you know *what* my style is, Blake?" she said, fluttering her eyelashes at him.

"I know what suits you and what doesn't and I know he's not the man for you."

No, this man in front of her was the man for her.

"Oh, so you're an expert on me now, are you?" she flirted, thrilled beyond her wildest dreams that he was finally noticing her. It was this dress. She had so much to thank Erica for. The other woman had...

"I'd like to think I know you very well, Samantha," he said, suddenly looking very superior, very arrogant. "You wouldn't be happy with Remy. Trust me."

Thud.

Clarity hit her like a bolt of lightning. What a fool she was in thinking anything had changed. This wasn't about Blake wanting her. This was about him being his usual conceited self. The man wasn't jealous. He was merely trying to stop her having a relationship with another man over the next two weeks so that she wouldn't inconvenience *him*. Frankly, she deserved better than this.

"That's your considered opinion, is it?" she said coolly now.

"Yes, it is." His eyes told her he'd noticed her change in tone. "Are you going to tell him you're leaving soon?"

She tried to think. She was *so* disappointed. "I'd prefer to keep that to myself for the time being. It's no one's business but my own."

"And mine, of course," he pointed out dryly. Then, "But you're probably right in not telling him. I doubt he's after a long-term relationship anyway."

"Neither am I," she said, taking pleasure in the way his face hardened. "In the meantime, I'm sure Joel and I will both manage to enjoy ourselves."

He looked all-knowing. "I doubt you'll have anything in common."

She raised one eyebrow. "Really? Don't forget I worked in a doctor's office before coming to work for you. And my family runs a medical transcription business, so I used to have quite a bit to do with doctors."

Blake's lips twisted. "So you'll talk about deciphering his handwriting? That'll be a laugh a minute."

Her fingers tightened on her clutch purse. He thought he was being clever, did he? She needed to wipe away that smirk. She gave him a sultry look. "Oh, I'm sure we'll have plenty of...*other things* in common."

The smirk fell off his face. "Dammit, Samantha, you shouldn't—"

The doorbell buzzed.

Samantha glanced over at the front door a few feet away and saw Joel through the glass panel. She tossed Blake an expressive look before going over to open it.

Joel stepped inside, his eyes sliding down, then up. "Wow! Don't you look like a million dollars." He grinned at Blake a few feet away. "I can't believe this beauty is going out with me."

"Neither can I," Blake muttered, then as quickly gave a smooth smile but Samantha heard him. "I mean, she's usually picky about who she goes out with."

She blinked. Was that still an insult? Joel had a puzzled look that said he might be thinking the same thing.

She hurriedly forced a smile. "Thanks for the compliment, Joel." She stood and looked him up and down, too. "For the record, you look like a *billion* dollars," she joked, then realized she'd overplayed her hand when Blake sniffed, though she suspected it was more of a snort. She turned her head slightly so Joel couldn't see her stabbing her boss with her eyes.

Blake ignored her. "So, where are you two dining tonight?"

Samantha was immediately suspicious. "Why do you want to know?"

He smiled. "No reason."

Joel then mentioned a restaurant in the center of Aspen. "It's only just opened and I know the owner. It'll be very hard to get a reservation in another month or so." He didn't sound like he was bragging, at least not to Samantha, but she saw a glint in Blake's eyes that told her he wasn't in agreement.

She smiled at Joel. "That sounds lovely."

He looked pleased. "And you, Blake? You're off to dinner, too, by the look of things."

Wearing a dark suit, Blake was the one who really did look like a billion dollars, Samantha had to admit, unable to stop herself from wishing she was going out with him instead of Joel, in spite of the fact that Blake was being an overbearing jerk.

"Just a business dinner in town." Blake looked at his

watch. "As a matter of fact, I'd better call a cab. I need to be on my way."

Joel frowned. "A cab? Don't you have a car?"

"I noticed it was leaking oil this afternoon so I thought I'd better not use it tonight."

Samantha sensed Blake was manipulating the situation for his own benefit again. Did he think she was stupid? He was doing this on purpose to try and keep her and Joel apart as much as possible to spoil her night.

She stared at him. "But you only bought the vehicle a few months ago and it's barely been used. How can a luxury Cadillac SUV have an oil leak already?"

He looked totally guileless. "I agree. It's the darnedest thing."

"We could give you a lift, if you like," Joel said, making Samantha want to rattle him.

"Oh, I'm sure Blake doesn't want to ride with us." She was determined not to give her boss any satisfaction. "The resort has a chauffeur service."

Joel frowned. "No, that's okay. I don't mind. We're going that way anyway."

She would have sounded mean-spirited to refuse. As Blake well knew, she decided, watching the satisfaction in his eyes. He was Joel's boss and he knew Joel wouldn't deny doing a favor for him.

She passed her coat to Joel. "Would you mind helping me on with this, please?"

"Of course." Joel held it open while she slipped into it, then he helped lift her hair out from under the collar so that it was once again bouncing around her shoulders. It was somewhat intimate and Samantha felt a little awkward at having a man touch her hair, but she soon felt better when she saw the steely look in Blake's eyes after he noted it, too.

"Thanks," she said, smiling brightly at her date, then deliberately linked her arm with his. She gave Blake a sweet smile as he put on his black evening coat, letting him know she didn't care that he wasn't pleased. Too bad!

"My car's out front," Joel said.

They left the lodge, then Samantha slipped onto the front passenger seat before Blake could take it himself. She wouldn't put it past him to try and make her sit in the back, and she wasn't about to let him play at being boss while she was on a date. This was *her* night out. Blake may have been the reason for it, but right now she wasn't about to give him an inch.

Soon they were driving off into the night.

"This is very good of you, Joel," Blake said, sounding grateful from the backseat, which didn't sound right to Samantha's ears. Blake *never* sounded grateful like other mere mortals.

"We don't mind, do we, Sam?" Joel said, shooting her a sideways smile.

"No, of course not. We have to keep the boss happy, don't we?" She smiled back at Joel, knowing Blake could see her from his diagonal viewpoint behind the driver's seat.

"By the way, *Samantha*," Blake said, placing the slightest emphasis on her name, making her realize that Joel had called her "Sam" again—the name Blake had never called her.

"Yes, Blake?" she said, keeping her tone idle.

There was a tiny pause before he spoke. "Don't worry about that very important phone call I was waiting for tonight. One of the resort staff will sit in the office and wait for it."

"Good." She took her job seriously, but Erica's suggestion had been a good one, so she wasn't about to feel guilty about it.

"But I did have to give them your cell phone number, as well. Just in case. I hope you don't mind. Someone has to take the call if by chance it's missed at the hotel, and I'll have to turn my cell phone off so it won't interrupt the guest speaker tonight."

She could feel herself stiffen. He was trying to take advantage of her good nature for his own purposes again. This wasn't about taking the call. He wanted to put a spoke between her and Joel's budding relationship, freeing up her time for the job.

She turned her head to face him. "Actually I *do* mind. This is my night off. I don't want to work tonight."

He raised an eyebrow, like he was surprised. "I'm sure Joel won't have a problem with it. He's a doctor. He's used to being on call. You understand, don't you, Joel?"

"Sure I do." Joel glanced at her and smiled. "Leave your cell phone on, Sam. I don't mind if you take the call."

Her mouth tightened but she didn't reply. Her cell phone was already off and she intended it to stay that way. And Blake knew this had nothing to do with Joel anyway. Blake was just trying to make sure the job was in her face tonight.

Joel must have sensed something amiss because he started talking about general things for the rest of the way. Samantha could feel Blake's eyes on her from the backseat but she ignored him as she responded to Joel, relieved when the car slid to a halt outside a restaurant.

"Thanks for the ride." Blake opened the back door then paused briefly. "And don't worry about how I'll get home. You two have a good time, okay?"

Samantha bit down on her irritation. His sincerity was so false. He was just trying to get a ride back to the lodge to make sure nothing sexual happened between her and Joel. Ooh, it would do him good to wonder and worry what she and Joel were getting up to later in the evening.

She smiled tightly. "We'll be very late, so you'd best get the car service. Good night, Blake."

His lips flattened and he shot her a dark look. "Good night." He waited a second, but when Joel said good night, he got out of the car and shut the door. The last Samantha saw was him striding into the restaurant.

Then they drove off and she looked ahead, hoping Joel wouldn't say anything. He didn't, at least not until they were seated at their table and the waitress had left with their order.

"Excuse me for asking, but don't you like Blake?" he said.

She smiled to soften her words. "Of course I do, but I've worked with Blake a couple of years now. Sometimes he thinks everyone is there purely for his benefit."

Joel grinned. "As a successful businessman, he's probably right."

She laughed. "Yes, that's true." Then she forced herself to relax against the back of her chair. "Now let's talk about something else. I really don't want to talk about the boss tonight."

Joel smiled. "I'm more than happy to oblige, Sam. Now tell me…"

They had a pleasant evening after that. As predicted, they talked about her family's business and her experience in transcribing, though Blake's earlier derogatory comment about deciphering handwriting spoiled the discussion for her. Did Blake always have to be there at the back of her mind?

Unfortunately by the time the evening was half over, Samantha knew Joel wasn't for her. He was handsome and he was a nice guy, but they really *didn't* have anything else in common, much to her disgust. Not like her and Blake. She grimaced. No, she and Blake had nothing in common either—except the job and an attraction that she hated to think was really only on her side. Shades of Carl came to mind.

"Sam?"

She pulled herself back from thoughts of the past. "Sorry, I remembered something I forgot to do," she fibbed, then she smiled. "But it can wait. Now, what were you saying?" She would have a good time if it killed her.

It nearly did.

Her social life and her work life were the same thing, so she'd never lacked for company at business dinners and parties. But she wasn't used to being on a date and having to tune in to one person for hours on end. It was very draining.

Unless of course that person was Blake. He never bored her. Every minute of every day he challenged her like no other person on earth. Life with Blake was the adventure she'd always been after. One she soon had to leave, she remembered, her heart constricting. She pushed the thought aside. She would get through this.

"We should do this again, Sam," Joel said, holding open his car door for her on their return to Pine Lodge.

It was strange, but for some reason an evening of being called "Sam" had started to get on her nerves. It wasn't Joel's fault at all, but it was as if the shortened version of her name was an issue between her and Blake and therefore belonged only to them now. And that was rather pathetic.

"I've got plans tomorrow night," Joel said, dragging her from her thoughts. "But I'm free after that. Would you like to go to a movie on Monday night?"

She hesitated, feeling a little bad in using him. She didn't want to go out with him again, yet if she didn't continue with her plan to try and make Blake jealous, then Blake would think he'd won. She wouldn't give him the satisfaction now.

She got out of the car, with Joel doing the gentlemanly thing and assisting her. "I'd like that, but let me get back to you tomorrow, if that's okay."

"That's fine."

All at once she felt his hand move from her elbow to her chin. It was a smooth move and said this guy knew what he was doing, so perhaps using him shouldn't really cause her concern after all.

"But first…" he murmured.

She didn't resist even though his kiss wasn't something she wanted, and not because he wasn't an attractive man. Despite still being angry with Blake for trying to manipulate the situation earlier this evening, she wanted it to be Blake's lips—and *only* Blake's lips—on hers.

Suddenly scared that she might never want another man to kiss her, she raised her mouth to Joel. Perhaps Blake's attraction for her was merely in her mind? Perhaps she needed to be kissed by another man just to remind her—

"Don't let me interrupt," a male voice muttered.

Blake.

Samantha jerked back guiltily and Joel stopped, and they watched their employer stride past them and go inside Pine Lodge. He'd been walking from the direction of Jarrod Manor, where he must have gone after dinner.

"That was good timing," Joel said, over her thudding heart. Unfortunately her heart's thud wasn't for her date. It was for another man.

"Now, where were we?" Joel murmured, lowering his head and placing his lips on hers, making her conscious of one thing. She'd have to stretch her neck higher if it was Blake kissing her.

Blake sat on the couch and tried to get the image of Samantha about to kiss another man out of his head. She'd been swaying toward the doctor like she'd needed a shot in the arm. If she didn't get inside here pretty damn quick he was going looking for her. On the pretext of her safety, of course.

And he *was* concerned for her safety. That and other things. She was clearly ready to jump into bed with the first man who looked twice at her, and all to get back at *him* for not letting her walk away from her job. Hell, if he'd agreed to that she would have already gone from his life. His gut twisted at the thought.

The front door opened right then and in she walked. His pulse began to race when he saw she was alone.

Good girl.

She seemed distracted as she headed for the stairs, undoing the buttons of her coat as she walked. Then she saw him sitting on the couch and her eyes flared with pleasure before she seemed to catch herself.

For a moment his breath stalled. She'd never shown any sort of emotion toward him before. They got on well together but it had always been business between them. He should be perturbed, yet he knew he could use it to his advantage.

Then her mouth tightened as she came toward him. "Are you waiting up for me?" she said, her tone less than friendly, making him question if it had been a trick of the light before. He mentally shook his head. No, he knew what he'd seen.

"Can't a man have a drink before bed?" he drawled, relaxing. She was home now...with him...and that's all that mattered.

Her top lip curled. "You certainly didn't have to worry about drinking and driving, did you?"

He pretended ignorance. "No, I didn't." He indicated another glass of brandy on the coffee table in front of him. "I poured a nightcap for you. Sit with me."

An odd look skimmed across her face. "Perhaps I'd prefer to go straight to bed."

If one of his dates had said that he would have taken it as a come-on. But Samantha was a challenge in a different way. Did she know what she was inviting in that dress? Did she have any idea what she actually did to a man's libido? All at once he was enjoying what he now suspected to be her sexual naïveté.

"One drink," he coaxed. "And you can tell me all about your evening."

She paused, then put down her evening purse and began undoing the rest of her coat buttons. Slowly she began taking it off in an unintentional striptease, exposing the sexy pink material beneath. How had he never before noticed what a stunner she was?

She sank down on the opposite chair and gracefully picked up the glass, indicating the already poured brandy. "You were so sure I wouldn't take Joel up to my room, were you?"

He hadn't been, no. "Yes."

She took a sip then considered him. "You certainly tried hard enough to make it *not* happen."

"Did I?" He was feeling rather proud of himself for putting obstacles in her way tonight. It must have worked or she wouldn't be here now. With him.

"You know you did, and I don't appreciate it. You're trying to make sure you get every last bit of work out of me before I leave."

Is that what she thought? "Maybe I was protecting you?"

She gave a short laugh. "From what? Having a good time?"

He looked over at her kissable lips that had recently been beneath another man's...and something became even more determined inside him. If she was going to have fun, she was going to have it with *him*.

He forced a shrug. "I just think you need to look at who you go out with in future."

Her lips twisted. "Thanks for the tip."

He'd never known her to be sarcastic, not like she was lately. It was...energizing, he admitted, watching as she eased back in her chair, the soft silk stockings making a swishing sound as she crossed her legs. He'd give anything to reach out and smooth those long legs with his hands. Or perhaps his lips…

Before he could put words to action, he told himself he had to slow it down. He didn't want to frighten the lady by going too quickly. Time was running out but he had to let her lead. Tonight, anyway. Tomorrow—when she was in a friendlier mood—was another day.

He took a sip of his brandy and let it soothe his throat. "So. Did you have a good time tonight?"

Her eyes darted away briefly. "Yes, I did. Very much."

She was lying. "I bet."

She arched one of her elegant eyebrows. "I hope you didn't put much money on that bet, Blake."

"I didn't have to." He knew women, both in the business world and out of it. She was lying. And he was intensely relieved.

A soft smile curved her lips. "Joel really knows how to treat a woman."

She was still lying. And he found that fascinating. "Sure he knows how to treat a woman. The guy's a womanizer."

"I suppose it's easy enough to recognize one's own sort."

He had to chuckle. She made him laugh. Then he saw a touch of real amusement in her eyes and something connected between them. She quickly looked down at her glass, hiding her eyes for a second.

He started to lean forward. "Samantha…"

Her head snapped up. "For your information, Joel's a

very nice man," she said, making it clear she was trying to ignore the sudden sexual tension in the room.

It was a wasted effort. "I'm sure he is. Ask *any* woman in Aspen."

She sent him a defiant look. "Don't think I wouldn't go to bed with him if I wanted to, Blake."

She was all talk, but his gut still knotted at her words. "Obviously you didn't want to, or you would be in bed with him this very minute. Am I right?"

"No, you're wrong. I mean, yes… I mean, mind your own business." Her lips pressed together. "I'll sleep with whoever I want *when* I want."

"You're being very contradictory tonight, Samantha. They'd eat you alive in the boardroom with that attitude," he mocked.

She stiffened. "Listen, Blake, I'll sleep with any man I want when I'm good and ready. Tonight I just wasn't ready. And in case you didn't notice, this isn't the boardroom."

No, but he did want to eat her alive right now. He wanted to kiss her and take away the imprint of another man's lips, his hands itching to slide up over her hot dress and lift that hair off her nape himself, exposing the soft skin beneath to his lips.

Adrenaline pumping through him, he knew it was time to take action. He'd had enough playing games tonight. He wasn't one to sit on the sidelines for long. He needed to know if her lips were as good as they looked, if her body would curve to his touch, if the skin at her nape was soft and sensitive.

Surging to his feet, he removed the brandy glass from her hand and put it on the table. He heard her intake of breath as he pulled her to her feet, but nothing would stop him now. Already he could feel a mutual shudder pass between them.

"Blake?" she said huskily as he brought her into the circle of his arms, leaving mere inches between them. He'd never been this close to her before. Not close enough to see the rush of desire in her blue eyes. It knocked the breath from his body.

And then a sudden flash of panic swept her face and before he knew it, she had pushed against him and spun away. Scurrying toward the stairs, she left him standing there, his arms never feeling as empty as they did right now.

As hard as it was, he let her go. He could follow her and she would take him as her lover, but he knew all he needed to know for the moment. She wanted him. And he wasn't giving up. His plans for seduction were still very much alive.

Samantha closed the door behind her and pressed herself back against it, willing her racing heart to slow down so that she could let herself think. She'd gone and panicked just now. Blake had finally reached for her and she'd blown it.

What was wrong with her! Being in Blake's arms and in his bed was what she wanted most, wasn't it? So why had she run away like a frightened deer? He must think her green when it came to relationships, which of course she was. One lover in high school, then falling in love in her mid-twenties, did not constitute experience. Not unless that included the pain of rejection, she decided, quickly pushing that thought away.

Then she knew.

Despite the spark of electricity when he'd grabbed her

arm last night, this evening she'd managed to convince herself that his meddling was actually about the job and nothing more. But just now the desire in his eyes had thrown her for a loop again. He really *did* feel passion for her, and when he'd touched her they'd both felt that zip of attraction. It had overwhelmed her, that's all.

Oh, Lord, what did she do now? Go back downstairs and beg him to make love to her? She couldn't. She'd reached the limit to her little seductress act tonight. She didn't have it in her to face him again so soon.

She took a steadying breath. Right, she'd messed this one up tonight, but something positive had come out of this. She now knew that Blake really *did* want to have sex with her. So if she wanted Blake, and he wanted her, then next time there should be no further problems.

She hoped.

Four

"Blake, did you get a chance to read those documents I gave you?"

Blake was in a good mood as he leaned back against the marble countertop. It was eight on Sunday morning and one of his younger brothers had come by Pine Lodge to discuss an upcoming project, but it was Samantha who was on his mind. Anticipation coursed through him as he remembered how sexy she had looked last night. Soon she would be *his*.

"Blake?"

Reluctantly he dragged his thoughts away from his assistant who was still upstairs sleeping in her room, to look at the man propped against the kitchen doorjamb. He hid a smile as he raised the coffee mug to his mouth. Gavin may look laidback but *he* knew it was all a facade. Taking on the job of building a new and exclusive high-security bungalow for Jarrod Ridge meant a lot to his brother.

"Yes. I've put them in the safe up at the Manor," he said, deliberately misunderstanding him.

"And?"

Blake chuckled and put him out of his misery. "And I think you've done an admirable job of running with this project."

Gavin began to smile with relief. "You do?"

"The intensive feasibility studies, as well as the building site and sustainability analysis reports you've put together, are impressive. But then, so were the ones you did for my Vegas hotels."

Gavin's grin widened. "It means a lot to hear you say that."

Blake indicated the coffeepot on the bench. "Grab yourself a coffee."

Gavin straightened away from the door and went to get a mug. "You know," he said, pouring himself a drink. "I've really welcomed this challenge."

"I can see that."

Gavin shrugged shoulders made impressive by many hours working with his crew on various construction sites. "It's nice to be home and together again as a family after so long, but I'm glad I don't have to pamper people on a daily basis. It really isn't my style."

Blake nodded. "You're a first-rate construction engineer, Gav, but I agree. There's nothing like doing something you love."

Gavin smiled, looking pleased. "You said it, brother."

"Seriously. I'm proud of you."

"You getting soft in your old age, Blake?" he teased.

"Probably." Blake was proud of all his brothers and sisters. Well, his half sister, Erica, was another matter.

All at once, Gavin's smile left him. "You realize Dad would never have said such a thing."

Blake grimaced. "I like to think I'm not quite as cold as the old man."

There was a moment's silence as they both remembered their father. Blake refused to feel anything for the passing of a man who had shunned his children's emotional well-being and so badly let them down. Donald Jarrod's legacy had been more than the Jarrod Ridge Resort. It had been a legacy that his children keep their emotions on ice, avoiding personal commitment. And while both Guy and Melissa had found true happiness with Avery and Shane, Blake couldn't see it happening for himself. Not at all. Nor for Gavin or Trevor either. That was just the way it was.

"That reminds me," Gavin said. "You're working out of Dad's old office now you're CEO, so wouldn't it be more convenient to be living at the Manor, as well? Why are you staying here at Pine Lodge instead?"

Blake shrugged. "Actually it's more convenient to be staying here. That way I can keep my hotel operations separate from the resort stuff." His hand tightened around the coffee mug. "Besides, even though Erica's moved into Christian's place, they both spend most of their time at the Manor during the day. I don't want to encroach on their territory. You know what newly engaged couples are like."

Gavin shot him a mocking smile. "Since when have

you ever taken a backseat to anyone, big brother? Or are you still scared of our new half sister?"

Blake knew Gavin was riling him, getting him back for stringing it out a few minutes ago. "I was never scared of Erica, as you well know."

"You're going to have to get over your dislike of her one day, buddy."

Blake felt an odd jolt. "I don't dislike her. I just don't totally trust her."

Gavin's eyes narrowed. "She really doesn't have to prove anything more to us, Blake." He paused. "But I guess it's all for the best that you stay here anyway. Your new assistant might not get on with the rest of the family as well as Samantha does." A speculative look entered his eyes. "Yeah, whoever is coming in as your new PA, it'll be much easier for them to keep the two businesses separate if you both stay here."

Blake's jaw clenched. He refused to even think about Samantha leaving, or someone coming in to replace her. And why was he surprised that word had gotten around the family? Samantha had said she didn't want anyone to know, but obviously she'd told one person at least. It had to have been Erica. No doubt the two had shared some girl talk yesterday while they'd been shopping together.

"Samantha is *not* leaving," he said tightly.

"That's not what I'm hearing."

"Shut up, Gav." He slammed down his half-empty coffee mug. "Now, if you'll excuse me, I have some work to do." He strode past his brother and out of the kitchen.

As he entered the living room, he heard a noise outside. He glanced through the picture window.

Samantha wasn't in bed asleep like he'd thought. She was standing on the bottom step of the lodge, dressed in warm clothes and a woolen hat, talking to a man who no doubt was one of the guests at the hotel. She must have gone up to the Manor to eat breakfast, probably with her doctor friend, and this guy must have followed her back like a lost puppy. No, make that a raccoon.

He heard her give a lilting laugh and his mouth flattened. The guy was in his forties and looked sleazy to Blake. And hell, Samantha looked like she was flirting with him. Didn't she have any sense when it came to men? The sooner he showed her what it was like to make love to *him,* the better.

"Look at that," Gavin murmured in his ear. "I think someone else may be working today...*on* Samantha."

Blake glared at him, then strode over and pulled open the front door in a rush. If she was going to flirt it would be with *him*.

"How about us going for a scenic drive?" the man was saying. "Maybe even do lunch in town? I know it's pretty quiet at this time of year, but we should be able to find somewhere to eat. What do you think?"

"I—"

"I think I need to speak to my assistant," Blake cut across her as he stepped out on the porch. They spun to look up at him. "Samantha, I need you to make some calls to Vegas for me."

She sent him an annoyed look, making it clear she didn't like the interruption. "Blake, it's Sunday and most of the offices are closed. It'll have to wait until tomorrow."

He had the urge to remind her that last night he could easily have taken her to his bed. She wouldn't have minded *that* interruption, he was sure. "Then I need you to help me with something else."

Her lips tightened. "So I'm not going to get any time off now until I leave?"

"No." He turned to go inside and waited but realized she wasn't behind him. "Coming, Samantha?"

Her chin tilted stubbornly. "I'll be there in a minute."

Blake saw Gavin's look of amusement as his brother pushed through the doorway then descended the stairs two at a time, calling out a greeting to the pair as he left.

Blake went back inside. He didn't hear her following. Counting to ten, he waited but he could see her still standing there chatting. At that moment something occurred to him. Wasn't it strange that she'd been jumpy with *him* last night, yet she seemed perfectly at ease with Mr. Sleazy down there? And what about last night with the doc? She hadn't seemed nervous around the guy.

So what did that tell him? That she was flirting with men she considered *safe?* Which meant she must feel nothing for them, he mused. Nothing at all. The thought filled him with relief.

As for what she was feeling for him…there was definitely something between them. Yeah, she knew they'd be explosive together in bed.

And that begged the question. Just how far was she prepared to go to fight her desire for him? More importantly right now, did she have any idea what she was inviting by leading those other two men on?

Making a decision, Blake pulled on his jacket and boots, grabbed his car keys and strode back out into the chilly air. "I need to go check on something," he said, going down the stairs, "and I want you to come with me, Samantha." He bared his teeth at the other man in the semblance of a smile. "Sorry, buddy, but I need my assistant."

"Blake—" she began.

"This is important." He cupped her elbow and began leading her toward the side of the lodge to the garage where he kept his black Cadillac SUV.

She glanced over her shoulder and called out to the other man. "I'll talk to you when I get back, Ralph."

Blake gave a snort as he clicked the remote to open the garage door.

"What was that for?" Samantha hissed, hurrying to keep up.

"I hope you're not thinking of dating *Ralph*. The guy's old enough to be your father. Hell, he's even got a name to match."

She hid her satisfaction. "Perhaps I'm attracted to older men?"

He sent her a knowing look. "Then you'd better not dress like you did last night. He doesn't look like his old ticker could handle a woman, let alone a sexy one like yourself."

Her own "ticker" jumped around inside her chest and she tried not to blush. She loved hearing that Blake thought her sexy, though she wasn't sure why he was looking so confident all of a sudden. Still, this time she wasn't going to run away from him if he made a move on her. No repeat of last night, she told herself firmly.

They entered the garage, but it was only after she slid onto the passenger seat of the SUV and was putting on her seat belt did she remember something. "Didn't you say this vehicle had an oil leak?"

Blake smirked at her. "Here's the thing. I took another look earlier and it wasn't leaking after all. The problem must have been with someone else's car."

"Now there's a surprise."

"It was to me, too," he drawled, starting the engine.

No wonder he looked pleased with himself, she decided. He'd orchestrated the "poor me" routine last night over the oil leak, and now he'd put a stop to her going out with Ralph. Not that Ralph was her type, though he seemed very nice, but he *was* a man and one she could flirt with for Blake's benefit.

Once the vehicle had warmed up, she took off her gloves as he reversed out of the garage.

"Where are we going?" she asked, when he started along the narrow road lined with thick trees, and it became clear they were heading for the main entrance to the resort.

"You'll see."

For a second she dared hope this might be about spending some time alone together away from everyone else. "Is this really about work?"

"What else?"

Disappointment wound its way through her. They were clearly still employer and employee. Had last night merely been an aberration on his part because of the late night and close proximity? Was this once again about Blake trying to stop her from leaving her job, rather than him actually wanting her?

Back to square one.

Soon Blake was driving past the two stone pillars with the brass Jarrod Ridge Resort sign, and turning the SUV onto the main road but in the other direction of town. At this time on a Sunday morning there wasn't much traffic and further along he took another turn onto a side road. She wondered where they were going as they drove through stunning natural scenery filled with golden fall colors that would soon disappear under winter-white, but it was no use asking him again. Blake only did what he wanted to do and he would tell her only what he wanted her to know.

Remembering Gavin had visited Pine Lodge this morning, she suspected then where they were going. Farther along, Blake pulled over onto a slot of land that looked out over the Roaring Fork River weaving its way through a lush green picturesque valley between towering snow-dabbled peaks. The Jarrod Ridge resort was nestled like a crown jewel amongst it all.

He stopped the vehicle and cut the engine.

He didn't speak at first, just stared straight ahead, so she had to ask the obvious. "Why did you bring me here?"

He nodded his dark head at the majestic mountain panorama before them. "I wanted to show you where the new private bungalow will be built."

"I see." Her suspicions were correct, but the way he spoke made her heart sink. It was as if he had acknowledged she was leaving now. Like he was showing it to her—while he still could.

"Let's take a closer look." He started to get out of the car then glanced back at her, his gaze going to the woolen hat on her head. "Put your gloves on first. There's no wind but it's chilly."

A couple of seconds later they were standing in front of the black SUV, looking at the breathtaking alpine backdrop in front of them.

He pointed to a wooded area near the bottom of the

mountain to the right of the resort. "See that over there? That's our silver mine where we used to play as kids. One of my ancestors started up the mine but it's been out of use for over a hundred years."

"How interesting," she said, meaning it.

"The bungalow will be farther up the mountain but not too close. We don't want to destroy the historical significance of the mine."

She'd briefly seen the documents Gavin had given Blake, and heard them discussing it at times, but Gavin was the one running with this project. He was keeping it very much between himself and Blake at this stage, though she knew they were keeping the rest of the Jarrods up to date.

"See that rocky outcropping?" Blake continued. "That's close to where we'll build the bungalow. It's going to be super luxurious with top-of-the-line security. There'll be iris-recognition scanners plus the usual cameras and motion detectors. Personal safety will be a must, as will our guests' privacy."

She could picture it in her mind. "I'm really impressed. It'll be great."

He nodded. "It's just what Jarrod Ridge needs to stand out above the rest," he said, a proud look about him as he appraised his family's empire.

An odd tenderness filled her as she glanced up at his familiar profile. There was something so attractive about a man confident with himself. An aura that pulled a woman close and made her want to get under it, to become a part of the man no one else knew.

All at once he turned toward her, his gaze fixing in on her. "Why are you looking at me like that?" he asked quietly.

Caught!

She cleared her throat. "I was thinking how much you enjoy a challenge. You're suited to these mountains."

He looked pleased. Then, "You could be a part of all this, too, you know."

Her heart stumbled. Had he brought her here for another reason? "Wh-what do you mean?"

"You love it here. You won't be happy anywhere else." He paused. "Think carefully before you walk away from your job, Samantha."

The job.

She groaned inwardly at her stupidity. Had she really thought this confirmed bachelor had been about to pop the marriage question to his personal assistant? What on earth was the matter with her? Hadn't she learned her lesson with Carl? The thin air must be making her imagine things that weren't and could never be. Not that she'd ever consider it anyway.

She took a shuddering breath before speaking. "I *have* thought about it, Blake." Very much so. She hadn't stopped.

He turned to face her. "Stay, Samantha."

"I...I can't." If it had been a plea, she might have considered it. As it was, she knew this was basically still about him being inconvenienced.

She went to turn away. She couldn't face him fully. The last thing she wanted was him seeing she'd mistakenly assumed he was talking marriage a minute ago. What a fool she was for even thinking it, let alone believing he might be thinking it, too. This wasn't about anything more than desire, she reminded herself.

His fingers slid around her arm and tugged her back. "Why are you being so obstructive?"

She couldn't feel the pressure of his fingers through her thick jacket but she knew they were there. "Obstructive to what?"

"To me being concerned for your well-being."

She ignored the thud of her heart. "Oh, so *that's* why you won't let me finish up my job early?" she scoffed, knowing this was the only way she could handle him. "You're *concerned* for me?"

He froze.

Silence surrounded them.

Then, he said quietly, "I am, actually."

She gasped midbreath. "Why, Blake? Why are you concerned for me?"

"Why wouldn't I be?" As he spoke she could feel his eyes almost pulling her toward him.

"Um…Blake…"

He drew her toward him and bent his head. He was kissing her before she knew what was happening, instantly destroying any defenses she may have drawn on, regardless that she wanted him so very much. Like an avalanche rolling down a mountain, she fell—and it was just as devastating.

Then he slid his tongue between her lips and she opened her mouth to him fully. Hearing his husky groan, she wound her arms around his neck and held on to him, trusting him, knowing where he took her she would follow.

Time blurred.

And then, amazingly, he was slowing things down, giving her back herself, letting her regain focus. Finally, he eased back and they stared at each other.

"Oh, my God!" she whispered, awed by the sheer

complexity of the kiss that should have been simple and wasn't. It left her trembling.

He was feeling something equally as powerful. She could see it deep in his eyes. He truly desired her. Her dream of being in his arms was finally becoming a reality.

His cell phone began to ring.

He remained still, not moving, and she knew why. Nothing could take away from the strength of this moment between them. Here in the mountains it was like they were the only two people alive.

Then as quickly as she thought that, he blinked and turned away, breaking the moment. She heard him answer it, but she couldn't seem to move. She understood why he had turned away. Why he had broken the moment. It had been too much for him. For her. For them both. Without him looking at her, she could take a breath again.

She did.

And then she found she could move. She swiveled to go get into the SUV, needing to sit down for a minute and feel something solid beneath her.

She took a few steps but as she went to reach for the door handle, her feet slipped from under her on a patch of ice and, with a small cry, she felt herself falling backward…backward….

She frantically made a grab for anything within reach, but there was only the air and she felt her legs going up and her body going down, her back hitting the grass, then her head on something harder. She literally saw stars….

The next thing she knew Blake was dropping to his knees beside her. "Thank God!" he muttered, when he saw her eyes were open.

"What happened?" she managed to say.

He glanced back to where she'd been walking. "You must have slipped on that ice back there."

She started to lift her head, then winced at the pain.

"Take it slowly." He put his hand under her shoulders to help her up. "Is your back sore or anything? Are you hurting anywhere?"

"No."

Then he swore. "You're bleeding."

"I am?"

His hand came away with some blood on it. "You've cut your head." He helped her to sit up, then he checked the back of her head. "It's only small but it's bleeding like the devil and might need a stitch. There's a lump starting where you hit it, too." Snatching up her woolen hat that must have come off during the fall, he placed it against the cut. "Hold that on it. It'll help stem the flow of blood. We need to get you to a doctor."

"Joel?" she said, without thinking, not meaning anything by it.

His mouth tightened. "Yes." He waited. "Do you think you can stand up? Are you dizzy or anything?"

"A little, but I'll be fine."

He helped her stand, then walked her the few feet to the car. Soon they were heading back to Jarrod Ridge.

"How do you feel now?" he said a few minutes later.

"Okay."

They drove a little farther. "Talk to me, Samantha."

"I don't really feel like talking," she said, calling herself an idiot for slipping. If only she'd looked where she was going, then—

"I want you to stay awake. You may have a slight concussion."

"Oh." She realized this was the correct procedure.

"Come on, you can do better than that," he said, a serious look in his eyes.

"Okay." She tried to think. "What do you want me to say?"

"I don't know. Anything. What's your favorite color?"

She didn't need to think about that. "Yellow."

His brow rose in surprise. "Yellow? Any particular reason?"

She winced a little as she adjusted the woolen hat against the injury. "Because it's bright and happy."

He glanced at her again, noting her wince, his mouth turning grim. "Okay, so what's your favorite flower?"

"Tulips."

Another look of surprise from him. "Why?"

"They're so beautiful."

There was a tiny pause. "Like you," he murmured, and her breath caught, then she moved her head and winced again. "Not long now," he assured her.

After that Blake drove straight up to the clinic at the spa lodge. The middle-aged nurse immediately took control, putting Samantha in an exam room. She checked her over, mentioning it wasn't too bad but that she'd need to call the doctor anyway.

"No need to get Joel if he's busy," Samantha said, feeling bad for interrupting his Sunday morning.

Blake nodded at the nurse. "Get him."

The nurse nodded in agreement then looked at her. "The doctor really should see you," she said, then went and picked up the wall telephone as Samantha glanced at Blake.

He gave a short shake of his head. "He's paid to do his job, Samantha. Let him."

Before too long, Joel strode into the exam room, nodding at Blake and giving her a chiding frown. "What have you done to yourself, Sam?"

Samantha didn't look at Blake, but she sensed he'd noted the shortening of her name. Joel was professional in his examination. She didn't need stitches but he tidied up the cut and it finally stopped bleeding. Thankfully he hadn't needed to cut any of her hair in the process.

"I don't think the lump on your head is anything to be concerned about," he assured her, "but we still need to keep an eye on it for any signs of concussion." He considered her. "If you like, I can come to Pine Lodge and check on you a couple of times throughout the day."

"I'll take care of her," Blake said firmly. "I know what signs to look for."

Joel glanced at Blake, held his gaze a moment, then nodded. "Fine. But I'll drop by the lodge and check on her this evening. Call me sooner if you have any doubts."

"I will."

Samantha looked from one to the other. "Do either of you mind if I have a say in this?"

Blake shot her an impatient look, but it was Joel who spoke. "Sam, this has to be taken very seriously. Your brain's had a knock, and sometimes things can develop later on. You need to rest up and you need to have someone keep a close eye on you for at least twenty-four hours."

She swallowed, not sure she liked hearing that, but before she could say anything the clinic door opened and someone called out for help, saying something about a twisted ankle. The nurse and Joel excused themselves to go check.

Blake came to stand in front of her. "I intend to look after you whether you like it or not."

"But—"

"It's my fault you were out there today," he cut across her, his eyes holding firm regret. "No arguments, Samantha. I owe you this."

She melted faster than snow under a heat lamp. "All right."

There was nothing in his eyes that said he remembered their kiss, and right now she was grateful for that. She would have plenty of time to go over it once she was alone.

He picked up her jacket. "Come on, then," he said gruffly. "Let's get this on you and get you back home."

Home?

Why did that sound so good to her?

Five

By the time Blake brought her back to Pine Lodge it was almost noon. Not that Samantha was hungry. She wasn't. She was glad now that he'd decided to stay close today. She wasn't feeling ill, but she was still a little shaky, so she was appreciative of him cupping her elbow as they walked.

That shakiness increased as they went up the staircase and he told her that tonight she was to sleep in the spare bedroom in his suite—a spare bedroom separated from his bedroom by only a connecting bathroom.

Her stomach dipped as they reached the top stair. "I'm only across the landing there, Blake. It seems silly not to stay in my own room."

"No. I want you near in case you need me."

She *did* need him, but not in the way he meant. He was being nothing more than caring right now, while she was still stunned by the impact of their kiss back on the mountain.

"Fine," she murmured, not up to arguing anyway. She was a bit of a mess. Her jacket had mud on it, her slacks were still slightly damp in places where she'd fallen on the wet grass, and parts of her brown hair felt like it was matted with blood. Yuk! She must look a wonderful sight.

"I need to change my clothes," she said, wrinkling her nose. "Actually I might have a shower. My hair feels sticky."

He shook his head. "Not a good idea. You might faint in there."

Her heart thudded and she could feel her face heat up as she pictured him coming in to rescue her. She looked away as they walked toward her room. "You're right," she said, then could have kicked herself. Any other woman would have used that to her advantage, but no, not her. What was the matter with her? Then she remembered. That's right, she'd had a bump on the head, she excused herself, wincing.

"Are you in pain?"

"A little."

He pushed open her bedroom door and led her inside. "Here. Sit on the chair and let me help you take off your jacket."

"Thanks." She did as he said.

"Your sweater's got dried blood down the back of it," he said, after he'd eased her out of the padded material. "I don't know how you're going to get it over your head without causing pain." A small pause. "I'll have to help you off with it."

She gulped. "You will?"

"Yes." His voice was nothing but neutral.

She tried to appear nonchalant, too. "Trust me to wear a tight-necked sweater today," she joked, feeling dizzy again but not from her injuries. It was the thought of him undressing her, even though it made sense to do it this way. She didn't think she'd be able to get the sweater off without him. She had a long-sleeved T-shirt underneath to cover herself, but that had a wide neck and she could easily take it off herself.

"Right. This won't take long." His voice sounded tight and she wondered… "Keep still now."

He slid her arms out of the sleeves, then she felt him touch the hem of her sweater, and almost like it was in slow motion he started to lift it upward. She could feel him move close…closer still as he inched it up higher and higher…. She could feel his breath change as he neared her breasts, though not once did he touch her in any intimate way.

"Okay, careful now," he said, as he reached her nape, his voice huskier. "This will be a little tricky." He moved closer…. "There. That's it. Now let me ease it over your head." He moved around to the front of her and eased the knit material gently up over her head, and suddenly it was off and she was sitting there, her gaze level with his belt buckle. And then she raised her eyes to his, saw him looking down at her, and she dropped her eyes to where her T-shirt had ridden up and was revealing her breasts cupped in her lacy blue bra.

She lifted her head again and their eyes locked together. Something dark flared in his, and in retaliation her breathing became practically nonexistent as she remembered their kiss. Until that moment back there on the mountain none of this had been purely about *them*.

Things had changed.

Now it was.

All at once he twisted jerkily toward the small table and placed the sweater on it, saying over his shoulder, "I'll leave you to do the rest, but I'll be back soon to check on you." His voice sounded rough as he headed for the door. "You should get into bed."

She realized he was trying to be a gentleman and keep it all under control because she was injured, but what if she wasn't injured? Would he take her?

The thought was moot, she told herself, swallowing hard and concentrating on what he'd said. "I'm not staying up here all day, Blake. I can sit on the couch downstairs and do some work." It didn't feel right to go to bed in the middle of the day. Not unless…

He stopped at the door, his eyes firm. "I won't let you work, but you can lie on the couch."

"Good of you," she joked, trying to ease the tension in the room.

He didn't smile. He had a hard flush on his face. "I think so," he muttered, then left her to it, shutting the door behind him and giving her some privacy.

Swallowing, she had to move or he might come back and decide to help her undress the rest of her clothes. And that wouldn't be such a bad thing on her part, but clearly he didn't want to right now. She appreciated that he was thinking of her, even as her body craved to be a part of his.

First, she went into her bathroom, groaning when she saw a streak of blood on her cheek and the mess of her hair. Carefully she lifted the T-shirt over her head.

Unable to stop herself, she stared at her lace-clad breasts, her cheeks reddening as she thought of Blake seeing the invitation of her body like this.

Filling the sink with warm water, she grabbed a washcloth and cleaned as much of the blood out of her hair as possible, then very gently combed it into place over the cut. She was pleased with the result. If she didn't know better, and if her head hadn't been sore, it would be hard to believe she'd just had an accident.

But if she was going to be an invalid today, she may as well be comfortable. She changed into denim jeans and a long-sleeve blouse that buttoned up so she didn't have to lift it over her head. Blake tapped on the door as she stepped into a pair of slides.

"Come in," she called out, half-surprised he'd knocked, considering he'd appeared to have taken charge of her welfare.

He pushed open the door then stood there, inspecting her from the face up. "You look much better."

"I feel better. Thanks."

Then his gaze traveled downward and a curious look passed over his face. "I don't remember seeing you in jeans before."

One glance from him and she could feel how much the jeans hugged her figure. Her stomach fluttered. "I usually only wear them at home." If they were staying at a hotel, Pine Lodge included, she wore stylish clothes even when going casual. She considered dressing right a part of her job.

"You should wear them more often," he said, his eyes blank but his voice tight again. He stepped back. "Come on. There's a couch waiting for you downstairs."

She avoided his gaze as she walked forward, then

went past him in the doorway, but she could feel his presence like a soft touch.

Thankfully soon she was lying on the couch with cushions behind her back and a throw over her body. Did she want a book to read, he asked. A movie on the DVD player? A magazine?

"Perhaps some magazines," she said, though she didn't actually feel like doing anything but lying there and being with Blake. "You don't have to do this," she said as he went to get them from the rack.

He came back with a selection, his mouth set. "I told you. It's my fault you were injured in the first place. I shouldn't have taken you with me."

"But you were only wanting to show me the bungalow location before I left Aspen," she said in a flood of words, then saw his mouth tighten further. She understood. She didn't want to be reminded that she was leaving soon either. "Anyway, what's done is done. I don't blame you but if you want to make it up to me, then I'd love a hot drink. A hot chocolate would be nice. With marshmallows."

"No."

She blinked. "Why not?"

"Because you shouldn't be drinking or eating for a few hours. It could make things worse."

She realized he was right, but, "I'm really thirsty, Blake, and I'm feeling fine now. How about some peppermint tea? That shouldn't hurt." She watched him consider that.

He nodded grudgingly. "Only a very weak one, then."

She smiled. "Thanks."

He set off for the kitchen and she could hear him

moving about in there. Her family used to cosset her like this at times, and she had to admit she liked being taken care of by Blake.

He soon returned with her hot drink, then he moved to the table in the corner where they'd set up the office. For a time it remained quiet as she flipped through the magazines and sipped at her tea. Then she began feeling sleepy. Eventually she finished her drink and made herself more comfortable, being careful with her sore head as she curled up on the couch. Her eyes closed and she found herself thinking about her and Blake back on the mountain. She could still remember the feel of his lips against…

The phone woke her with a start and she heard Blake swearing as he snatched it from the handset. She sat up and tidied herself, listening to his conversation, knowing someone in his family was inquiring about her. He soon ended the call.

"Sorry about that," he told her. "It was Guy checking to see how you were. He'd heard about the accident from Avery."

"Oh, that's nice of him."

The phone rang again and Blake reached for it. "Yes, she's fine, Gavin, but I'll be keeping an eye on her anyway." She saw Blake listen, then dart a look at her, before turning away. "You're a funny guy, Gav." Then he hung up.

Curious, she asked, "What did he say?"

"Nothing much."

Had Gavin made a brotherly comment about keeping an eye on her? Not that she minded. It might work in her favor. "That's good of your family to be checking on me."

"You're supposed to be resting. I don't want them interrupting that."

His comment warmed her as she glanced at the wall clock, surprised to see the time. "I must have been asleep a while."

"An hour."

So he'd been keeping an eye on her. "That long? I didn't realize."

"I did."

The phone rang again and he muttered something low. This time it was Trevor. No sooner had he hung up than they heard car doors slam shut and Blake strode over to look out the window.

"Who is it?" she asked.

"Melissa and Shane."

She watched him start toward the front door and quickly called his name. He stopped to look at her. "You *will* let them in, won't you?"

His mouth tightened. "For a short while."

"Be nice," she chided gently, and he shot her a look saying that was a given. "You know what I mean, Blake. I think it's wonderful of your family to be concerned for me."

His mouth softened a little. "Yeah, they're pretty good when they want to be."

Soon Blake's sister Melissa and her new fiancé, Shane McDermott, came into the lodge, bringing a breath of crisp, fresh air.

Melissa's long, wavy, blond hair flew behind her as she made a beeline for the couch. "Samantha! We heard you'd had an accident. Are you okay?"

Samantha was touched that they'd thought to drop by. "I'm fine, Melissa. Thank you for thinking of me."

"She's fine for the moment," Blake said, standing closest to the door, as if ready to open it in a moment's notice. "But she needs to rest as much as possible."

Shane stood beside him but he at least smiled at her, unlike Blake. "Good to see you, Samantha," he said, inclining his head in the cowboy way.

Samantha smiled back at the handsome man. Shane was the architect who'd designed the resort's riding stables. He might look urban and sophisticated, but he'd been raised on a nearby ranch and his cowboy status couldn't be disputed. "You, too, Shane."

Melissa sank down on one of the lounge chairs and frowned at Samantha. "You do look pale. So tell me. What happened?" Without giving her time to reply, she glanced at the men. "Blake, I'd love a hot chocolate so be a dear and make me one, won't you?" She darted a look at Samantha. "What about you, honey?"

Samantha wrinkled her nose. "Blake won't let me."

Melissa seemed to consider that, then darted a look at her brother before nodding at Samantha. "Yes, that's probably best." She looked at her fiancé. "Shane, darling, would you mind helping Blake in the kitchen? I'm not sure he knows his way around it," she teased.

Blake eased into his first smile since they'd arrived. "You'd be surprised, Melissa."

Melissa patted the small hump of her stomach on her slightly curvy figure. "You'd better hurry. This baby is getting hungry." She winked at Samantha.

Samantha smiled but as the men left them alone and she looked at Blake's sister, she felt a tug deep inside her chest. Melissa had a radiant glow about her. She'd only recently announced her pregnancy to Shane and they were soon to be married. They'd had a few ups and downs but now all was well.

Samantha was very happy for Melissa, and yet she felt sad for herself, with this inexplicable ache in the region of her heart. One day she wanted a baby and a family of her own, but she couldn't imagine any man she wanted to father them—except for maybe Blake. That would mean he would have to marry her, but he didn't believe in happily-ever-after, and she wasn't ready for that either.

Still, she couldn't shake off the thought of cuddling Blake's baby in her arms. It was natural for a woman to think about having children with the man she was attracted to, right? Strangely, she didn't ever remember thinking about having Carl's children. Her notion of being married to him had merely been about them traveling the world together. It hadn't progressed further than that. Thank the Lord!

"Are you okay, Samantha?"

She managed a smile. "Apart from a small headache, I'm fine."

Melissa's piercing blue eyes suddenly seemed so like Blake's. "I hear you're leaving us soon?"

This was why the other woman had got the men out of the way. Melissa wanted to question her.

Samantha tried to look at peace with her decision. "Yes, it's time to move on to new pastures."

"Blake will miss you."

"So everyone keeps telling me," Samantha said wryly, but was grateful that Shane came back in right then to ask Melissa a question about how hot she wanted her drink. Once he left again Samantha changed the conversation to the ranch where Shane had grown up. Melissa was more than happy to talk about her fiancé.

The other couple stayed for a while, until Blake shooed them out, reminding them that a certain person needed to rest up.

"Right," Blake said, once they'd gone. "I'll get some more work out of the way, then how does an omelet sound for dinner? I don't think you should eat anything too heavy, just in case. It's not a good thing to have a full stomach."

She looked at him in mild amusement. "Is this Doctor Jarrod speaking?"

He didn't seem to find that funny. "Yes, so take note."

"I would, only you won't let me work," she quipped.

"Funny," he muttered, then went back to his paperwork. She sighed. He was taking it all so seriously, and while that was sweet of him, it wasn't necessary.

After that, Samantha was itching to get up and move around but knew it was best she take things easy. For something to do while she was waiting for Blake to finish working, she popped a movie in the DVD and began watching it with earphones so that she didn't disturb him. It was a romantic comedy she hadn't seen before and it made her giggle. She didn't realize she'd been laughing loudly until suddenly she became aware of Blake standing near the couch.

She paused the movie and looked up at him as she pulled out her earbuds. "I'm sorry. Is this interrupting your work?"

"No." He went still. "It's good to hear you laugh. You don't do it often enough."

Her pulse was skipping beats. "The job isn't exactly a laugh a minute," she joked. Then realized how that might sound. "That came out wrong. I didn't mean—"

"I know what you meant," he said easily enough as he leaned over and pulled the earplug cord out of the television. Picking up the remote, he turned the movie back on, only instead of going back to his work he sat down on the other chair.

She blinked in mild surprise, then tried to concentrate as he began watching the movie with her. He'd only missed about fifteen minutes of the story, so they both watched it together. It was amusing enough that she could feel herself relax, and when it was finished even Blake looked relaxed. She was glad about that. He worked too hard at times, and took his responsibilities too seriously.

Later, in spite of him telling her to stay on the couch, she followed him into the kitchen where he was going to prepare dinner. "I need to walk. My legs are getting numb."

His brows immediately drew together on full medical alert. "They feel numb? Are you getting any pins and needles? Is it hard to walk or are—"

"Blake, I was merely trying to say I wanted to move around," she cut across him, somewhat bemused by his agitation.

He grimaced. "Okay, so that was a mild over-reaction."

"Mild?" she teased.

He gave a self-deprecating smile, then jerked his head toward the bench. "Go sit over there and take it easy."

She ignored that and turned toward the cupboard.

"I'll put out the place mats and cutlery first. We can eat in here."

He must have known it was a waste of time to argue because he nodded, then went back to preparing the omelet. It was a strange feeling watching him cook for her. It would be another memory to take away when she left.

Soon they were sitting down on the tall stools to eat and the next hour flew by as they chatted. As if they both didn't want to ruin the moment, neither of them spoke about her leaving.

Then he mentioned Donald Jarrod in passing, and that made her think. Blake had never spoken about his father while they were in Vegas, but now they were in Aspen she'd managed to put two and two together. "Your dad was pretty hard on you, wasn't he?"

He tensed even as he gave a light shrug. "After my mother died, he was hard on all his children."

She considered him. "But harder on you."

A flash of surprise crossed his face. "Yes. How did you know?"

"You were the eldest. He seems to have been a man who had set ideas about the order of things and didn't give an inch."

"He was. Very much so."

"Tell me more."

He paused and for a moment she didn't think he would tell her. Then, "Guy was only younger by a few minutes but it could have been years in my father's eyes. I was the oldest, so it was up to me to make sure I took responsibility for everything. None of us ever really got to play while growing up, but I suppose I got even less time than the rest."

The thought upset her. "That's sad."

He shrugged. "My father actually did us a favor. We grew up being very independent. We don't need anyone."

She could see that. And that was even sadder, but she didn't say so. She tilted her head. "It still would've been hard losing your mother like that when you were just a small boy. And then having your father distance himself would have made it far worse. Children don't understand why love has been withdrawn. They just know."

His expression suddenly bordered on mockery and she knew she'd touched a nerve. "And you understand the way a child's mind works when he loses a parent, do you?"

She pulled a face. He knew very well both her parents were alive. "Well, no, but—"

"I rest my case."

"Blake, I don't think it's too hard to comprehend what you must have gone through."

Anger flashed across his face. "Enough, Samantha. I don't want or need your sympathy for something that happened a long time ago."

"But—"

The telephone rang and he snatched it up from the wall beside him, almost barking into it. His mouth tightened. "Hang on, Erica. I'll put her on." He handed the phone over to Samantha.

"I see Blake's being his usual talkative self," Erica mused down the line. She didn't wait for Samantha to agree. "I heard about your accident and just wanted to see how you were doing."

Samantha appreciated her concern. "I'm fine, thanks,

Erica." She forced herself to sound cheery. "Blake and I just had dinner. He cooked me an omelet."

An eloquent silence came from Erica's end. "A man of many talents," she finally said. "I'd better let you go, then. I'll talk to you tomorrow." She hung up before Samantha could respond.

Samantha took her time placing the receiver back down, hiding her expression from him. She wouldn't tell Blake what Erica had been thinking. That his half sister was delighted the two of them were bonding, even if Blake did sound like a grouch. "That was really nice of her to call."

His lips twisted. "I wonder if I have any relatives left who might like to interrupt us tonight?"

Her brow creased with worry. "You really should give Erica a chance."

"To do what?"

Anger stirred the air, though she knew it wasn't directed at her. She tilted her head. "Do you blame Erica for your father's affair with her mother?" she said, coming right out and saying it.

He didn't look pleased by her comment. "I'm not blaming Erica for what my father did. I just don't want her coming in here and splitting up the family. I'm not convinced she'll stay in Aspen."

She didn't know how he could say that. Was he blind? "She and Christian are so in love. And she's in love with everyone here at Jarrod Ridge, too. Their hearts are here, Blake. They won't leave you."

He swore. "I don't give a rat's ass if they leave or not. This isn't about what *I* feel anyway. It's about her causing problems for the family and then walking away without a care in the world."

"I'm sure that won't happen. Erica isn't like that."

One eyebrow shot up. "You know her so well, do you?"

"Do you?"

A muscle began ticking along his jaw. "Thank you for your opinion, but I don't need it." He pushed to his feet and began collecting the plates, taking them over to the dishwasher. "Go into the living room. I'll bring in the coffee."

For a few moments she didn't move. She watched his rigid back and felt depressed by his remoteness and abruptness. She'd pushed him hard just now and she wasn't sure why, except that she somehow felt she was fighting not just for Erica's sake but for Blake's, as well. If she could at least get him to relent toward Erica then maybe when *she* left, her time here would have been of value. Maybe then something good would have come from all this. She sighed. Or was she simply looking for something to make herself feel good about leaving Blake?

And that brought her back to what she'd said before about Erica leaving him. Was that the crux of the matter? It occurred to her then that Blake may have abandonment issues with his mother dying, and now that made it difficult for him to get close to his half sister. Or to get close to anyone, including herself.

Someone rang the doorbell and Blake swore again.

"That'll be Joel," Samantha reminded him. "He said he would check on me."

"Stay there," he muttered and strode past her to let in the other man.

A couple of seconds later Joel breezed into the kitchen. She noticed he took in the homey scene, but he was all professional while he checked her over and announced he was pleased.

Then, "We have to get you better for tomorrow night," he teased, but she saw him dart a look at Blake and she suddenly had the feeling there was more to this. He seemed to be letting Blake know he was staking a claim.

"Tomorrow night?" Blake asked in a menacing voice.

Joel closed up his medical bag. "Samantha and I have a date for Monday night." He winked at her. "We're going to the movies."

Samantha wanted to say she hadn't actually accepted the invitation but the displeased look in Blake's eyes kept her quiet.

"Let's see how she feels first," Blake said grimly, then stepped back in clear indication that the doctor should precede him to the front door.

Joel hesitated, like he wasn't about to take orders, then he must have remembered that Blake was his boss. He inclined his head at Samantha. "I'll call you in the morning," he told her, picking up his bag.

He left the room and Blake saw him out, and Samantha couldn't help but wonder once again if Blake might be jealous of Joel. The thought made her heartbeat pick up speed. Blake had certainly *wanted* to kiss her back there on the mountain and surely that had to mean something.

Didn't it?

All at once she needed to know what he felt for her. "Joel finds me attractive, don't you think?" she said dreamily as Blake came back in the kitchen looking anything but relaxed.

His eyes filled with meaning. "Sure he does," he said cynically.

She couldn't let him get away with that. "What does that mean?"

"Just that any woman with the right equipment can attract a man. And believe me, you've got the right equipment," he drawled, slipping his hands into his trouser pockets, all at once looking very much in charge of himself, making her want to bring him down a peg or two.

"Thanks for the assumption that I'm only good for sex," she said with faint indignation.

His hands came out of his pockets and his complacency vanished. "I didn't say that," he retorted, then strode over to check on the coffee. He spun back around. "Dammit, what the hell are you doing with those men anyway? You don't need them. They're beneath you."

Startled, she gathered her wits about her. *This* was more like it. "Maybe I *want* them beneath me," she joked.

"Don't talk like that."

She hid a soft gasp. It *did* sound like he was jealous. She needed to push more. "I don't understand how you can say a doctor isn't good enough for me, Blake."

"That's because he's *not* good enough for you."

Her spirits soared. "What about Ralph? You don't even know what he does for a living."

"And you do?"

She did, then realized she'd set herself up here. She had to cough before she said, "He's a car salesman."

"Huh! That explains the slime rolling off him."

"Blake!" She hadn't expected quite such a response. "What's got into you?"

His mouth drew down at the corners. "Those guys aren't after you for your intellect."

She screwed up her nose. "How nice of you to point that out."

"You know what I'm saying."

Yes, she did. Unfortunately she knew it was true. And that would have been fine if she'd been the least bit interested in the other men. As it was, she still felt a little guilty using them, though no doubt they were big enough to look out for themselves.

She tilted her head and knew she had to say this. "If I didn't know better I'd think you were jealous."

"And if I am?" he challenged without warning.

She felt giddy but she couldn't let herself get her hopes up. "I'd have to ask why. Is it because you know I'm leaving soon and you only want what you suddenly can't have?"

"What the—"

"Or is it because you might actually want *me?*"

For a moment he looked like he would move in close. "You ask me that after the kiss we shared?"

Her breath came quickly. "I—"

And then something changed in his expression and his jaw thrust forward. "This isn't the time to discuss it. You need your rest. You should go lie on the couch."

Her throat blocked with disappointment, but then understanding dawned and she realized he was pulling back for *her* sake. If it hadn't been for her accident, she was sure he would be making love to her right now.

Frustration weaved through her, despite appreciating that he was doing the right thing. "I think I'll go read in bed. It's getting late." He went to come with her and she put her hand up. "No, I can manage by myself. Good night, Blake. And thanks."

He nodded. "Make sure you sleep in the spare bedroom. I still want you close to me."

She could feel heat sweeping up her face. Did he have to say it like that? "Okay."

He seemed mesmerized by her reddening cheeks. "I'll be checking on you a couple of times in the night." His voice had a gravelly edge to it now. "So I apologize in advance for disturbing you."

She looked away; the thought of him coming into her room during the night was enough to disturb her *now*.

Then she went up to bed with stars in her eyes. And they weren't from the hit on the head either. Unfortunately she knew he wasn't about to take advantage of her while she was injured, and certainly not during the night when she was sure he'd remain a perfect gentleman. But he'd better watch out when she was back on her feet.

Six

Blake looked at the bedside clock and grunted to himself. It was almost seven o'clock and still dark outside, but he needed to get up and check on Samantha before he did anything else this morning. Today he planned on working from Pine Lodge so he could keep an eye on her, but he needed to go to the Manor and get some things out of the way first.

He'd spent a restless night, getting up every couple of hours to check on a sleeping Samantha in the bedroom next door. Of course it was easy for her to sleep so peacefully. She didn't have to stand over an attractive member of the opposite sex who wore satin pajamas and looked deliciously alluring in bed. And she didn't have to reach out to touch that person's shoulder to shake them awake, nor rigidly ignore the urge to slide into bed next to her warm body and pleasure her senseless.

He would have done it, too—if he hadn't had to

wake her and ask questions to make sure she wasn't suffering any sort of confusion. Even now the thought of her having any sort of aftereffects from the head injury still managed to clench his gut tight. He'd hated seeing her hurt. If he hadn't been so focused on getting her away from that Ralph, then none of this would have happened.

Not even the kiss.

No, that kiss *would* have happened—if not there, then somewhere else. There was something going on between them now. It had started happening the night she'd handed him her resignation and it hadn't let up.

And it wasn't one-sided either. She'd dissolved in his arms so quickly yesterday he'd thought the marrow had melted in her bones. No woman had ever reacted quite like that for him before. It certainly made a man feel good.

Remembering the feel of her lips beneath his, he was tempted to just lie there and think about her, but he knew he'd never get out of bed if he did. And then Samantha would be bringing *him* breakfast in bed. The thought was more than pleasurable.

Giving a low groan, he tossed back the covers and shoved off the mattress in his pajama bottoms, then headed for the bathroom to take a shower. But as he opened the door and went to reach for the light switch, the light flicked on anyway and Samantha came through the connecting door.

She jumped back with a gasp. "Blake!"

A lick of fire sizzled through his veins as his eyes slid down over her slim contours, registering that what he thought had been green satin pajamas was an emerald midthigh nightshirt. It looked so sexy on her, suiting her complexion and rich brown hair.

He lifted his eyes back up to her face. "How's the head?" he asked huskily.

She seemed to become flustered. "Er…it doesn't feel too bad." Awkwardly she spun to face the mirrored wall, going up on her toes to stare at her reflection. "I came to see if it was okay." She lifted her long tousled strands to check the injury. "Yes, it looks fine," she chattered. "There's a bit of a bump and no sign of bleeding."

He appreciated that she was okay, but did she know that stretching up over the sink like she was, the side split of her nightshirt was showing him more of her long silken legs than he'd ever seen before? All the way up her thigh to the line of her panties.

Suddenly she seemed to freeze in position as she stretched up at the mirror like that, and he realized right then she was looking at *him* in the mirror, with a hungry look that drifted down over his bare chest and the pajama bottoms he'd worn last night for her benefit. He tensed with arousal and she must have noticed. Their eyes locked together in the glass.

And then she slowly pushed back from the sink and turned to face him with her body, her chin tilting provocatively, her eyes inviting him to take her. Caught off-guard by such an unfamiliar look from her, he swallowed hard. His assistant was certainly showing him a new side of herself lately.

"Samantha," he said thickly, galvanized into taking a step toward her. "Do you know what you're—"

"Yes, Blake, I do."

He reached her and she tumbled against him, her hands flattening against his chest, her mouth seeking his, her lips parting beneath his without any pressure at all.

Their kiss was hot and urgent and demanding, their bodies pressing closer and closer together, reveling in each other. Then a soft moan of hers breathed into him, and in a haze of desire, he deepened the kiss until he finally had to break away to suck in air.

But only for a moment, until he began planting quick, soft kisses down that creamy throat, before coming back up again to her lips, needing to be inside her mouth once more, needing to breathe her in once more.

He pulled her harder against him, running his hands hungrily over the satin material and feminine curves. She quivered all over from head to toe, wildly gripping his shoulders like she needed to hold on to him.

Mouth to mouth, he backed her to the full-length sink and lifted her up onto a folded fluffy towel. Her thighs fell open and he heard a button pop from the front of her nightshirt. He gave a groan of approval and wedged himself between her legs….

And the coldness of the marble touched his erection through his pajamas.

The shock of it made him still. Heaven knew he could do with cooling down…slowing down…but Samantha sat in front of him with her head tilted back and her eyes closed. Her cheeks were overheated, her breathing unsteady, and despite that come-to-me look she'd given him a short while ago, she appeared to be about to lose control. God knows he'd felt the instantaneous spiral of desire himself, but this was more and he really had to wonder just how inexperienced she actually was. He swallowed hard. Could she even be a *virgin?*

He wasn't sure how he felt about that, but he did

know he couldn't continue this right now. His previous lovers knew the score but this woman may not. And if he was playing with more than her body…if her emotions were more than involved…he could cause her a lot of heartache. He didn't want to do that to Samantha.

Yet this wasn't the moment to talk about it, with her looking all sexy and ready for the taking. There was too much hunger in the air in here. It would only confuse things. He liked her too much to do this to her.

Unwrapping her arms from around his neck, he lifted her down off the bench, hating that he had to walk away from her. "I'm sorry, Samantha."

Bewilderment spread over her face. "What's the—"

"I just can't do it," he rasped. "Not like this." As hard as it was to leave her side, he turned and went back to his room.

He badly wanted to turn right back around, sweep her up in his arms and carry her to his bed. He shuddered as he closed the door between them.

They would talk later and perhaps it would turn out that he'd have to keep the door closed permanently between them. Maybe she would be his road not taken. But he had to think what was best for Samantha. She deserved better than becoming his temporary mistress.

Samantha didn't know how she made it back to her own room. Humiliation scorched through her. She'd done exactly what she'd wanted to do and given Blake a come-on. She hadn't deliberately gone into the bathroom to entice him in there, but the opportunity had presented itself and she'd thought it had worked. Then he'd just upped and walked away and, despite his obvious arousal, he said he couldn't do it.

Couldn't make love with her.

She knew it had nothing to do with her having a minor head injury this time. He might say it was, but she knew this was about him not wanting her enough. His body had automatically responded to a female in his arms, but his mind had been elsewhere. As he'd said the evening before, any woman with the right equipment could attract a man. Unfortunately the attraction he felt for her hadn't been enough. Not for him.

It was Carl all over again.

She plopped down on her bed as her legs gave way. Had she unwittingly done something wrong back there? Something to annoy him physically? Clearly he hadn't been invested in the moment like she'd been. It had been wonderful in his arms but she hadn't realized he'd been feeling different. She thought he'd felt the same way. It was obvious now that he could turn himself on and off at a whim—just like he had after their kiss on the mountain.

Unlike her.

Her emotions whirled like a spinning top let loose on the floor. Oh, God, what was she going to do? How was she going to face him? Worse, would he insist on letting her out of her contract now? She had the feeling he would tell her to leave sooner rather than later.

At the thought, her emotions stopped spinning. They stopped dead. Her chin lifted. Right. Okay. If she was being given the heave-ho, then she would certainly leave without protest. It's what she needed to do anyway, she told herself. She regretted she would leave with this between them, but things had gone too far. It was a good lesson in being careful what she wished for. Now she simply wished this nightmare would go away.

Samantha took a shower and carefully washed her hair, but wasn't sure if she was dismayed or relieved after she came out of the bathroom and heard Blake's car leaving. Going over to peek out her bedroom window, she saw him driving toward the Manor in the early morning light. Evidently she was okay to be left alone now, she thought with a stab of hurt.

Then her heart dropped to her feet. Perhaps he was going to tell his family that she was leaving sooner? Would he tell them why? That she'd made a play for him and put him in an awkward position? Her cheeks heated at the thought and she wanted to curl up in a ball and not see any of them again.

Yet pride wouldn't allow her to do that. She'd held her head high when Carl had rejected her and she would do it again now. She would go up to the Manor and finish her tasks, and she would arrange her replacement. If she smiled at the others and acted carefree, then no one would know how bad she felt.

No one except Blake.

Half an hour later she sat at her desk at the Manor, relieved not to have seen anyone she knew on the way here. She didn't want to answer questions about her accident, or anything else for that matter.

Thankfully the door to Blake's office was shut, though the red light on the telephone told her he was making a call. Quickly she got herself organized, then found the number she was after and reached for the phone, hoping someone at the employment agency would be at their desk early like her. She knew that as soon as the red button on his phone lit up with her extension, Blake would learn she was here, but it couldn't be helped.

She got the answering machine. Having dealt with this employment agency before for other office matters, she decided to leave a message. At least that would get the ball rolling. "Yes, this is Samantha Thompson calling on behalf of Blake Jarrod Enterprises. Could Mary Wentworth call me back as soon as possible…" The red light on Blake's phone went off. Her heart started to race as a second later his door was flung open. "It's about a position that's become available." He strode to her desk. "It's—"

He pressed the button to disconnect the call, his eyes slamming into her. "What are you doing?" he demanded in a low tone.

She angled her chin as she looked up at him. "I'm trying to work."

"I thought you'd have enough sense to rest up today."

"I don't need to rest up. I did plenty of that yesterday." Calmly, she placed the telephone back on its handset. "I'm perfectly fine now."

His eyes narrowed. "And why the hell are you calling someone about your job?"

"You need a new assistant."

"I'm happy with my old one."

She arched one eyebrow. "Really? It didn't seem that way to me this morning," she said, staying cool when all she wanted to do was fall in a heap and cry her eyes out.

He swore.

"Don't worry, Blake. I'll be leaving Aspen soon, so

you don't have to worry that I'll attack you. I know you're not that into me."

He blinked, then, "What the hell!" He swore again. "We need to talk."

"It's a bit late for talking, don't you think?" She went to pick up the phone again. He grabbed her hand, not hurting her but not letting her make the call either. "Stop manhandling me, Blake."

He tried to stare her down. "No."

"Blake, this isn't getting us anywhere."

"Listen, Samantha. You're—"

Erica walked into the office and stopped dead, blinking in surprise as her gaze went from one to the other, then down at their hands gripped together. "Er... Blake, your car is here to take you to the airport."

He casually let go of Samantha's hand. "Thanks, Erica."

Samantha felt the blood drain from her face. "You're leaving?"

Like Carl?

He looked at her oddly. "Something cropped up overnight at one of the hotels and I need to go to Vegas and sort it out. I'll tell you about it later."

As fast as it had tightened, the tension unscrewed inside her. So he *was* coming back. It had been crazy of her to even think he wouldn't. Blake wouldn't give up all this because of *her*.

She went to get to her feet. "I'll come with you." Once she was in Vegas, she would start bringing her life there to a close.

"No, you stay here. You shouldn't be flying with a head injury," he said firmly, surprising her. She'd have thought he'd be eager to get her out of Aspen now.

He cast his half sister a look. "Erica, can you keep an eye on Samantha and make sure she doesn't stay here too long today? I don't want her overdoing things."

Erica looked startled then pleased. "Of course." It was obvious she valued being asked by her brother to help out, but Samantha was still surprised that Blake wanted *her* to stay in Aspen.

He nodded. "Thanks. I'll just grab my stuff." As he spoke he headed back into his office before coming out with his briefcase and coat. He looked at Samantha. "I'll be back tonight. I'll explain everything then." He started toward the door then hesitated. "You *will* be here when I return, won't you, Samantha?"

It hadn't occurred to her to leave behind his back, though she couldn't discount that it might have. Then she remembered how she'd thought he might have issues with feeling abandoned over his mother's death. Did he think *she* was about to abandon him, too? Tenderness touched a part of her that wasn't reeling by the latest events. "I promise."

He looked satisfied then he gave Erica a jerky nod as he passed by. He left behind a meaningful silence.

After a couple of seconds, Erica came toward the desk. "Are you okay?"

"My head's fine now, thanks."

She tutted. "You know I mean more than that."

Samantha grimaced. "Yes, I suppose I do." Then as she looked at the other woman, she wondered if Blake would eventually discuss her with his family. Would he even tell them she had made a play for him? Her breath caught. She'd never known him to talk about his affairs before to anyone. Huh! Affair? There *was* no affair. That was the problem.

"He's concerned for you, honey."

"He's concerned for the job."

"You're wrong." Erica paused. "Give him a chance to explain whatever it is he needs to explain."

The telephone rang then, and Erica said she had to go check on something but would be back later. Samantha answered it and heard Mary Wentworth's voice, and knew she needed to slow everything down a little. So she apologized to the other woman that she couldn't talk right now and would call her back tomorrow. By then, she should well and truly know the score between her and Blake. Either way, she still had to leave. It was just a matter of when.

After she hung up, the workday began with the phone ringing, then the mail arrived. Samantha worked through it all, but a part of her mind was on Blake's reaction earlier. He'd said he was perfectly happy with his old assistant.

Her.

And that made her wonder if he might still want her to work out her contract. Her heart raced at the thought, then came to a shuddering halt when she remembered this morning in the bathroom. She probably couldn't stay at Jarrod Ridge past tomorrow, but at least on his return tonight she might learn what had turned him off her. It may not be something she wanted to hear, but she needed to know or she would always wonder.

Erica returned an hour later, but Samantha still felt physically fine and convinced her not to worry. She'd decided to work until lunchtime, then she got a ride back to the lodge, where she made herself a light lunch. Afterward she felt tired, so she stretched out on the couch and took a nap.

The front doorbell woke her sometime later. It was a florist with a vase filled with the most gorgeous yellow tulips she'd ever seen. Something flipped over inside her heart. Her family wasn't into sending flowers, and only one person here knew she loved yellow tulips.

There was a card with them. "Dinner tonight. Pine Lodge. All arranged. See you at seven."

Her throat swelled with emotion as she carried the vase over to a side table and set it down. They looked so stunning that she was about to race upstairs to get her camera, but then wondered if that was a good idea. Did she really want to take away more memories of Blake?

The telephone rang then.

It was Joel. Oh, Lord. She'd forgotten her date with him tonight. The tulips caught her eye and she knew she'd rather spend her last hours here in Aspen with Blake than go to the movies with Joel.

She opened her mouth to speak but before she could say anything, he apologized and told her that his cousin was in town overnight and this was his only chance to catch up with her. Did she mind? No. Could they go to the movies tomorrow night instead? She said she would let him know. She had no idea whether she would still be here tomorrow night. Then he mentioned that he was in town right now and would get the nurse to check on her later today, but she thanked him and said it wasn't necessary.

More than relieved, Samantha looked at the tulips as she hung up the telephone, Joel already relegated to the back of her mind. Blake might just want to discuss her job tonight, but right now she didn't care. She needed to know where it had all gone wrong this morning. More importantly, she wanted to know if there was even a slim chance it was something that could be fixed.

Seven

Samantha hadn't been sure what she should wear for tonight. While the flowers and the dinner were very thoughtful of Blake, and while he'd said he would give her an explanation as to why he walked away from her this morning in the bathroom and that sounded promising, none of that meant he *wanted* her.

In the end she decided to keep it fairly low-key, just like she would if she were dining with him for business reasons. She wore a thin brown sweater over cream slacks and a pair of low-heeled pumps, adding a gold chain at her neck to make it a little more stylish.

Just after six-thirty one of the hotel staff arrived as sunset spiked through the lodge. He placed a cooked casserole in the oven to keep warm, dessert in the refrigerator, then lit the log fire before beautifully setting the table in the small dining alcove. Had Blake requested the two candles on the table? She was about to ask the young waiter when Blake came in the front door.

"Blake!" she exclaimed, her pulse picking up at the sight of him. Realizing she might be giving herself away, she pulled herself back and toned it down. "You're early," she said more sedately. "I didn't expect you quite so soon."

"We had a tailwind." He nodded at the waiter. "It looks good, Andy. Thanks."

Samantha wasn't surprised that he knew the man's name. Blake was good with people—as long as you did the right thing by him.

"No problem, Mr. Jarrod." Andy's smile encompassed them both. "I'll come and collect everything tomorrow." He nodded good-night, then went through to the kitchen.

Blake stood there for a minute looking at Samantha, his eyes flicking down over her outfit then away. "I could do with a shower," he muttered, and made for the stairs.

She felt nervous all of a sudden. She twisted away herself. "I'll just make sure the food's okay." She left the room and went into the kitchen, glad that Andy was still gathering a couple of things together before he left. It brought the world back into focus and took it away from her and Blake. She needed the balance.

Andy left and she busied herself unnecessarily checking on the casserole, then poured herself a glass of water and stood there sipping it to calm her nerves. She could only stay in there so long, and soon she wandered back into the lounge area and drew the drapes against the encroaching night, before switching on the lamps.

It was too quiet, so she put on a CD to fill the silence

and sat down on the couch to wait. The wood scent from the burning logs in the fireplace wafted throughout the room, and after a few minutes, she could feel the soft music begin to ease the tension inside her. And then it hit her and she realized how romantic the whole place looked. She groaned slightly. It hadn't been intentional but would Blake believe that? It all looked so intimate.

Panicking that he might think she was trying to seduce him, she was about to about to jump up and turn off the music when she saw Blake coming down the stairs. He wasn't looking at her and she ate up the sight of him. He was so handsome in light gray pants and a navy crewneck sweater, but it was his magnetic aura of masculinity that caught her breath.

He reached the bottom step and all at once he glanced up and his gaze quickly summed up the ambiance in the room. She could feel warmth steal under her skin. This guy never missed a trick.

"You must be tired," she said, hoping to ignore what he might think was obvious.

"A little. It's been a long day."

And then their eyes met—memories of this morning between them.

She moistened her mouth. "Blake, I—"

He shook his head. "Not yet, Samantha. Let's eat first. I'm starving and I need to relax a little."

"Of course." She swung toward the kitchen. "I'll serve the dinner."

"I'll pour the wine."

She hurried away, expelling a shaky breath once she reached the privacy of the kitchen. Blake wouldn't discuss the matter until he was ready, so she would just have to have a little patience. Perhaps it would be best if she had some food in her stomach first.

When she came back carrying the plates of chicken casserole, he was sitting at the table, having poured the wine. He stood up as she approached and took the plates from her. He'd always been a gentleman where she was concerned, holding out her chair or opening doors for her. She knew it was something he did on autopilot.

"You lit the candles," she said for something to say. "They look really nice."

He put the plates down on the table. "Andy knows his job."

She wasn't sure if that meant Blake had asked for them or if Andy had merely improvised. Did it matter, she asked herself as he held her chair out just as she'd expected.

As she sat down, she glimpsed the tulips on the side table. That was probably why he'd looked at her strangely before going upstairs to change. He must think her so ungrateful.

"Oh, Blake, I should have said something earlier. Thank you so much for the tulips. They're absolutely gorgeous."

"You like them, then?" He looked pleased as he sat down opposite her.

"I love them."

He considered her. "You getting hit on the head was very good for me."

She blinked. "It was?"

"I learned two things about you. What your favorite flower is, and your favorite color."

"Want to know my favorite perfume, too?" she joked, touched by his words.

Only he didn't laugh. "It's Paris by Yves Saint Laurent," he said with an unexpected thickness to his voice that made her nerves tingle.

"You know?"

"You bought some the first time we went to Paris together, remember?" He made it sound like they'd been together in Paris for something other than business.

Surprised he remembered that time two years ago when she'd first gone to work for him, she dropped her gaze and fanned her napkin over her lap, though she rather felt like fanning her face instead. "This looks delicious."

There was a slight pause. "Yes."

She could feel his eyes on her as she picked up her fork and finally looked at him again. "So, what was the problem in Vegas that you needed to go there in such a hurry?"

A moment ticked by then he picked up his fork. "There was a problem with one of the chefs. He was being a bit too temperamental, and the kitchen staff was threatening to walk out. It was beginning to escalate into a big commotion with the unions. It started to get ugly."

"And it's sorted out now?"

"Of course."

She had to smile. "Naturally. You wouldn't have come back otherwise, right?"

Suddenly there was an air of watchfulness about him. "What happened to your date with Joel tonight?"

She'd wondered if he'd mention it. And then something else occurred to her. Could he have arranged to get Joel out of the way tonight? The thought made her pulse race. "His cousin's in Aspen for the night and he wanted to spend time with her." She tilted her head. "You didn't have anything to do with that, did you?"

His brow rose. "Me? Am I that good?"

"Yes!" she exclaimed on a half chuckle.

A flash of humor crossed his face. "Believe me, I'm not *that* clever."

It did sound silly now. Blake could make things happen, but this time he'd have to find Joel's cousin and get that person to come to Aspen. Why would he bother? He knew he merely had to send her flowers and arrange dinner and she'd capitulate like every woman before her.

"Anyway, how are you feeling?" he asked.

"Terrific."

He searched her face, then inclined his head as if satisfied. "At least you only worked half the day."

Her eyes widened. "How do you know that?"

"I checked with Erica. She said you'd left at lunchtime."

She smiled wryly. "Did she also tell you she checked on me nearly every hour after that?"

"She promised me she would."

Why was she *not* surprised? "That was a bit over the top, wasn't it?"

"I don't think so."

She tried not to look more into it than there was. He probably wanted her all better so he could get rid of her faster. Then she knew that wasn't fair of her and she pulled her thoughts back into line. "You always were concerned for your staff, Blake. Thank you."

He looked at her strangely, as if he couldn't understand why she was putting herself in with the rest of his staff. But if that were the case, didn't that mean he was thinking she was something more to him than she actually was?

God, she had to stop thinking so much!

She picked up her wineglass. "You know, Blake. Erica isn't as bad as you imagine her to be. I suspect she'd still have kept an eye on me even without you asking her." She took a sip of her drink but watched him carefully over the rim of her glass.

His brows furrowed. "I guess so." As much as he appeared to concede the point, he didn't look totally convinced about Erica's intentions.

Samantha understood why. "You think she's only doing something nice for a reason, don't you?"

"Maybe."

"Has it occurred to you that the reason is *you?*" She let him consider that, then added, "Maybe she wants to get to know her brother, and she knows the only way she can do that is to show him she is willing to help him out?"

"Maybe." He paused. "But she cares for you, too."

She felt a rush of affection for Erica. "And that goes to show she's a nice person and worthy of your friendship… if not your love."

His lips twisted. "The hit on the head seems to have muddled your brain. You think you're a psychoanalyst now, do you?"

"Where you're concerned I have to be," she said without thinking, but knew it was her mention of the word *love* that had got his back up. Love and Blake Jarrod did *not* go hand-in-hand.

And neither did Samantha Thompson.

Not with love.

Certainly not with Blake Jarrod.

A curious look passed over his face. "Why would you want to psychoanalyze me anyway?"

This time she thought before speaking. No use giving away more of herself than she needed to. It was best she keep up a wall. He would appreciate her more for that.

She managed a thin smile. "A person likes to figure out how their boss's mind works. It helps with the job."

He leaned back in his chair. "Yes, you were always good at that."

Then…just as she thought she had it all under control, all at once everything rose in her throat. She couldn't take any more of this subterfuge and talking around things that mattered. "Blake, don't you think it's time we talked about last night? You took such good care of me, and then this morning…"

He stilled. "Yes?"

She swallowed hard. She had to ask the next question and she had to be prepared to accept the answer. "I'd like to know what I did wrong."

His face blanched as he sat forward. "Nothing, Samantha. You did nothing wrong."

"Then what—"

He drew a breath. "Samantha, are you a virgin?"

She felt her cheeks heat up. "No."

He looked surprised. "I thought you might be."

"Well, I'm not," she said, hunching her shoulders, wondering where this was going to lead.

His expression softened a little. "But you're not very experienced, are you?"

Okay, so it led to further embarrassment.

She could feel her cheeks redden further. "You must know I…er…haven't been with a lot of men."

"How many?"

Her eyes widened. "None of your business."

"You made it my business this morning."

She hesitated, then, "One lover when I was a teenager."

His brow rose. "And none since?" He must have read her thoughts. "You can tell me. I'm not going to tell anyone else."

So, okay, she would accept that. "Well, there was a man back home…."

He didn't blink an eye but she knew she had his attention. "And?"

"We didn't become lovers, but I was in love with him."

"What happened?"

Her lips twisted with self-derision. "He wasn't in love with me."

Blake nodded. "That explains why you haven't had any relationships since I've known you," he said, almost to himself. Then his eyes sharpened. "Are you still in love with him?"

"No. Carl left to go overseas and ended up marrying someone else. I realized I'd been in love with the *idea* of love and that's all it was." She sighed. "But it was a good lesson in learning that you can never be sure of another person's feelings." Realizing that she was suddenly giving too much away, she tried to be casual. "So, you see, I can only lay claim to one lover and that was a long time ago."

"I could tell."

Her composure lurched like a drunken sailor. "I'm sorry. I thought my enthusiasm might make up for any lack of experience."

"Don't apologize. Your enthusiasm was great. Damn great," he said brusquely. "I had a hard time walking away from you."

Her heart faltered. "You did? I thought you didn't want me."

He expelled a harsh breath. "Did my body *feel* like I didn't want you?"

She remembered the tense cords of his body burning her flesh through her nightshirt. "No," she croaked, then had to clear her throat before speaking again. "But what do I know anyway? I thought a man could easily turn it off and on." Carl certainly had been able to put a stop to anything beyond a few kisses.

"I'm not made of stone like that other guy," Blake scoffed, reading her mind, but his voice had gentled. "And all this goes to prove to me that I did the right thing this morning. I'm the experienced one here and that means I have a responsibility to you. I'm glad now I didn't take something from you that you might regret giving later on."

"You mean my virginity?" Her heart rose in her chest at the respect he'd afforded her.

"Yes."

"But I'm *not* a virgin," she pointed out.

"I know that now."

He'd rejected her all for nothing? It was admirable, but… "You should have asked me at the time."

He pursed his mouth. "It's not only that," he said, sending her stomach plummeting.

"I see."

"No, I don't think you do." He clenched his jaw. "You were so damn generous, Samantha. You were giving me everything and I was worried that you…er…might look more into this than you should. I just wasn't sure you could handle any emotional involvement."

She appreciated where he was coming from with this, but her heart still managed to drop at his words. What *was* it about her that every man felt they had to warn her off?

"Don't worry," she assured him. "I'm not planning on repeating history and losing my heart to anyone in the future."

His eyes searched hers. "Are you sure?"

"Positive." Suddenly she felt all-knowing. "Maybe it's *you* who can't handle it, Blake."

He looked startled, then scowled. "I admit it. I can't. And to be blunt, I don't want to even try." He paused. "But this isn't about me. I'm thinking of *you*, Samantha. Not me."

Her heart tilted. She appreciated his honesty but she could look after herself. And to be equally as honest, how could she give him up without a fight now that she knew he wanted her?

"Blake, thank you for that but you're doing me an injustice. I'm a grown woman. I know sex doesn't always mean commitment. I have needs and I know my own mind. I know what I want, and while I'm here…" She looked him straight in the eye. "What I want is *you*."

"Hell."

She flinched. "I'm sorry if that makes things more difficult."

"Don't be. It's your directness, that's all. It blows me away."

She felt a rush of warmth. "I do want you, Blake. Very much."

"Your head—"

"Is on the mend." She paused, preempting him. "And yes, I'm sure."

His eyes flared sensuously. "Then do me a favor."

She moistened her mouth. "What?"

"Go upstairs and put your nightshirt on for me," he said, his voice turning heavy with huskiness.

She blinked in surprise. "My nightshirt?"

"You looked so sexy in it this morning. I've been thinking about it all day. It's been driving me crazy."

Sudden awareness danced in her veins. "Does this mean we're going to—"

"Have sex? Yes." A tiny pulse beat in his cheekbone. "But only if you're sure you can handle a purely sexual relationship," he said, giving her one last out.

Excitement washed over her. He still wanted her.

She nodded. "I can handle it, Blake."

"Then go change."

She got to her feet. It was now or never. And right now *never* definitely wasn't an option.

Samantha couldn't deny she was nervous as she came out of her room in her nightshirt and descended the staircase in a pair of high-heeled gold sandals she'd put on at the last moment. The bottom button was missing from her nightshirt, but the material covered her and what did it matter now anyway?

Blake had turned the lamps off and stood by the log fire, watching her in the flickering light with the same look he'd had on his face last Saturday night when she'd dressed for her date with Joel. She'd been trying to capture Blake's attention that night to make him jealous. Tonight she'd definitely caught more than his attention.

Tonight they both knew they would be a part of each other. The power of that thought stunned her.

"Come over here, Samantha," he said huskily when she reached the bottom step. The air throbbed between them and she quivered, moving forward without a falter as she made her away across the carpet to him.

His blue eyes moved slowly down over her, and something flared in them. "You're still missing the button," he said, as if to himself.

She blinked in surprise as she reached him. "You knew it was missing?"

"Oh, yes. It came off this morning in the bathroom… when I lifted you up on the sink."

She could feel herself go hot all over. "Oh. I hadn't realized."

"I know you didn't," he said, with a pointed look. He pulled her up against him. "God, you're so damn sexy, Samantha Thompson," he murmured, gathering her close. "My very sexy lady." His body was hard and she trembled. "Now, does that feel like I can turn myself off so easily?" he said thickly, his breath stirring over her face.

The solid warmth of him pressed against her stomach. "No." The word emerged on a whisper.

"There's no going back this time," he said, reassuring that this time he would not walk away.

The deepest longing stirred within her. "Kiss me, Blake."

He did.

Once…twice…long and slow…

And then he eased back and looked deep into her eyes.

She looked back at him.

Blue on blue.

"I want you in front of the fire," he murmured, sending her pulse jumping all over the place. "Here. Lie down on the cushions." She saw he had placed two big cushions near their feet. "Be careful of your head," he said, helping to lower her to the thick rug, so sweet and caring. She wanted to say it was too late, that she was about to lose her head anyway, only the words wouldn't come.

Soon she was lying there in her nightshirt and her gold sandals and he was standing over her in the firelight, his gaze scanning the full length of her, before stopping at the junction to her thighs. "You left your panties on," he mused throatily, telling her the front of her nightshirt must have fallen open at the hem.

She moistened her mouth. "I wanted to take them off, but…"

"I'll be happy to do the honors…" he said, and her heartbeat quickened, "but in a minute."

All at once she wanted him so much. "Take off your clothes first, Blake. Don't make me wait."

His eyes darkened and he dragged his sweater up over his head, along with his T-shirt, tossing them aside. He kicked off his shoes and his hands went to his belt.…

He hesitated.

"Your trousers, too." She was desperate to see him fully as a man for the first time, the thought making her lightheaded.

Another second, then his hands dropped away from the buckle. "Not yet." He dropped to his knees beside her, and let his gaze slide along the full length of her, like he was committing her to memory.

But his bare chest beckoned her and she reached

out to touch him, her fingers tingling as she came into contact with the dark whorls of hair over hard muscle. He groaned and slammed his hand over hers, stopping it from moving.

"Not yet," he repeated, putting her hand back down beside her.

And then with slow deliberation he began to undo her top button. She gasped as he undid another and slid her nightshirt off her shoulder a little. "I've wanted to do this since this morning," he murmured, lowering his head and trailing a kiss from the curve of her shoulder to her throat, then down to the valley between her breasts.

He inhaled deeply, then lifted his face and undid another button, exposing her breasts. Soon he was leaning over her, using his mouth to possess the tip of one nipple before moving to the other, gliding his tongue back and forth over them, imprinting them with his taste.

"Oh, my God," she muttered, shuddering at such an exquisite touch. "I…"

"Steady, my lovely." He shifted back a little. Another button undone allowed him to drift kisses along the exposed skin to her belly button. She shuddered again when he stroked his palm over her stomach, before the rest of the buttons were unfastened and the material finally parted, falling away to her sides and revealing her near-nakedness to him.

"Beautiful," he murmured, dipping his fingers under the waistband then peeling the panties down her body. By the time he'd finished, he'd moved to kneel between her thighs. She moaned faintly, suspecting a blush was rolling all the way down to her feet.

"So beautiful." He slowly reached out and slipped a

finger through the triangle of curls, making her gasp. "You like that?"

She moaned again. "Oh, yes."

For long, heart-stopping moments he toyed with her dampening skin, sending tremors through her. And then he slid his hands under her, cupping the cheeks of her bottom and tilting her lower body up to him, the satin material of her nightshirt falling away fully as his head lowered to the dark V at her thighs.

But before he touched, he stopped and looked up again, his eyes catching hers, holding still. He didn't speak or move a muscle, but there was a primitive look in his eyes that swept her breath away.

Slowly he lowered his head again and sought her out, his mouth beginning a slow worship of her femininity. She gasped as his tongue slid between her folds, teasing and tantalizing her, stroking her in erotic exploration, taking her to the brink, then bringing her back…once… twice…then finally he took her right over the edge, any remnants of her control disintegrating as she pulsed with the purest of pleasures.

Long moments later, she was still trying to recover when he rose to his feet and stripped off his trousers. She watched mesmerized as he put on a condom, thrilled that she had the power to make this man so hot and hard for her.

He was soon kneeling back down between her legs, and kissing his way right up the center of her until he found her mouth. He gave her one long kiss, then suddenly he was part of her.

In her.

She held him deep inside, finally one with Blake

Jarrod. She'd been waiting so long. It was the most wonderful feeling in the world.

He kissed her deeper as he began to thrust, long strokes time after time. Soon she began to tremble around him, toppling over the edge again, the flickering of the flames in the fireplace nothing compared to their own fire burning within.

Samantha lay amongst the cushions in front of the fire and watched Blake stride toward the downstairs bathroom. He'd covered her with the throw from the couch, and she enjoyed lying there watching his bare back and buttocks that were all firm muscle and arrestingly male.

She smiled to herself in the gentle glow from the fireplace. She couldn't believe it. She'd made love with Blake. She felt marvelous. He'd been so generous and loving and...

All at once, she found herself blinking back sudden tears. Their lovemaking had been so much more than sex. She hadn't admitted it to herself until now lest she back out, but when he'd said earlier they were having sex, something had gnawed at her as she'd gone up the stairs. It had sounded like they would merely be having sex for sex's sake. And while that was somewhat true, that wasn't what she was *only* about.

She'd known the same was true for Blake. He'd already proven that by not taking advantage this morning when he'd thought she was a virgin. She'd "made love" with Blake, despite love not being involved. There was respect between them and that was more important to her.

Right then she heard him coming back and she

quickly blinked away any suggestion of tears. He wouldn't want to know. Otherwise he'd think she *hadn't* been able to handle it, when it was merely because she hadn't expected to be quite so touched by all this.

He gave a sexy smile as he dropped down and leaned over to kiss her. "How do you feel?" he murmured, pulling back and looking into her eyes.

She was fully aware of his nakedness next to her. She could easily reach out and touch him. "Wonderful."

He looked pleased as he lifted the throw and slid under it to lie on his back, pulling her against his chest and kissing the top of her head but being careful of her injury. "Is that better?"

She was glad he couldn't look into her eyes. "Much."

He chuckled, his breath stirring her hair. "Who knew, eh?"

"What?"

"That we'd be so good together."

She'd never doubted it. "We work well together in business, so why not in bed?"

"True."

After that, they lay in quiet. The fire crackled and the clock on the wall ticked the seconds by. Samantha began to feel sleepy. There was no place she'd rather be in the world right now, she thought, as her eyelids drifted shut and she listened to the tick tock...tick tock...tick...*she loved him*...tock.

Startled, she jumped. Dear God, *she loved him*.

"What's wrong?"

Her brain stumbled. Panic whorled inside her. The ability to speak deserted her for a moment...and then somehow she pulled herself together. "What? Oh, nothing. I think I fell asleep too fast."

"Don't worry. There's no chance of that happening again just yet." He put his hand under her chin, lowering his head and lifting her mouth up to his. She quickly closed her eyes, hiding them from him, hiding her deepest secret. She'd betrayed him by falling in love with him. And she'd betrayed herself. She hadn't wanted to love him. She had never intended for that to happen.

Then he kissed her and the slow, delicious process of making love to her started again. She prayed to God for the strength not to reveal her love for this man who was leaving his mark on her like no one had ever done before. She couldn't afford to give her feelings away, or their relationship would be over before it had really begun. Wanting Blake had been hard enough.

Loving him was going to be intolerable.

Eight

Blake made love to her many times during the night, both downstairs and in his bed. Samantha had never known such bliss, but by the time the next morning rolled around and she'd gone back to her own room to get dressed for work, she had a thousand worries inside her head. She loved Blake and that presented so many problems. She'd virtually promised him she wouldn't fall for him. Now it seemed like she'd gone back on her word.

Worse, somewhere along the line she hadn't exactly "fallen" for him. No, she'd skipped that bit and had progressed straight to loving him. They'd worked together so closely these past two years, she already knew Blake was the type of man she admired and respected. And falling "in" love implied she could fall "out" of love with him—like she'd done with Carl. With

Blake, she knew there would be no retracting her love for him.

If only she could.

Oh, God, loving Blake had taken her further with her emotions than she'd ever dared venture. And now she had to survive until she could leave for good. She had to remain tough. She would constantly have to keep something of herself back. Last night during their lovemaking, she'd only managed to keep a lid on it through sheer terror—only by telling herself he would run in the other direction if he knew how deep her feelings went. Talk about emotional involvement on her part!

And now more than ever she had to leave at the end of her month's contract. She couldn't stay permanently. Blake had been honest enough to admit he couldn't handle emotional involvement and she believed him. If he discovered she loved him, he'd be horrified. He'd probably have her on the next plane out of Aspen before she could blink. Even if he didn't, she couldn't risk giving him such a strong emotive power over her. A power he might use in and out of the bedroom to get her to stay.

For all the wrong reasons.

Yet would Blake manipulate her in such a way? He was, after all, the man she loved. An honorable man. Would he really do any of those things? Her heart remembered his generous lovemaking and said no. Her head remembered the hard businessman and said maybe.

Making love to a woman certainly changed things, Blake decided as he watched Samantha eat breakfast in the hotel restaurant. He'd sat opposite her like this many times in the last two years but it had always been about work. Now all he could think about was being inside her again.

She'd been so generously tight last night when he'd finally buried himself in her softness. It had almost sent him straight into orgasm. Only the need to give her more pleasure had held him back. Never before had that happened to him. He'd always made sure his partner had been fulfilled before taking his own pleasure, but this time her pleasure had been totally his. It had been the ultimate experience for him. How could that other man—that Carl—not have wanted her in his bed? Idiot!

"Tell me something, Blake," she said, cutting into his thoughts as he buttered a slice of toast.

"Anything." Well, not quite anything. He wasn't up for a meaningful discussion this morning. He merely wanted to sit here and soak up this beautiful woman in front of him.

She tilted her brunette head to one side. "Did you tell Andy to add the candles last night at dinner?"

He was relieved at the simple question. "Sorry, no. I wasn't planning on seduction. At least, not until I was sure you could handle becoming my lover." He smiled. "I'll light you some candles tonight, though."

A feathery blush ran across her cheeks but she looked pleased. "I've just realized something. You're a romantic, Blake Jarrod."

"Sometimes." He liked to romance a woman as much as the next guy. "But don't get the wrong idea that I'm a softie."

She nodded. "Got it. Hard in business. Good in bed."

He gave a low laugh. "I like that assessment." He also liked to think he was both things in and out of bed, but he wouldn't embarrass her further. Not here.

But tonight...

"I keep forgetting to mention this," she said, "but I haven't thanked you for taking such good care of me the other night."

"Oh, I think you did thank me," he said pointedly. "And you can thank me again later."

"Blake!" she hissed, but he could see she was enjoying this sexual interplay.

"What?" he drawled. "I'm just saying—"

A figure appeared at their table. "There you are, Sam," Joel said, giving them both a smile but causing Blake's mouth to clamp shut. "I'm glad I caught you. How are you this morning? How's the head?"

"Fine, Joel. No aftereffects at all," she assured the doctor.

"You're taking things easy, I hope?"

Her eyes made a quick dart across the table then back up at the other man. "Yes." Her cheeks had grown a little warm and that in itself appeased Blake.

"Good. Then how about we take in that movie tonight?"

She looked at Blake again. "Oh, Joel, I'm sorry, I can't."

"Tomorrow night, then?"

Blake held his tongue. He wanted to lay claim to Samantha and tell the other man to shove off, but he'd first give her the opportunity to do it.

"Um, Joel. Perhaps not." She shifted in her seat. "I'm returning to Vegas in less than two weeks' time and then I'm going home to Pasadena for good once I wrap things up there. So, you see, there's a lot to be done here right now. I need to work full-on with Blake until then."

Blake was dumbfounded.

"You're leaving?" the other man said, sounding shocked, echoing Blake's thoughts. "I can't believe that."

Another echo of his thoughts.

She looked slightly uncomfortable. "Yes, I know. I'm sorry I didn't tell you, but it was something that hadn't been finalized until now."

Joel gave a small nod. "I understand. Maybe we can get together in Pasadena sometime in the future? We'll at least have to get together for coffee before you leave."

She slipped him a smile. "That would be lovely."

Blake was vaguely aware of the other man walking away from the table, but he only had eyes for one person. "Samantha," he growled. "What the hell is going on?"

Her look seemed cagey. "I didn't want him knowing the truth. Our affair is our business and no one else's."

Anger stirred inside him. "I'm not talking about our affair, and you know it. Dammit, don't tell me you don't know what I'm talking about."

She lifted her chin. "You're talking about me still leaving," she clarified. "I'm sorry, Blake. Did you think that I would change my mind?"

"Yes, I damn well did." He'd expected her to stay now, not because he'd enticed her into staying but because she *wanted* to. And hell, she didn't seem to understand that he'd made a big concession in not seducing her in the bathroom yesterday morning. Now it felt like she'd slapped him in the face. He'd given. She'd taken. And now she was giving nothing back.

"But why, Blake? Our lovemaking hasn't changed

anything. We both decided it would only be physical and nothing more. No commitment, remember?"

Her words appeared to be reasonable, but for all that she had a peculiar look in her eyes he couldn't decipher. "That's still got nothing to do with you leaving."

"Doesn't it? I was leaving before we made love and I'm still leaving, so what's changed?"

Damn her. She was right. Even so, he couldn't explain it. He just knew something *had* changed and he didn't want to decode it. He just wanted her to stay and enjoy what they had for a while. They could at least get a couple of months together. Why leave while the going was good?

She shot him an unexpected candid look. "Blake, you asked me if I could handle a sexual relationship, and I said I could. It sounds to me like *you* aren't handling it."

His mouth tightened. "I'm handling it."

She shook her head. "No, I don't—"

"Blake," a male voice called out, and Blake instantly knew who it was. He stiffened. Damn the world! His twin brother was the last person he wanted to see. Guy had always understood him—sometimes more than he understood himself. Right now wasn't a good time to put that to the test.

He shot to his feet, turned and headed for the private elevator. "It'll have to wait until later, Guy," he muttered, striding past his brother.

Guy's steps faltered as he approached the table. Then as he came closer, he looked at Samantha with mild amusement. "Was it something I said?" he quipped in that easygoing way of his.

Samantha couldn't smile if her life depended on it. "He's got a lot on his mind."

Guy sobered. "Yeah, I know." He sent her a penetrating look that reminded her of Blake. "I hear you're leaving."

She nodded, still surprised word had gotten around the family so fast, and even more surprised that they were genuinely sorry to see her go. It wasn't like she was a friend of the family...or marrying into it.

"I'm glad I saw you," Guy said, drawing her back to the moment. "Avery and I would like to have you around for dinner before you go."

Somehow she managed a faint smile. "That would be very nice."

"Blake, too, of course." Silence, then, "He'll miss you when you leave."

"Maybe." *Maybe not.* "I'll find him an excellent replacement."

"It won't be the same."

Her throat constricted. "He'll get over it." She stood up. "You'll have to excuse me, Guy. I need to start work. There's a lot to do."

Guy stepped back and let her pass, but he was frowning and she could feel his eyes on her all the way out the eatery. Thankfully she had a few moments of privacy as the elevator took her to the top floor.

If only Blake wanted her to stay because he loved her, then things would be perfect. But for him this was only about two things—the job and sex. It wasn't about love. She sighed. She'd have to be crazy to think he would make a commitment. And she hadn't wanted a commitment before anyway, so why the heck was she even considering it now?

She must have rocks in her head.

Or have been hit *on* the head with a rock. It must have caused more damage than she'd thought. Why else would she be unwise enough to love a man who wouldn't let himself love in return? That bruise must have addled more than her brain. It had addled her heart.

Thankfully Blake's door was shut when she entered her office so she sat at her desk. Come to think of it, she felt a little better knowing she had hoisted Blake with his own petard. That was rather clever of her. He'd sprouted all that talk about not getting emotionally involved, but clearly his emotions *were* involved, albeit not enough and not the ones that mattered most to her.

They didn't entail love.

God was merciful just then, when not only did the phone start to ring but one of the staff who had a meeting with Blake walked into her office. Samantha got busy, putting on her professional persona as she placed the caller on hold, buzzing Blake on the intercom to tell him his first appointment was here. At his request, she ushered the staff member into his office, all the while keeping her face neutral whenever she looked at her boss. He seemed equally as disinterested in her, though she knew otherwise. What he was and what he seemed were two different things. She could recognize that in another person. After all, wasn't she an expert at the same thing?

Midmorning while Blake was busy at a staff meeting in the Great Room, Samantha picked up the telephone with a heavy heart and did what she had to do. She called Mary Wentworth back and spoke to her about a replacement. The other woman was surprised to hear she was leaving, but was more than happy to help. Mary promised she would e-mail some résumés of suitable applicants within a few hours.

Blake returned after the meeting, formally asked if there were any messages, then strode straight into his office. Samantha's heart sank at how cold he was, but there was nothing she could do about it. She still had to leave.

At lunchtime she had some sandwiches sent up from the kitchen, and Blake made it apparent that he preferred to eat at his desk by himself, with his door closed between them. Usually they ate together while discussing work. Or if they ate at their own desks, the door remained open.

Not this time.

And that was fine with her, she decided, growing more and more upset. She needed a filter to stop the waves of anger coming out of his office anyway. To clear her head, she went for a walk in the fresh air. Blake didn't ask where she'd been when she returned and she didn't offer. It was plain to see he was no longer concerned about her.

By late afternoon, Samantha had had enough of his attitude. He'd chastised her after she'd put through a call he hadn't wanted to take. He'd found fault with a letter she'd typed up for his signature. And he'd told her to go recheck some figures on a report that she knew were correct.

When she brought the report back, she deliberately placed another folder on top of it.

His head shot up. "What's this?"

"Résumés. They all come highly recommended."

His lips flattened. "I didn't ask you to do this."

She angled her chin. "It's what you pay me to do."

"I pay you to do what you're told."

She gasped, then held herself rigid. "That's unfair of you. You don't mind me being proactive in other things with my job. It's why I'm such a good assistant and you know it."

"We're talking fairness now, are we? *You're* the one leaving *me*. How fair is that?"

"I'm not leaving *you*, Blake," she lied. "Anyway, don't take it personally, remember? That's what you said to me when you reminded me of my contract obligations."

He muttered a curse, but for Samantha the last straw had already broken the camel's back. "I can't continue under these conditions, Blake. If you won't treat me right, then I'll pack my things and leave tonight. And I don't care if you take me to court for breach of contract either." She hesitated, but only for a second. "I believe I could make a good case for justifying my leaving anyway, considering the personal turn our relationship has taken."

There was a lengthy silence.

His eyes challenged hers. "Would you go that far?"

She gave a jerky nod. "If pushed I would. Don't doubt that."

He held her gaze with narrowed eyes.

And then suddenly something happened and a suspicion of admiration began to glint in them. "Way to go!" he said softly, startling her. "You're a tough little madam. I always knew you could hold your own in your job, but I never thought to see the day when you used it against *me*."

A little of the tension went out of her. "So things will return to normal?" she asked cautiously.

"No."

Her heart dropped.

"Things can never be normal between us again. Not since last night." He drew a long breath, as if taking a moment before making a decision. "I don't want to see you go, but I don't want to keep you here against your will either. If you want to go then I have to accept it."

It wasn't what she wanted at all.

It was what she *had* to do.

"Thank you, Blake."

"But at least stay until your contract runs out." He waited a moment. "I'm not asking for the job and I'm not asking for the sex. I'm asking for *me*."

She caught her breath. This was the best she could hope for, the best it could get, and she wasn't about to argue with that. She would take her happiness where she could.

A whisper of joy filled her. "Okay, yes. I'll stay until my contract runs out, Blake," she said, and watched him let out a shuddering breath that touched her greatly. He really *did* want her to stay so that he could be with her.

Clearly satisfied now they were back on an even keel, he leaned back in his chair with a look she had no trouble translating. "Go over there and lock the door."

A tiny shiver of anticipation went down her spine. "Blake, I can't… I don't…"

"You can." His eyes turned deeper blue. "I seriously need to make love to you, Samantha."

Her heart tilted. Oh, she wanted that, too. She darted a look at the door. "The others—"

"Will think we don't want to be disturbed." He gave a crooked smile. "And they'd be right." He waited a moment. "You can always race into my washroom if anyone comes."

Wanting this…wanting him…she went and locked the heavy wood door, but ducked her head out into her office first to make sure no one was there. "I can't believe I'm doing this," she muttered, turning the lock.

"Don't think about it." He looked amused and she decided that if he wanted her, then he was going to have her. And she would wipe that amusement right off his face.

Fingers going to the buttons of her long-sleeved blouse, she began to undo each one as she approached him across the plush carpet.

One eyebrow lifted. "Are you teasing me, Miss Thompson?"

"Actually I think I am."

He smiled, and she smiled, then his smile started to slip as she completely undid the blouse, leaving it hanging open over her black bra. She marveled at where this seductress in her was coming from, but didn't let it deter her. She wasn't about to waste a minute of it.

She reached the side of the desk. "More?"

"Oh, yeah."

"You're the boss."

Her hands were shaking a little as she slid the zipper of her slacks down, pushing them and her panties all the way to the floor, then stepped out of them. She heard a rasping sound escape Blake's throat and there was a blaze in his eyes that seemed to emit from his whole body.

Gratified by his reaction…satisfied by his amusement now turned to desire…she climbed onto his lap, knees on either side of his thighs, her blouse covering her bra—and then only just.

After that, passion overtook all rational thoughts and the air hummed with soft, sensual sounds.

Nine

They dined together back at Pine Lodge, then made love again that night, and when Samantha woke the next morning she lay there and wallowed in a sense of occasion. Her memories of them together like this were all she could take away with her. Her heart, she would leave with Blake.

He woke up then and made slow love to her again. Afterward she put on a bright face and they went about their business as usual, neither of them showing any outward sign to the others that they were lovers. They hadn't discussed it, but Samantha was glad about it. Already his family seemed to have taken a special interest in them, and she didn't want anyone guessing she loved him.

Late morning, Samantha left her office and went down to the hotel kitchen to get some fresh milk for their coffee. She could have phoned down for it but she needed to stretch her legs.

In the hallway, she ran into Erica. They chatted a few moments but Samantha could see the other woman was preoccupied. "Erica, is something wrong?"

Erica wrinkled her nose. "Yes, unfortunately. I've been arranging a surprise party for tonight for this man who lives in town. It's for his wife's fortieth birthday and she thinks she's coming here for dinner." She clicked her tongue. "I've been working on this for weeks."

"So what's the problem?"

"We've got a DJ for later in the evening, but the husband particularly asked for someone to play piano music in the background during the meal, and now the piano player has come down sick." Her smooth forehead creased as she began thinking out loud. "The DJ could probably play some soft music as an alternative, but I really don't want to disappoint the husband. He said his wife loves the piano and he wants to give her the best party. I was hoping there might be someone in town I could find, but it's probably too late."

All the while she was talking, Samantha's heart began thumping with a mixture of excitement and panic. "You may not believe this," she said, not believing she was actually saying this, "but I can help."

Erica's eyes brightened. "You can? Do you know someone who plays the piano?"

"Yes." *Did she really want to say this?* "Me."

Erica stopped and blinked. "*You* play the piano?" She grimaced. "Sorry, that came out wrong. I just mean—"

Samantha smiled a little. "I know what you meant."

Regardless, Erica still looked doubtful. "You *really* play the piano?"

Samantha nodded. "Yes, *really*."

"You're sure?"

Samantha chuckled as her anxiety faded. "Lead the way to the piano and I'll show you. Just don't expect perfection. I have to tell you I'm a bit rusty."

Erica began to grin. "As long as it's not 'Chopsticks,' then I'll be happy. Follow me."

A few minutes later, Samantha did a warm-up then started playing a quick medley of popular tunes. Her fingers felt a bit stiff because she hadn't played since last Christmas at home in Pasadena, but she was soon enjoying herself—and enjoying the look on Erica's face.

"That's wonderful!" Erica murmured, once the music ended.

Samantha smiled with relief that she hadn't lost her touch nor made a fool of herself. "Thanks, but it's nothing special."

Erica shook her head. "No, you're very good."

"Not really."

"Yes, *really*," Erica teased. "Good Lord, I didn't know we had Liberace living here at the resort."

Samantha laughed. "Just be grateful my mother made me take piano lessons growing up."

"Oh, I am. Play some more, Samantha." All at once Erica's eyes widened and she chuckled. "Oh, my God, I don't believe I'm about to say this but 'play it again, Sam.'"

Samantha laughed. She knew she needed the practice so she was happy to oblige and felt more confident with each touch of the keys.

Afterward, they talked for five minutes then Samantha continued on her way to get the milk. Blake had a business lunch in town and had already left by the time she returned to the office, so she didn't get to tell him about it all until late afternoon.

He fell back in his chair. "*You* play the piano?"

A wry smile tugged at her mouth. "Why is that so far-fetched?"

"I don't know." Then he shook his head as if he wasn't hearing right. "Let me get this straight. *You're* going to play the piano at a party here at the resort tonight?"

She shrugged. "It's just background music during dinner." But she wasn't quite so calm inside, and talking about it now was making her kind of nervous.

He tilted his head at her. "Why didn't you tell me you could play the piano?"

"It wasn't a job requirement," she joked, more to calm her growing anxiety than anything.

His mouth quirked. "No, I guess it wasn't."

Her humor over, she bit her lip. "Actually, do you mind if I leave a little early? I need to get myself ready and I'd like some time to myself."

He gave a wayward smile. "You creative types are all alike."

"Blake—"

"Feel free to leave early," he agreed. Then his eyes slowly settled on her mouth. "But before you go…" Hunger jumped the distance between them. "I do think there is one requirement of your job that needs revisiting."

She knew what he was getting at. Her heart raced with a growing excitement. "Blake, we can't make love in here every afternoon."

"Who said we can't?"

"But I have to go now," she said, knowing she was weakening.

"In a minute," he murmured, sending her an intimate look across the desk. "Come and give me a kiss goodbye first."

She wagged a finger at him. "That's all, Blake. One kiss and no more."

"Trust me."

She moved toward him. "Okay…"

Half an hour later she left the office a very satisfied woman, amused at how easily she had fallen for his trickery. Of course, she couldn't fully blame her boss. She'd *wanted* to fall for it.

"Lady, you're far too dangerous to let loose on our male guests," Blake said, watching Samantha step into high heels. She wore a beaded jacket over black evening pants that flattered her slim figure, and she'd curled the brunette strands of her hair into a bubbly halo around her gorgeous face.

"You think I look okay?"

"More than okay. You'll knock 'em dead." He stepped closer and went to pull her toward him but she put a hand against his chest, stopping him.

"Wait! You'll mess up my lipstick."

Blake was amused. "I'd like to mess up more than your lipstick, beautiful."

Her blue eyes smiled back at him. "You already did that this afternoon. 'Trust me,' remember?"

He gave a low chuckle. "I remember." Even now he felt the stirrings of desire, so he stepped away from temptation. "Come on. I'll drive you up to the Manor."

"I can call the valet."

"That's okay. I want to look over those documents Gavin gave me about the new bungalow. It'll be a good chance to study them without the phones ringing." It was an excuse but she looked so good that he wanted to make sure she got home okay. If anyone hit on her they'd be sorry.

Ten minutes later they walked down the corridor toward the ballroom, but as they got closer she suddenly stopped. "Blake, please. Don't come in with me. You'll only make me more nervous."

"Okay. I'll be in the office until you're ready to go home."

"But—"

He leaned forward and dropped a kiss on her forehead. "I'll wait for you."

He looked up and saw Erica and Christian coming toward them. They were a distance away so he nodded at them then turned and walked in the other direction, taking the private elevator up to the office. He didn't care that they'd seen the kiss. He *did* care that they might think Samantha was his weak spot.

Christian had proven his integrity months ago, but the other man had his own weak point—Erica. It could make him blind to whatever his fiancée was up to, Blake thought, then winced. She may not be up to anything at all, he corrected, aware his hard attitude toward his half sister was diminishing with each passing day.

Yet he couldn't discount Erica was fooling him as well as Christian, though he was feeling less and less that was the case. He was usually a pretty good judge of character—when emotions weren't involved. Unfortunately finding out he had a half sister *had* brought out an emotional response in him. He hadn't liked that.

And he didn't like the emotional response he was feeling now as he sat down at his desk and saw the file with the résumés. It all came back that Samantha was actually going to leave. It had either been let her go in three weeks' time or lose her now. He hadn't been able to bear the thought of the latter.

And he wasn't up to reading those résumés right now either, he decided, putting them to the side. He would deal with it when he had to and not before.

He wasn't sure how long he'd been working when he heard piano music drift up from the bottom floor. He sat back in his chair and listened. Samantha was clearly talented as she went from one tune to another, even throwing in some classical music. He heard clapping at the end of that one, though whether it was for Samantha or in honor of the birthday guest, he wasn't sure. The music started up in another medley of popular tunes, so he figured it was for Samantha.

And rightly so.

Unable to stop himself, he knew he had to see her play in person and not merely listen from afar. He got up from his desk and went downstairs, hearing the clink of glasses and cutlery and the murmur of voices, but it was the music that drew him as he approached the ballroom.

Pushing open one of the large doors, he slipped inside and stood at the back, watching people half listening and half talking as Samantha played another piece of classical music. She didn't see him, but she appeared totally at ease at the piano, concentrating on the music, her hands flowing across the keys, looking very feminine and beautiful. Suddenly he was so proud of her that a lump rose in his throat.

"She's good," a female voice murmured, and he glanced sideways at an attractive woman in her late thirties who'd come to stand beside him.

He wasn't interested. "Yes," he said, looking back at Samantha.

"You're new here." She thrust a manicured hand in front of him. "I'm Clarice, by the way."

It would have been rude not to shake her hand, but he still wasn't interested. "Blake." He wished the woman would leave him alone so that he could concentrate on Samantha.

"Do you know the guest of honor?"

For a moment he thought she meant Samantha, then he realized she was talking about the birthday lady. "A casual acquaintance." He didn't feel the need to explain.

"I went to boarding school with Anne. We've been lifelong friends."

"That's great." The music ended on a high note and everyone started to clap and it gave him the chance to move away. "Excuse me," he said, taking a step.

Clarice put her hand on his arm, stopping him. "Would you care to have a drink later?"

He'd been approached like this many times but for some reason now he found it distasteful, though he hid it. He only wanted to see Samantha. "I'm sorry," he said, being as nice as possible so as not to offend. "Not tonight." He walked away.

And headed straight for Samantha getting up from the piano. She was laughing as some people rushed to talk to her, and as Blake weaved his way through the tables he could only think how much she lit up the room.

Then she saw him. "Blake," she murmured, her blue eyes lighting up *for him,* sending an extraordinary feeling soaring inside his chest.

He reached her and put his hand on her elbow. "I think the lady needs a drink," he told the group at large, making no apologies as he led her away.

"What are you doing here?" she said as he took her over to the bar.

"I could hear the music upstairs. It drew me to you." He paused. "I'm totally in awe of you," he murmured, pleased to see a hint of dusky rose color her cheeks.

"Thank you," she said in a breathy voice.

For a moment they held one another's gaze.

"Samantha," Erica said, rushing up to them and kissing Samantha on the cheek. "You were wonderful!" In her excitement she kissed Blake's cheek, too. "Isn't she wonderful, Blake?"

For a split second he froze at Erica's friendliness, but then he found himself relenting toward her even more. Anyone who liked Samantha so much deserved a little more consideration.

He gave his half sister his first ever warm smile. "Yes, she's pretty wonderful."

Erica seemed a little taken aback at his friendliness, but her self-possession soon returned as she spoke to Samantha. "The minute you started playing this afternoon, I knew you were good."

Samantha laughed as she looked from one to the other. "Do either of you have an ear for music?"

"We know a class act when we see it," Erica said, then winked at her half brother. "Don't you agree, Blake?"

Blake nodded, his gaze returning to Samantha and resting there. "I couldn't agree more," he said, as everything inside him went still.

Samantha was class all the way.

Just then, the real guest of honor and her husband came up to thank Samantha for playing so beautifully. Then Anne asked Samantha if she'd play her a special piece of classical music.

And as Blake watched Samantha start to play the piano again, he realized this woman could be destined for better things than being his assistant. He wasn't an expert at piano playing by any means, but he knew when something sounded good. It hit home then that he had no right to keep her here and hold her back from what could be her true vocation. He really did have to let her go. Somewhere at the back of his mind he'd still believed she wouldn't leave. Now he knew different.

"You're amazingly good at playing the piano," he said later, once they were inside Pine Lodge and alone together.

She sent him an amused glance as she took off her coat. "Don't start that again."

He frowned as he took off his own coat and hung it on the rack. "I don't understand why you didn't take your music further. I'm sure you could be a world-class pianist."

She lifted her shoulders in a shrug. "I'm an average pianist. I know my limitations."

He'd been raised to push himself to the limit. "Aren't you putting those limitations on yourself?"

She shook her head. "No, I don't think I am. There are lots of mildly talented people who don't take it all the way. It doesn't mean they're wasting their lives. They can use it in other ways. Some people teach. Some people play for themselves. Others play at parties," she said, her lips curving wryly.

"But—"

She put her hand against his chest. "I don't have the passion for it, Blake. Really, I don't. I like to play occasionally but that's all."

He finally understood what she was saying, but the world had better look out if she ever decided to further her talent.

He felt her palm still against his chest. "What *do* you have a passion for?" he said huskily, bringing it back to the two of them as much as he could. That's what he would focus on from now on. Them and only them.

She rubbed herself against him, seeming to delight in making him aware of her. "Right now? You."

By the time they reached the bedroom they were both naked. After they made love, he pulled her into his arms and let her sleep, but listening to her soft breathing, he admitted to himself that never before had he felt as comfortable after making love to a woman as he did right then. This woman felt right at home in his arms.

And he wasn't sure he should like the feeling.

Ten

One advantage of sleeping with the boss was that she didn't have to jump out of bed and hurry to get to work, Samantha thought lazily, after she woke late the next morning and lay in Blake's arms. He was still asleep.

Then he moved a little and she tilted her head back to look up at him. "You're awake?" she said unnecessarily.

He opened his eyes. "I have been for a while."

That surprised her. Usually the minute he woke up he made love to her.

"Is something wrong?"

"No," he said, but she felt his chest muscles tighten beneath her.

She saw that he had a closed look about him. Something must be on his mind, though she didn't know what. He'd been fine when they'd made love last night. Now he seemed…distant.

She could only think something had occurred to him during the night and upset him. For some reason a wall had been erected between them now. Then she remembered how Erica and Christian had seen him kiss her on the forehead before the party. It hadn't been a passionate kiss but it was clearly more than friendship. So perhaps Blake minded that his family knew about them now? As far as she could tell, it was the only thing that had changed overnight.

"Erica and Christian probably realize we're lovers now," she said, testing the waters.

"They'd be stupid if they didn't." It wasn't said nastily, but it still made her wonder.

She tilted her head back a little. "You don't mind?" He'd looked more at ease with Erica last night. He'd actually seemed to like his half sister.

"Why should I?"

"True." She swallowed. "I'm leaving soon so it doesn't matter anyway, does it?" she said, trying to get a reaction out of him. *Any* reaction. One that didn't lock her out.

There was nothing.

Feeling disheartened, she pushed herself out of bed and hurried to the shower, a tightness in her throat. Their remaining time together was so short. She didn't want to spend it like this.

No sooner had she stepped under the spray than he opened the sliding doors. "What's the matter?" he said, frowning at her.

She thanked goodness the water streaming over her head hid any tears that threatened. "Nothing."

His look said he didn't believe her as he stepped inside the cubicle and joined her. He didn't say a word, and he had a fixed look about him as he soaped them both up and then made love to her with an urgency that startled her. By the end of it she was none the wiser, but at least she knew he still wanted her.

Her heart twisted inside her then. As much as it was a compliment to her, was he still refusing to accept that she was leaving? If so, he was only making it harder for himself. They *both* had to accept it, she thought, her heart aching at the thought.

She managed a blank face as they went to the manor for breakfast. It was either that or cry, and she couldn't allow herself that luxury.

As they entered the lobby, a woman practically jumped out at them. "Blake Jarrod!" she exclaimed, in a you-are-a-naughty-boy tone. "You didn't tell me you owned this hotel." Her gaze slid to Samantha, "Or that your assistant was the piano player."

Blake put on a practiced smile but Samantha could tell he didn't like the woman. "It's Clarice, isn't it?" he said, making it clear he wasn't interested. "This is my assistant *and* piano player," he mocked, "Samantha."

Samantha inclined her head and the woman gave her a cool smile. "I'm Clarice Richardson. Mrs. Clarice Richardson, but I'm *divorced*." Her gaze slid to Blake, instantly dismissing Samantha. "I was wondering, Blake. How would you like to have that drink tonight?"

Blake shook his head. "Can't do, I'm afraid. I have a prior commitment tonight."

"Then how about a cup of coffee now?" the woman said, not giving up. "I have a free morning. In fact, I'm free for the whole day. I'm looking for someone to take me for a drive to Independence Pass."

"Sorry, but I have to get to work."

Clarice gave a tinkle of a laugh that grated on Samantha's nerves. "But you're the boss."

"Which is exactly why I'd better do some work," he said smoothly, then put his hand under Samantha's elbow. "If you'll excuse us."

"Oh. Of course," Clarice said, but Samantha saw her mouth purse with irritation as they walked away.

Then she realized Blake was walking her to the elevator instead of the eatery. "Aren't we having breakfast?"

"We'll get something sent up."

She gave a soft laugh. "Don't tell me you're scared of Mrs. Richardson?"

He shot her a wry look that said he wasn't scared of anyone. "No, but I don't want to deal with her."

"She's persistent, that's for sure." Samantha paused, thinking about something as they stepped inside the elevator and the doors shut. "So you're going out tonight?" She didn't want to sound demanding like Clarice, but as his lover she hoped *she* had a temporary claim on his time right now.

"No, I'm staying home. *You're* my prior commitment."

"I am?" Relief went through her.

He slipped his hand around her waist and pulled her hip against his. "And if I go for a drive to Independence Pass it will be with only one lady."

"Melissa?" she teased.

"You." He kissed her quickly on the mouth just as the doors started to open.

They met Erica as they stepped out of the elevator and into the corridor. She came hurrying forward with a big smile on her face. "Samantha, I want to thank you once again for the fabulous job you did last night."

Samantha returned the smile. "You're very welcome, Erica. I enjoyed it."

Erica considered her. "You know, I've already had a call from the president of the local music school. They heard about you and want to meet with you," she said enthusiastically, making Samantha's heart sink. "They have this huge summer festival where nearly a thousand students and faculty come together from far and wide. There's orchestral concerts and chamber music and—"

Samantha had to stop her there. "I'm sorry, Erica. It wouldn't be any use. I'm leaving soon." She felt Blake stiffen beside her.

Erica's eyes widened. "Oh, I thought—"

Blake muttered something about starting work and stalked off. For a moment Samantha wondered if he was still thinking about her not taking her piano playing seriously, but she soon dismissed it. This wasn't about her not playing the piano. It was about her leaving.

Erica looked at her and winced. "Sorry if I said something out of place."

Samantha tried to smile. "You didn't." She started to follow him. "But I'd better get to work."

Blake was closing his door behind him as she entered her office, and Samantha's heart sank. So. They were back to that again. Talk about a temperamental boss!

Shortly after, he buzzed her for coffee. When she took it into him he seemed okay if a little preoccupied, and she realized she was reading more into this than she should. He had the resort issues to concentrate on and was trying to get the feel for it, that's all. Besides, just because she was now his lover, it shouldn't upgrade her status from his assistant. On the contrary, here at work she'd be upset if it did.

Around eleven he opened his door and strode through her office, scowling. "I'll be with Trevor in his office." He left before she could make any acknowledgement.

Getting to her feet, she went to empty Blake's out tray. There were some letters he'd signed and…all at once she noticed he'd been reading through the files with the résumés. Her heart dropped. That file had sat on his desk untouched all day yesterday, but now he must be thinking ahead.

She should be pleased he wouldn't be left without an assistant, but she could only feel upset. And that was made worse as she went back to her desk and opened the agenda for tomorrow's meeting and saw one of the items was to discuss her replacement.

Oh, God.

So she didn't need Clarice to make a sudden appearance in her office about fifteen minutes later. "Mrs. Richardson, how did you get up here?" she asked, as the woman came toward her desk. A card key was needed for both the private elevator and the back stairs.

"I told one of the staff that I urgently needed to see the person in charge. And I do."

After seeing how Clarice had operated downstairs with Blake, the other woman would have refused to take no for an answer. More than likely she'd even given the staff member a monetary "donation."

Samantha frowned. She would deal with the security breach later. "This is a private area. You shouldn't be here at all. If you needed anything, you should ask at the front desk."

The woman sent her a haughty look. "I'd prefer to deal with Blake, Miss…"

"Thompson." Samantha recognized being put in her place. "Blake's not here at the moment," she said his name deliberately, "but I can pass on a message when he gets back. Now let me walk you to the elevator."

Clarice looked disappointed. Then, "I'll give you my room number." She picked up a sticky-note pad from the desk and wrote on it. "You'll make sure you tell him Clarice called, won't you?" she said, tearing off the slip of paper and handing it to Samantha.

"Of course."

Clarice went to turn away then spun back. "Tell him that I have a proposition for him," she said in a breathless voice.

"Fine." There was nothing to worry about with Blake, but it annoyed Samantha to have to deal with another woman who threw herself at him. There had been so many of them over the years. Clarice was very attractive, but so were the other women who had chased Blake.

Samantha stayed at her desk and waited for Blake to return for lunch. Knowing she was being contrary, she was still upset that he was looking at replacing her, and now she just wanted to spend more time with him. But he didn't return until after lunch, and she spent a quiet lunch break by herself.

"There's a plate of sandwiches on your desk," she said when he walked back through to his office.

"I ate lunch with Trevor."

It would have been nice to be told, she decided, then admitted to herself that as her boss, Blake didn't owe her his time.

She followed him into his office. "Here are your

messages. You'll see there's one from Mrs. Richardson." When his face remained blank, she said, "Clarice."

He let out a heavy sigh. "What does she want?"

"For you to call her. She delivered it in person."

He scowled. "How did she get up here?"

Samantha told him. "I've passed on my concern to the front desk. They're going to look into it."

He nodded. "Good."

"By the way, Clarice left her room number for you to call her back. She says to tell you she has a proposition for you."

"A proposition?" He grimaced. "I bet she does."

Samantha picked up the plate of sandwiches and put them in the refrigerator near her desk, feeling better that Clarice hadn't fooled him. Not that she expected he wouldn't see through it all. He knew more about women than she did herself.

It was fairly quiet for the next two hours as Blake returned messages and she typed up some reports. Then, he came out carrying his coat. "I have to go into town for a meeting. It'll take a few hours."

She almost asked if she could go with him, then stopped. Her place as his assistant was here.

Suddenly he came over and kissed her hard. "I'll see you later at the lodge. We can go out for dinner if you like."

She shook her head, pleased. "No, let's eat in. I'll get something from the hotel kitchen on the way home."

His eyes flickered, and she suspected he'd noticed her mention of the word *home*. "Okay." He left.

Not long after that, Samantha decided to go down to the kitchen to see about tonight's dinner. She took the plate of sandwiches down to the front desk, as one of the staff might appreciate them for later, rather than throwing them in the trash.

She was walking through the lobby toward the front desk when out of the corner of her eye she happened to glance over at the bar. Her heart stuttered. Blake and Clarice were sitting in there having a drink. Both of them were focused on each other, though she noted Clarice was leaning toward him and doing the talking, more with her cleavage than not. Was this where the other woman offered her "proposition?"

So much for his appointment in town, Samantha thought, not sure what she was doing as she spun around and headed back to her office, giving herself time to adjust to what she'd seen. She had to put this into perspective.

Okay, so there was probably nothing to it, but she just didn't like that Blake was telling her one thing, then doing another. And wasn't he getting Clarice's hopes up even by sitting with the woman? Then again, he was a free man and once *she* left Aspen he would get lonely. The other woman was certainly beautiful.

Samantha threw the sandwiches in the trash, unable to face going back downstairs again. Instead, she phoned the kitchen and ordered two meals for dinner, though she wasn't sure she would feel hungry.

Blake seemed lost in thought when he returned to the lodge that evening, so Samantha didn't mention it straightaway. Besides, she didn't want to sound like a harping wife.

She managed to wait until they had almost finished dinner before saying offhand, "By the way, Blake. Next time you *don't* plan on having a drink with Mrs. Richardson, don't do it in the bar."

His eyes narrowed. "What does that mean?" he said coolly, thankfully not looking the least bit guilty.

"I saw you with her," she said, still keeping her voice casual.

He frowned. "So?"

She lifted one shoulder. "I just thought it odd that you weren't 'free' to spend time with her...and then you were."

He had an arrested expression, before a look of male satisfaction crossed his face. "You sound jealous."

She tried not to look flustered. If he thought she was jealous then he might realize she was more emotionally involved with him than she was letting on. "It's not in my nature to be jealous," she lied, quickly disabusing him of that.

His eyes sharpened. "So you don't mind if I go out with other women, then?"

"While I'm here in Aspen, I *do* mind," she said, seeing his jaw tense. "I think a person should show respect for their lover, don't you?"

There was a moment's pause before he gave a brief nod. "I totally agree, Samantha. Lovers should be true to each other."

"Thank you."

He broke eye contact and took a sip of his wine. "Anyway, you have nothing to worry about with Clarice. She waylaid me as I was leaving for my meeting in town and I felt I had to hear her out. Her proposition is a business one. She owns a chain of high-end boutiques and she wanted to know if she can put one here at Jarrod Ridge."

Samantha digested the information. Now she felt foolish for jumping to conclusions about Clarice.

Yet not.

"It's purely about business," Blake assured her. "I'm going to speak to the family about it at tomorrow morning's meeting."

Her heart constricted at the thought of what else was on tomorrow's agenda—the résumés for her replacement. She noted he didn't mention that right now.

Trying not to think about it, she concentrated on what the other woman's proposition would mean. "Clarice will be here in Aspen a lot, then." And *she* wouldn't be. Clarice would have a clear field with Blake.

He frowned. "I'm not sure. I'd say while it's being set up, she'll visit on and off from L.A." His eyes caught hers. "Why?"

She schooled her features. "No reason. I was merely thinking out loud." She planted on a smile. "And of course I won't be here anyway, so it doesn't concern me."

His eyes turned somewhat hostile. "That's right. What do you care anyway?"

"Exactly," she agreed, her heart breaking. She stood up. "I'll get dessert." She hurried out of the room, aware that he still didn't understand why she had to leave and thanking God he didn't. She took comfort knowing he had no idea she loved him.

Unfortunately the marvelous chocolate concoction in the refrigerator wouldn't lessen her inner pain. She doubted anything ever would.

"...And now that the Food and Wine Gala is completely out of the way for this year," Blake said the next morning, looking down the boardroom table at his siblings, "let's move on to the next thing on the agenda.

Gavin, can you give everyone an update on the bungalow project."

Blake already knew the details of the project, so he found his mind straying back to Samantha. Last night at dinner he'd actually been pleased that she might be jealous of Clarice. Never before had he wanted a woman to feel jealousy over him. Samantha had soon disabused him of that, but appeared to deliberately bring up the fact that she was leaving soon just to goad him. And he'd retaliated by lashing out with an I-don't-care attitude.

Only trouble was…he *did* care. And he couldn't shake that feeling. It kept hitting him in the face no matter where he turned. She didn't seem to realize how much he was going to miss her. If she did, would she still leave? He'd already made it clear he didn't want her to go. Hell, she should be here at his side right now taking notes. Instead, he deliberately told her not to bother attending the meeting today. Not when *she* was on the agenda.

"Blake, I've finished," he heard Gavin say.

He blinked and saw the others staring at him. He had to get back to business. "Right. The next item on the agenda is mainly for you, Trevor. One of the wealthy guests has approached me about opening a boutique here at the lodge." He explained further.

Trevor nodded as he listened. "Sounds good. We could see—"

There was a tap at the door.

Samantha came into the room, looking slightly apologetic. "I'm sorry for the interruption, but Trevor's assistant asked me to give him a message." She walked toward Trevor and passed him a piece of paper. "I ran into Diana downstairs," she said directly to him. "She was on her way up here, so I said I'd hand it to you and save her coming up." Then she gave a general smile and turned to leave the room.

Blake watched her walk away with a slight sway to her hips that emphasized the soft lines of her body, but as she closed the door behind her, he heard Trevor mildly curse.

"What's the matter, Trev?" Guy was the first to ask.

Trevor looked at the note and shook his head. "I don't know what's going on. It's some woman called Haylie Smith. She left a message the other day saying it's important she speak with me but that it's private and she won't discuss it with anyone else. I've never even heard of her."

"Maybe she's got a crush on you?" Gavin mocked.

Trevor shot his brother a look that wasn't amused. "I don't mind a novel approach but this is getting ridiculous."

"Perhaps you should call her back," Melissa suggested.

Trevor shook his head. "No, if it was that important she could leave a message as to why." He grimaced. "I'll have to let Diana know not to interrupt my meetings in future."

"Maybe you should get a tap on your phone," Christian said, ever the lawyer.

Erica looked at her fiancé. "Darling, the woman's only left two messages. Hardly enough reason to put a stalking charge on her."

"Hey, who said anything about a stalker?" Trevor choked.

"I think—" Melissa began.

"People, can we focus here," Blake cut across her. "We have other matters at hand."

A few seconds ticked by.

Then Trevor nodded. "Yes, of course." His forehead creased as he thought. "Now, where was I? Right. I think we can give this Mrs. Richardson a short-term lease and see how it goes. I'm sure she won't want a long-term lease anyway."

Blake agreed. "Good idea. Perhaps you'd like to check out her business practices and financial situation before we decide anything further."

"Sure."

Blake turned to Melissa. "How's the spa going, Melissa?"

Melissa launched into a brief report.

"And now we need to discuss plans for the upcoming ski season." Blake looked at his half sister. "Erica, I believe you were going to prepare a report on how the Christmas bookings and the hiring of staff are going."

Erica inclined her head, looking very efficient. "Yes, Blake, that's right. I've drawn up a presentation, so if you'll all just look at the screen..."

Blake glanced at the screen, immediately impressed by Erica's attention to detail, and he couldn't help but surreptitiously glance at Christian sitting down the table on his right. The other man was looking at Erica with pride and admiration. But Blake saw something in the other man's features that reminded him of how *he* felt whenever he looked at Samantha.

Samantha.

Something twisted inside him. In less than ten days she would return to Vegas to wrap up everything. Then in another two weeks she would be out of his life and gone for good. He swallowed hard. There was nothing good about her going, he decided, dropping his gaze to the paperwork in front of him in case the others saw his thoughts.

The next agenda item jumped out at him.

Samantha's replacement.

Dammit, he had to do this. It was time to bring to the table a list of suitable applications for her position. It was only fair he keep his family up-to-date. After all, the new applicant would be mainly working out of here now and he wanted everyone to—

Just then there was another tap at the door and Samantha stuck her head around it, then entered the room farther. "I'm sorry, Blake, but there's an urgent message here for you from Mrs. Richardson. She wants you to call her back as soon as you can. It's to do with her boutique."

Here was the woman who was leaving him. The woman who could so easily walk away from what they had. Resentment rose in his chest and up his throat. He was tying himself up in knots for her and she was standing there looking so damn poised and polite.

And so damn beautiful.

Something snapped inside him right then. "I'm sure whatever Mrs. Richardson has to say can wait. Please keep any other messages for us until we finish this meeting," he dismissed, hearing himself talk in that harsh tone like he was listening to someone else talk to her.

Samantha flinched, then went to leave but turned back and squared her shoulders, a rebuke in her eyes. "Of course, Mr. Jarrod," she said primly and left the room with quiet dignity.

The door closed behind her.

All eyes were turned on him.

"I don't think there was any need for that, Blake," Guy said quietly.

Blake felt bad. If she hadn't come in at that moment then he wouldn't have verbally attacked her. It had been a reaction to her leaving him, not a reaction to *her*.

He looked at them. They were staring back at him with reproachful eyes that reminded him of Samantha. His mouth tightened. "I know, I know, I'll apologize later." He put thoughts of that to the side. "Now. Speaking of Samantha, as you know she's leaving. I'm looking at other applicants and I think one of them will be eminently suitable to replace her."

Guy arched a brow. "Can anyone replace her?"

"Guy," Blake growled.

"Blake," Melissa began, "don't you think—"

"No, Melissa," he said firmly, without being rude, knowing what she was going to say. "All of you listen to me. This is private between Samantha and myself. It's none of your business. Now. Let's talk about finding me a new assistant so that we can end this meeting and get on with other things."

The tension in the air was palpable, but he ignored both it and the looks on their faces. He owed no one any explanation. Hell, what explanation could there be anyway?

Samantha wanted to leave.

Samantha *was* leaving.

And he hated himself for embarrassing her just now.

"I apologize, Samantha."

Samantha had heard him enter the office but she'd

ignored him. Now she lifted her head to find Blake standing in front of her desk. Anger and hurt rioted inside her. She had to keep busy.

She rose to her feet and went to put some papers in the filing cabinet. "I'm glad I'm leaving now."

"Don't be like that."

She spun around. "Like what, Blake? Standing up for myself?"

His eyes clouded over. "Look, I know I embarrassed you in front of the family. I shouldn't have done that. I'm sorry."

She lifted her chin. "I was only doing my job. I'm not a novice at this. The woman said it was urgent, and seeing that her proposal was on the agenda for the meeting, I assumed you'd want to know any important developments."

"I know. And you're right. You did the right thing." His expression turned sincere. "You may not believe this, but the reason I snapped was because of you. I was angry because I had to bring up mention of your replacement. I don't want a replacement. I want *you*."

Her heart skipped a beat and she began to soften. She didn't doubt him. She never doubted what he said. If he said something, he meant it. He wasn't manipulating her. He'd accepted that she was leaving and he had nothing to lose by being honest. Why fight with him when time was so precious between them?

She thawed. "Oh, Blake."

He came toward her and slipped his arms around her waist. "Forgive me for being a pig? The others know I feel bad. Their sympathy was all on your side, believe me."

"Let's forget it." But it was nice to know his family had stuck up for her, especially against their big brother.

He lifted his hand and stroked her cheek. "Are you sure you don't want to change your mind about leaving? It would be good between us."

She drew a painful breath. "No, I can't." He wanted short-term. She wanted forever. And he wasn't a forever type of guy.

His eyes shadowed with regret and he lowered his head and kissed her. She opened her mouth to him, knowing this was the only way she could let him inside herself.

The telephone rang just then and they both ignored it.

It stopped, then rang again.

She pulled back. "I should get that," she said, and Blake nodded with a grimace.

It was Clarice.

Samantha looked at Blake as she listened. Then, "Yes, I passed the message on, Mrs. Richardson."

Blake's mouth tightened and he held his hand out for the phone. "What's the problem, Clarice?" he said, after she handed it to him. There was a pause as he listened. "Look, I'm pretty busy right now." He winked at Samantha and her heart soared with love.

Another pause.

"It was discussed at a meeting this morning. My brother, Trevor, is going to work with you on this." He listened. "Yes. Fine." He hung up, shook his head at it, then kissed Samantha quickly. "I need to go see Trevor and fill him in before Clarice gets to him. Unfortunately I'm not sure he knows what he's coming up against with that woman."

Samantha considered him. "You really worry about your brothers and sisters, don't you?"

"Yes, I suppose I do."

She went up on her toes and kissed him briefly. He looked a little surprised as he turned and left the office. He was a good brother, she decided, her heart beating with love for him.

And a good man.

Eleven

Just before lunch, Melissa popped into the office as Blake was discussing a letter with Samantha. "I've booked you in for a spa treatment with me at four, Samantha. You need some major pampering."

Samantha blinked. "Oh, but—"

"No arguments. I don't give many massages these days but I've decided to give you one." Melissa smiled slyly at her big brother. "Anyway it's Blake's treat."

Blake lifted his brows. "What is it with my sisters bullying me?" Then he smiled at Samantha. "Keep the appointment."

"Okay, thanks." Samantha smiled at Melissa. "And thank you, too, Melissa."

"You're very welcome. See you at four." Melissa started to leave then stopped to consider her big brother. "It would do you good to have one, too, Blake." Her face lit with mischief. "You could share with Samantha. I'll even throw in a bottle of chilled champagne and some chocolate truffles. It's quite decadent."

"Not right now, thanks. I've got a lot to do."

"And that's exactly why you *should* have a massage."

"Soon."

"I'll keep you to that."

After she left, Samantha looked at Blake. "I wish you could come with me."

Heat lurked in the back of his eyes. "So do I, but I've got that meeting in town this afternoon."

His look warmed her through as she tilted her head. "You don't realize, do you?"

"What?"

"That you said *sisters* before."

Not *sister* and *half sister*.

Sisters.

Something flickered across his face, then he shrugged. "Yeah, well, don't make a big deal out of it." He went back into his office and Samantha went back to work, but she felt he'd made a big step in his relationship with his family and she was pleased for them all.

At four, Samantha walked over to the Tranquility Spa. Just stepping into a place that exemplified sophistication and sheer indulgence in a mountain setting relaxed her. It was gorgeous.

Melissa was waiting for her and led her to one of the treatment rooms that had serene music playing in the background. "I'll leave you to take off your clothes. Then slide under that sheet there and lie facedown on the bed. It's heated. I'll be back in a minute."

Samantha did as suggested and five minutes later, Melissa came back. "Good. Now I think a gentle massage should do the trick." There was the sound of her moving about. "Hmm, I'll have to be careful with your head. How is it, by the way?"

Samantha appreciated that Melissa remembered her injury. "Much better, thanks. It's healing well."

"I'm pleased. It could have been so much worse." Melissa started to rub oil on Samantha's back. "I hear Blake was quite upset about it."

"He blamed himself because he insisted I go with him for a drive."

"My brother's deep at times."

"I know." Samantha groaned as Melissa began long strokes to help soften the muscles.

"Am I hurting you?"

"No, not at all. It's exquisite."

Melissa laughed. "There's nothing like a massage." She continued working wonders, finding the right spots with unerring accuracy. Then, "Blake was pretty hard on you in the conference room today."

Samantha was glad she was lying on the bed with her face turned to the other side. "He apologized later."

"I knew he would. He's a man who knows when he's in the wrong."

"A rare boss," Samantha said, trying to make light of it.

"And a rare man."

"Right on both counts," Samantha just had to agree, then gave a little moan of pleasure as the massaging reached the base of her neck. She hadn't realized how badly she needed this.

Conversation ceased for a bit, before Melissa said, "I think Blake might be getting used to Erica."

Samantha wasn't surprised by the comment. "So you noticed that he said *sisters,* did you?"

"Oh, yeah."

"Erica's really nice."

"I love her already." Genuine warmth filled Melissa's voice. "It's like we're full sisters, not half sisters. We connected together right from the start."

"You've been really great at welcoming her into the family, Melissa. Erica must have appreciated that, especially when it came to the cool attitudes of her brothers."

"Those guys are so stubborn at times, and now look at them. They'll protect her to the death. I suspect even Blake would, too."

Back to Blake.

It always came back to Blake.

Time to change the subject. "So how is business doing at the spa?"

"Quiet right now, but next month it'll start picking up. And in December we'll be run off our feet. Of course, Shane worries about me and the baby, so I've promised him I'll put on extra staff."

"I can understand that."

There was a tiny pause. "This baby means so much to us," she said, with a little catch in her voice that tugged at Samantha's heartstrings.

"Pregnancy suits you. You're glowing."

Melissa cleared her throat. "Thanks. I can highly recommend it." All at once there was a slight change in the air. "What about you, Samantha? Do you plan on having children one day?"

Samantha swallowed the despair in her throat at the thought of having Blake's baby. She forced herself to sound natural. "Yes, I'd love to. But only when the time is right and with the right man."

There was no immediate reply. Then, "Forgive me for saying this, but isn't Blake the right man for you? Wouldn't you like to have his baby?"

Samantha's heart constricted as she was forced to face something she hadn't dared let herself think about now that she knew she loved Blake. This was dangerous territory for her. Loving him like she did and having his baby would be so absolutely wonderful, but knowing it was never going to happen was like a knife through her heart.

She swallowed hard again, then somehow said calmly, "You should know your brother by now, Melissa. Blake isn't into commitment, and having a baby would be a *huge* commitment."

Besides, Blake was already a father figure to his brothers and sisters, and he was already married to his job. There wasn't room for her, even if he actually *wanted* her to be a part of it all.

"Is that why you're leaving?"

She didn't hesitate. She couldn't afford to. "No. I'm leaving because it's the best thing for me."

There was a short silence, then, "I see."

Much to Samantha's relief, Melissa changed the subject and they talked about more desultory things on and off until the massage was over.

"Now," Melissa finally said, after she'd tidied up. "How do you feel?"

"Like I'm about to slither off the bed."

Melissa laughed. "That's what we aim for. Right, I'm going to leave you to get dressed. Take your time and don't rush. And make sure you drink lots of water for the next couple of hours. The massage releases toxins and if you don't flush them out you'll end up with a toxic headache."

"That sounds lethal," Samantha joked as she managed to push herself into a sitting position and wrapped the sheet around herself. "Thank you so much for this, Melissa," she said sincerely. "I didn't know how much I needed it. I really do feel wonderful."

Melissa smiled as she headed for the door. "Then I've done my job."

Samantha watched her leave, her smile fading as soon as the door closed, leaving her alone. Her body might feel better, but how did a person continue with a broken heart? Unfortunately no one could fix that.

"How was the massage?"

Samantha closed the front door behind her and saw Blake leaning against the kitchen doorjamb, as if he'd been waiting for her to come home. This was how it would be if she were to stay here with him. Yet how long would it last? Certainly not forever. Eventually things would become awkward between them and he would start to avoid her.

And then she'd know he would no longer want her.

"Wonderful," she said, giving him a smile that somehow felt empty.

"What's the matter?"

She looked at him and her heart felt sore. She couldn't seem to shake herself out of her despondency. "I think I need you to hold me, Blake."

"Why?"

"I just do, okay?"

He pushed himself away from the wall and came toward her, pulling her close. "Is that better?"

She slid her arms around him. "Yes." But a shiver went through her.

His brow wrinkled as he looked down at her. "What's going on with you?"

She drew a breath. "We won't have this for much longer."

He stiffened. "And?"

His reaction told her all she needed to know. "I feel… sad it's coming to an end."

"It's your choice to leave, Samantha."

She kept her face perfectly straight. "I know." He didn't understand and she couldn't say any different. "I want to go to bed, Blake. Let's make love until the sun comes up."

It could have sounded silly but he didn't smile and she was glad about that. It was as if he knew this meant a lot to her. And regardless of him avoiding any type of commitment, she hoped it would mean a lot to him, too.

In his bedroom she kept her eyes closed as she made love to him with everything in her heart. The thought of leaving him…of never having his child…of not sharing his life forever…was utmost in her mind. She'd never before felt such profound depth of emotion and she cried softly afterward. It would be so much worse once she left Blake for good.

Blake carefully eased out of bed the next morning just before sunrise, drew on his pajama pants and robe and left Samantha to sleep as he went downstairs to make himself some coffee. He felt restless, with a hard knot in his gut that he couldn't shake. Samantha had cried last night after they'd made love. She hadn't done that before. And it made him wonder. It was obvious she had strong feelings for him and he was certain now those feelings were the reason for her leaving. She hadn't said the words out loud, but he'd felt it every time she touched him and in her cry of release. Could she *love* him?

He couldn't love her back.

Hell, he should have seen this coming. *He* was the experienced one after all. Okay, so he'd invested more of himself in this relationship than he'd planned, but falling in love with Samantha, or any woman, wasn't on his agenda. It never had been and never would be. He'd never allow any person that much control over him.

Never.

So where did they go from there? Exactly nowhere. She'd leave and he'd let her go. End of story. There would be no happy ending for them. He couldn't give her that. He wished to heaven he could. He hated hurting her like this, especially knowing her last boyfriend had rejected her, too. She must feel so totally unwanted. Cast-off. Discarded and abandoned. God, how he hated to do this to her. It really pained him to do this. He shuddered, then reminded himself. He *had* warned her. And now that it came down to the crunch *she* had to be responsible for her own reactions.

Just then, the security light came on over the back decking and he saw a figure coming up the steps. The man was wrapped up to ward off the pre-sunrise chill, but he'd know that gait anywhere.

He opened the back door just as Gavin reached for the handle. "I see you smelled the coffee."

His brother smiled as he stepped inside the kitchen. "Sure did."

Blake went to get another mug down from the cupboard. "What are you doing out and about so early?"

Gavin began taking off his thick gloves. "I was going for a walk to clear my head and saw the light on."

Blake frowned a little as he poured coffee into the mugs. "Anything in particular bothering you?"

"Not really."

He handed one of the mugs to his brother. "Is the bungalow project worrying you?"

"Not at all." Gavin shrugged. "I guess it just feels strange being back home again. It hits me most at this time of the morning, and that means I usually need to get some fresh air."

Blake understood. "I know what you mean."

Gavin shot him a curious look. "I'm surprised. Don't you have a lovely lady warming your bed, helping keep those thoughts at bay?"

Blake kept his face blank. "Do I?"

Gavin shook his head. "You always were the same about never sharing your feelings with anyone."

Blake's lips twisted. "Yeah, like *you* do?"

"All I can say is that you must be losing your touch where Samantha is concerned."

"Why?" He knew he shouldn't bite, but Samantha was so much on his mind this morning.

"I thought for sure you wouldn't be dumb enough to let her go."

Blake immediately went on the defensive. "Why would I want her to stay?"

"You need to ask?" Gavin shook his head. "How about she's excellent at her job, she's a looker and a nice person to boot, and as much as I hate to say it, she's damn good for you, that's why. You'll never find an assistant who anticipates your needs the way she does."

Blake dropped his gaze to the mug of coffee in his hands. What Gavin said was true, except the bit about Samantha being good for him. He didn't need any woman to make him feel good.

And he didn't like his brother getting too close and figuring out something that didn't need figuring out. Certainly he didn't want his brother figuring out that Samantha was in love with *him,* and that he couldn't return her love. He had to protect her. He didn't want anyone talking about her even after she left here. He owed her that much.

"Yeah, she's more than competent at her job and she's beautiful, too, but so are many other women. As for being good for me…yeah, we've had some fun while it lasted but it's coming to an end now and I'm more than happy with that."

Gavin sent him a challenging look. "So you feel nothing more for her?"

"No," he lied, feeling like Judas.

"I'm sorry to hear that," Gavin said slowly.

Suddenly a figure stepped into the doorway. "Don't be, Gavin," Samantha said quietly, hurt in her lovely eyes but dignity in her face. "I'm not."

Blake's heart cramped. "Samantha, I—"

"No need to explain, Blake. I shouldn't have eaves-dropped but I'm glad I did. I would never have guessed you felt so little for me," she said, a catch to her voice.

He took a step toward her. "Samantha—"

She put up her hand. "No, Blake. You've said more

than enough." She turned and hurried away so fast all he saw was her shadow.

Shit!

Gavin lifted a brow. "Seems to me she might mean more to you than you think."

Blake tried to focus. "No, you're wrong."

Gavin stared hard, then put his mug down on the bench. "I'll leave you two to sort things out."

Blake gave a jerky nod as his brother headed for the back door and left him to it. He stood there in the kitchen for a minute as regret washed over him before he took the steps to follow her. He'd do his best to mend this damage as much as possible, but if he were to be honest, things between him and Samantha really couldn't be fixed. It was probably best this had come to a head.

Samantha could barely see as she fled up the staircase for the sanctuary of her room. After waking up, she'd gone downstairs in her nightshirt looking for Blake, surprised to hear Gavin's voice and never dreaming they were discussing *her*.

Oh, God. She couldn't stay in Aspen any longer. Not now. This was it. She was leaving as soon as possible, come hell or high water.

She grabbed her suitcases out of the wardrobe and threw them on the bed. She'd always been neat and tidy and fast at packing, but who cared anyway, she decided, swallowing a sob. All she wanted was to throw everything in her bags and get to the airport. She was going home to Pasadena where she would lick her wounds. Beyond that she couldn't think.

"Samantha?" Blake's voice came gently from the doorway.

Refusing to let him see her cry, she blinked back her tears as she carried her sweaters over to one of the suitcases.

"Samantha, stop. We need to talk."

She looked at him but continued what she was doing. "No. I'm leaving. It's time for me to get out of your hair."

And out of your life.

He swore low. "I'm sorry."

She dumped her clothes into the case. "You're only sorry that I overheard you," she said tightly, then took a shuddering breath as humiliation and hurt swelled inside her. "You made it sound so…cheap. You made *me* sound cheap. As if I don't matter."

"You *do* matter," he said, looking pained, but she knew better.

"Just not to you, right?" she derided, despair wrapping around her heart and not letting go.

"I didn't mean to speak like that about you. I just didn't want Gavin to know what was going on between us."

She snorted. "Of course. How silly of me? We can't have the great Blake Jarrod show any feelings now, can we? Not to his family and not to me." It was never about his feelings anyway, and that was the hardest part to take. She'd dared hope he might at least have a high opinion of her. "Your words show me that you never even respected me as a person, Blake. And certainly not as your lover."

His face blanched. "Don't say that," he growled. "I respect you. There's no one I respect more."

"It didn't sound like that to me back there." All at once she took a shuddering breath and admitted that she couldn't blame him for everything. "But I'm doing you a disservice. You made me no promises, I'll allow you that. You tried to warn me not to get involved with you."

His gaze sharpened. "And did you?"

What did she have to lose now? "Of course I did. I…" She couldn't say she loved him. She just couldn't. That would be too humiliating. "…I thought we had something special."

"We do."

She shook her head. "We *did*. It's over." Suddenly she caught a subtle change in his face—a change that Carl hadn't shown when he'd rejected her. She stilled. Her breath stopped. Did Blake have feelings for her after all? "Unless…" *Dare she ask?* "Can you give me one good reason to stay?"

Silence fell.

She waited. She couldn't say the words but he must know what she was asking. If ever there was a time he might let down his guard…a time when he could allow her into his heart…it would surely be—

His face closed up. "No, I'm sorry. I can't give you a reason to stay."

As hard as it was to pull herself together, she recovered her breath. "That's what I thought."

"Sam—"

A hard laugh escaped then. "Too late to call me that, Blake. Far too late." She held her head up higher. "Now, please leave me to pack in peace. It was good while it lasted but it's over between us now."

He stiffened, withdrawing into himself. "I'm really sorry I hurt you."

She held his gaze. "So am I. And as horrible as this

sounds, I wish I *was* capable of hurting you back." It would at least show she had meant something to him.

Turning away, he stopped and said over his shoulder, "The family jet is at your disposal. It'll take you wherever you want to go."

The words stung her heart. "Thank you."

He strode down the hallway to his suite, going inside and quietly closing the door behind him, shutting her out of his life. For good.

Samantha made herself move. She walked to her door and closed it, then went and sat on the bed and picked up a pillow to muffle her sobs. She figured this time she was entitled to cry.

Twelve

Half an hour later, Blake had showered and dressed and now sat in his office at the Manor, his leather chair turned toward the picture window. An early fall snow that wasn't unusual at this time of year had begun covering the resort, and now a weak sun was shining on the surrounding mountains. Usually at this time he was back at Pine Lodge making love to Samantha. All he could think now was that she was leaving.

God, she'd been so hurt back there. It had pained him to realize how much. And yet he hadn't been able to say the words to get her to stay. He'd known what she wanted, of course. She wanted him to say he loved her, but those words were no longer in his vocabulary. The last time he'd used them had been all those years ago to his mother—just before she died. He'd never said them again to anyone. He'd accepted he never would.

His upbringing—his whole life since—had been about avoiding commitment.

And now Samantha had to accept that, too.

Just then he heard a noise behind him and his chest instantly tightened. She'd come to say her final goodbye.

"What happened with Samantha, Blake?"

Erica.

He twisted his chair around, forcing his brain to work as he looked at the unhappy face of his half sister. Clearly she'd spoken to Gavin not too long ago.

He picked up a pen. "She's packing to leave."

"So you're just going to let her go?"

He gave a shrug. "She wants to go. I can't stop her."

She came closer to the desk, frowning. "What's gone so wrong with you two?"

He shot her a hostile look. "It's none of your business, Erica."

"You're my brother. I'm making it my business."

"Half brother," he corrected.

"I'm so sick of this," she snapped, drawing her petite frame up taller than she was, glaring down at him, standing her ground. "We have the same blood in our veins and that makes me a Jarrod, Blake. You're my brother, like it or lump it."

He stared up at her, a growing admiration rising inside him as he looked at this woman who was related to him, no matter how much he didn't like it. The angle of her chin. The light of battle in her eyes. That stubbornness in her mouth. Oh, yeah. Erica *was* a Jarrod, through and through.

"Blake, for God's sake, when are you going to drop your guard and let people in?"

He tensed. "I don't know what you mean."

"I mean, you won't let a half sister into your life because you think I might let you down like your mother did when she died. And you won't let Samantha into your heart because of the same thing. You're frightened you'll get hurt."

"That's ridiculous," he snapped. Sure, he wasn't willing to get involved with anyone and lay himself open to hurt, but that was only because he couldn't be bothered with the ramifications of it all. He was too busy to introduce any complications in his life.

"Then tell me why you're letting a beautiful woman like Samantha walk away from you?"

"She wants to go."

"No, *you* want her to go and she knows it."

His jaw clenched. "This has got nothing to do with you, Erica."

"Look at yourself, Blake. You're deliberately making it hard for Samantha to stay. You're pushing her away and abandoning her before she can abandon *you*."

He swore. "Just stay out of this."

"Think about it. Your mother died when you were six, so it stands to reason that you would be affected by her death. And what about your father? Donald Jarrod shut up shop with his emotions when his wife died, and the only way he could cope was by focusing on his offspring. He pushed all of you to be the best you could be, and none more than you as eldest."

"Erica…" he warned.

"I suspect he wanted his kids to be fully reliant on themselves. He didn't want any of you to get hurt. Not like *he* got hurt."

"That's enough."

"So you effectively lost not only your mother when you were little, but your father, as well. Is it any wonder you don't want to let anyone get close to you?"

He opened his mouth again....

And then somehow, without warning, her words began to hit him right where it mattered. But still he had to say, "What I want is not to listen to this drivel."

Her eyes said he wasn't fooling her. "People have their breaking point, Blake. Your mother's death was your—I mean, *our* father's breaking point. A person can do silly things in their grief. Everyone reacts differently. Our father turned to my mother, looking for solace. Who's to say you wouldn't do the same thing?"

"I would never want another woman after Samantha," he growled. "Never."

"Do you hear yourself?"

He stiffened and blinked. "What?"

She stood there watching him in silent scrutiny for a moment. "If Samantha died how would *you* feel?"

"Don't say that," he rasped, the thought slicing down through the middle of him.

"You love her, Blake."

His head reeled back. "No."

"Yes. Don't let yourself realize it too late. You may never get a second chance."

He swallowed as something deep inside him lifted up like a shade on a window and he finally admitted what was right there in front of him.

He *did* love Samantha.

And right then, he finally understood the depth of his father's loss. He still didn't understand how Donald Jarrod could have shunned the children who were a legacy of his beloved wife, nor how his father had turned to another woman, but the idea of Samantha dying squeezed his heart so tight he could barely breathe.

He surged to his feet. "I have to go to her."

"Thank God!"

He glanced at his watch. "She may not have left the lodge."

"She's already taken the valet car. I saw her leaving." Erica made a gesture toward the door. "Go. I'll make sure they stop the plane. And hey, take it easy getting to her, okay? We've got our first snow, and she'll want you in one piece."

"I will." He was almost at the door by the time she finished speaking. All at once he stopped, conscious that he had to take a moment more for something else. He returned to Erica to kiss her on the cheek. "Thanks, sis."

She beamed at him. "You're welcome. Just remember you'll have a few brothers and sisters who'll expect your firstborn to be named after them."

He grinned. "That's a lot of names."

"Well, maybe you can have a lot of kids."

He chuckled as warmth filled him at the thought of Samantha carrying his child. But first things first...he wanted only one person right now.

Samantha.

As he raced down to the lobby, he remembered how after their lovemaking the other night he'd felt so at home in her arms. Now he knew it was more than that.

In Samantha's arms he *had* come home.

"Is it going to be much longer, Jayne?" Samantha asked, after she'd boarded the Jarrod private jet and nothing seemed to be happening. They hadn't even taxied out onto the runway yet.

"I'm sorry about this, Ms. Thompson," the stewardess apologized. "It's the weather. There's a storm ahead. We have to sit tight until it passes."

Samantha swiveled her leather chair around on its base a little to glance out the cabin window to the snow-dusted airport. A few weeks ago, before she'd decided to resign, she'd been eagerly looking forward to the first of the snow falling over Jarrod Ridge. Now she had to return to the warm California weather and try not to imagine how magical it would have been here in Blake's arms.

Somehow she faked a small smile back at the other woman. "Okay, thanks, Jayne."

The stewardess smiled, then went to the back of the plane, leaving her alone to stare out the window. She'd done her best to repair her face after her crying session back at the lodge, but the longer she sat here the more likely she might burst into tears.

And if she did that she would be humiliated in front of Jayne. She wanted no one knowing how painful this was for her. Blake knew she'd been hurt, but he really had no idea at the depths of her despair. How could he? He didn't love her. He was going to move on. He'd probably already written her off as a bad debt, she thought with a touch of hysteria.

Oh, God. This was it. She was actually leaving Aspen…leaving Blake for good. Fresh tears were verging in her eyes when there was a sudden flurry of movement near the doorway. She quickly took a shuddering breath and glanced ahead to check what was happening.

Blake!

He stood there looking at her…so dear to her heart. And then he moved toward her through the wide cabin, and her thoughts kicked in. Was he here merely to make sure she left? She dared not think otherwise.

He stopped in front of her seat and looked down at her. "You didn't say goodbye, Samantha."

She moistened her mouth. "I didn't think you wanted me to."

"I didn't," he said, and her heart twisted tight at his honesty. "The fact is…I didn't want you to say goodbye at all. I still don't want you to leave. I want you to stay with me." He pulled her to her feet, looking at her with an emotion in his eyes that almost blinded her. "I love you, Samantha."

She knew in a heartbeat he was telling the truth. "Say that again," she whispered.

"I love you."

She threw her arms around his neck. "Oh, my God! I love you, too, Blake. So very, very much."

He kissed her then and she clung to him, loving him with every ounce of her being, feeling the pounding of his heart in time with hers. Forevermore.

Finally he pulled back, but kept his arms around her. "I love you, Samantha. I love you more than life itself."

She sighed blissfully. "I feel the same."

He gave her a soft kiss. "After we made love last night, I suspected you loved me."

At the time she'd hoped she'd masked her feelings well. "I gave myself away when I cried, didn't I?"

"Yes, I'm afraid you did, darling."

She went all sappy inside at the endearment, so she

could forgive him anything. "Yet you were still going to let me go."

"You can thank Erica that I didn't. She made me see sense about a couple of things."

"Thank you, sweet Erica," she mused out loud.

He smiled, then it faded on his handsome face, making him more serious. "I hope you can forgive me for what I said to Gavin. You were right. I didn't want anyone knowing my feelings for you. I was even hiding them from myself," he added with self-derision. "And I hope you can believe this, but I was trying to protect you. I didn't want them realizing you had feelings for me either." He lifted his shoulders. "Loving someone is a private thing."

She thanked him with her eyes. "I agree, though they probably suspected anyway. And yes, I do forgive you, darling," she said, loving the sound of that on her own lips and seeing his eyes darken. "If you hadn't said what you did to Gavin, then all this may not have been resolved."

He chuckled. "Erica would have made us resolve it, don't you worry about that. My sister is a very determined woman."

Her heart swelled. So he'd let Erica into his heart, too. How wonderful. Now he could be the man he was meant to be with his family.

And with her.

All at once there was so much to talk about. She'd have to tell him about when she'd actually realized she loved him, and she'd have to come clean about trying to make him jealous. He was bound to get a laugh out of that.

"Samantha," he cut across her thoughts. "I insist you

don't give up your music. I want you to contact that person Erica mentioned at the music school as soon as you can."

"Oh, Blake, I'm not giving up anything," she said softly, and ran her fingers along his chin, loving the feel of its masculine texture. "I've got all I ever wanted right here."

His brows drew together. "But—"

She smiled at the worried look in his eyes. "Okay, I'll contact them. Perhaps sometime in the future I'll be able to help out in some minor way, but please believe that playing the piano isn't important in my life. I enjoy it. I might even take some more lessons, or give lessons for that matter, but living here with you, and being part of your family, will be more than enough for me."

He gave her a searching look, then his shoulders relaxed. "While we're being honest…"

Her heart caught. "Yes?"

"I know you feel I'm letting you down in some way, but…"

She swallowed hard. "But?" What wasn't he telling her? Was he actually in love with someone else? Was she his second choice? Perhaps he—

"Forgive me, Samantha, but I don't think I'll ever be able to call you Sam."

It took a moment to sink in. She laughed and lightly punched his chest. "You think that's funny, don't you?"

He put his hands on either side of her face and looked at her lovingly. "You're Samantha to me. *My* Samantha. Do you mind?"

She blinked back silly tears of happiness. "Of course not." Not anymore. "It makes me feel very special."

"You *are* special, my darling." He placed his lips on hers, then, "Let's go to Vegas right now and get married."

She blinked. "Married?" As crazy as it seemed, she hadn't thought that far ahead. She'd been too busy taking in that he loved her. "You really want to marry me, Blake?"

He stroked her cheek. "Yes. I want your kisses for the rest of my life."

She drew his mouth down to hers and kissed him softly. "Here's one to start with."

When the kiss finished, he said, "Speaking of giving, you haven't *given* me my answer. Will you marry me?"

"Is there any doubt?"

"Not really."

"You're a conceited man, Blake Jarrod," she teased.

"And that's a good thing in this situation, right?"

She sent him a rueful glance, then something came to her. "But don't you want to get married in Aspen with your family present?"

"No. I'm an impatient man. I want to marry you now. Today." He scowled. "Unless *you* want a big wedding?" He didn't wait for her to answer. "I suppose I shouldn't cheat you of a wedding with your family."

She shook her head. "No, I don't need my family there. I love them dearly but they'll understand. All they want is for me to be happy."

"I can guarantee that."

"Then a wedding for two will be just perfect, my love," she murmured, a flood of emotion making her voice husky.

Blake lowered his head to place his lips against

hers. Outside the plane more snowflakes fell in a hush, blanketing everything in a fairy-tale setting. And that was appropriate. Their love was, after all, a fairy tale come true.

* * * * *

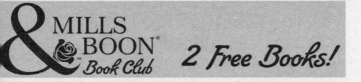

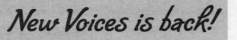